"[A] charismatic blend of insight, passion, and pulse-pounding action . . . *Eden* is a masterwork."

—Thomas

Born Burning

P
TO

Our Fourth of July gathering began as it always had, with an exchange of greetings, some sincere, some patently false. We had old rivalries some of us never outgrew, envy, embarrassments from past failures, even outright dislikes. Once a year, we did our best to put them aside for Helen's sake. We arrived, one family at a time in our expensive cars, to begin our annual ritual at Eden. That year we would soon learn the reunion would be our last as family. In months to come we would meet as adversaries, in lawyers' offices and in secret places, until our final gathering took place in a courtroom. Where one of us would be convicted of murdering our older brother.

Bantam Books by Frederic Bean

EDEN

Rivers West:
THE PECOS RIVER

and coming soon
THE RED RIVER

EDEN

Frederic Bean

BANTAM BOOKS

NEW YORK · TORONTO · LONDON · SYDNEY · AUCKLAND

EDEN

A Bantam Domain Book / November 1997

ISBN 0-553-57707-7

Published simultaneously in the United States and Canada

DECEMBER 1992

He leans forward in his chair, frowning slightly, peering at a stack of papers on his desk through wire-rimmed bifocals. The neighborhood is quiet outside his study windows. A fire crackles in the fireplace behind him but he does not hear it. His attention is on a legal brief. As he scans the pages his frown deepens.

He does not hear a door open across the room, nor does he hear the door close gently as someone enters his study. A shadow moves silently in front of the fireplace and the quiet hiss of flames covers the soft footfalls approaching his desk.

He looks up suddenly, turning, blue eyes round with surprise. Then he smiles and says, "I didn't hear you come in." His smile fades. "Why didn't you call?" His voice is thin, matching his frail appearance, and now his expression changes. He senses something is wrong.

No one answers his question. Behind the glasses, his eyes follow movement. His unexpected guest comes toward him without uttering a word and that, too, increases his alarm. He looks up at the face above him now, lips forming another question, until his gaze falls on the metal object in his visitor's hand.

The concussion of a gunshot abruptly ends the brief moment

of silence. His head is driven back against the soft upholstery covering his swivel chair. Blood erupts from a hole above his right ear, spurting across his desktop, crimson droplets falling on the legal brief, his blotter, an appointment book, his telephone. His glasses slide off his nose, tumbling to his lap, one wire earpiece drenched in blood. The room echoes with the gun's report.

His face is frozen in a moment of terror, eyes bulging in their sockets, lids quivering briefly in a death tremor. His hands form fists, trembling, twitching with neurologic activity gone out of control. His legs shake violently, stiffening, relaxing, and stiffening again. His bladder empties and the smell of urine wafts into the heated room.

Now his hands slowly relax. His head lolls to one side with blood pumping from a temporal artery—his heart refuses to stop despite the severing of supraorbital and temporal nerves in his brain, although it will stop soon, in minutes.

The twitching ends when his muscles no longer receive any commands they can identify. He is clinically dead as his visitor turns to leave the room. No one will find him for several hours. His family is away at a shopping mall buying gifts for Christmas, and during the holiday season malls stay open until midnight.

The killer hesitates when the doorbell rings.

Later, a figure comes over to the dead man's chair for a moment, and digs something from the upholstery with a letter opener. The door to the study opens and closes again. Later, the killer drives away from the house down a quiet street through a suburban neighborhood adjacent to White Rock Lake, home to some of the wealthiest residents of Dallas. No one has heard a gunshot or notices anyone leaving.

There are signs of forced entry at a side door and the dead man's wallet is empty. In the beginning, police investigators will conclude it was a burglary attempt gone awry . . .

PROLOGUE

I NOW BELIEVE WE ALL KNEW IT WOULD BE OUR last summer in Eden, although Helen never said so before we arrived. She could never have admitted something was wrong before we got there. We always discussed important matters face-to-face. We gathered at the old house for our annual Fourth of July celebration the way we had for years, just the family, including spouses who married into our mixture of love, hatred, jealousy, and avarice. I think we all sensed a difference that year, but no one could have identified what it was that made us edgy, suspicious, girded for a revelation that would change our lives forever. I think it must have been some intuition we shared that summer, a feeling that the very foundation of our lives was about to crumble. With the clarity of hindsight I remember misgivings, driving out to the ranch.

The ranch at Eden has always been home to the King family, a base of operations from which we launched our various careers, a place where we returned when things went wrong. That grand old house has been theater to countless scenes of sorrow and tragedy, a stage upon which admissions of guilt and failure and lust have been played out to the fullest, performances worthy of the best theaters on Broadway. There have been moments of great happiness and fulfillment too, the elation one feels over a promising beginning or the renewal of some fated enterprise after suffering a temporary setback. But no matter what the occasion or circumstance might be, sooner or later each of us returned to Eden with our successes and failures to lay them at Helen's feet.

We are a matriarchal family. Like homing pigeons, we come back to our mother's roost. Helen raised us this way, and it is as much a part of our nature as any other familial trait we share. She settled our disputes, supported us in moments of despair, and listened to our stories of triumph and tragedy. I think she has always known her children would be unable to manage their lives without mishap and she accepted it with grace, even dignity. From the very beginning, the sons and daughters of Helen King showed an inability to cope. We were shielded from harsh realities by money—enough money to resolve almost any form of distress—and perhaps this alone caused us to grow into men and women who believed our happiness could be purchased. Some of our spouses, both former and present, will also attest that we are incapable of giving love in a meaningful way to anyone other than Helen. I still believe this is not true of me.

On the surface we are successful people, some with families and children. We have expensive homes and cars and playthings. Some of us might be called distinguished in our chosen professions. Helen has seen to it that we each had every opportunity, every chance. Money can do that. Enough money.

Our mother understood us. We are so different and yet we are the same, the offspring of Lee and Helen King, heirs to wealth and the power that comes with it. When we fail, we have a safety net, a fortune made by our late father from Texas oil. Most siblings have a closeness, share feelings of loyalty and trust. Somehow, those bonds never formed between us. We were bonded to Helen in ways few people will understand. Helen was a loving mother by her own yardstick, although she never permitted it to show. At times, I wonder if she loved us too much.

Ours is a love story, although certainly not in a traditional sense. We have known love of a different kind, an overpowering feeling that has deeply scarred our lives. Five children tied by umbilical cords that became chains as we grew older. Each of us, in our own way, has tried to break free. Not one has succeeded. Until the summer of 1992. On that fateful Fourth of July day, we learned our mother was dying. And when she brought us together to inform us of her inoperable cancer, one that would claim her life within a few months, she added another revelation that would soon turn her children into strangers. Or mortal enemies. I think we all knew there would be some squabbling. I doubt that any of us believed things would turn deadly. After all, we are brothers and sisters, all sane and functioning, or so we believed. But one of us would become a killer. The motive, as it so often is, was money.

Our Fourth of July gathering began as it always had, with an exchange of greetings, some sincere, some patently false. We had old rivalries some of us never outgrew, envy, embarrassments from past failures, even outright dislikes. Once a year, although not at Christmastime as one might expect, we did our best to put them aside for Helen's sake. We arrived, one family at a time in our expensive cars, to begin our annual ritual at Eden. That year we would soon learn the reunion would be our last as a family. In months to come we would meet as adversaries, in lawyers' offices and in secret places, until our final gathering took place in a courtroom. Where one of us would be convicted of murdering our older brother.

PART

I

1

"**MY** DARLING MATTHEW," HELEN SAID, spreading her arms to me for our customary greeting on the front porch. As I got out of the car in the circular driveway I noticed a difference in the way she looked— thinner, and a heavy layer of makeup could not hide dark circles under her deep blue eyes. She was wearing a light-weight denim skirt and white blouse. I noticed she wasn't wearing her favorite jewelry, a marquise-cut diamond necklace with matching earrings our father gave her. My older brother Howard and I have always insisted she keep it insured for six hundred thousand dollars, what Lee paid for it before we were born.

"You look well, Mother," I said, opening the car door for Cathrine before I went up the steps to give Helen the embrace she expected from each of her children. My wife usually stands back until our greeting ends. Cathy doesn't care much for Helen. None of the husbands or wives who married into the King family enjoy these visits. Helen makes a point of showing them only passing interest, never unfriendly yet hardly what could be called affection. She makes a greater effort to seem warm with her seven grandchildren, but even then a touch of restraint is always there. If she has a favorite grandchild it is Matthew David, our fourteen-year-old son. David frequently tells Cathy his Grandma Helen should be named the Ice Queen. I guess he has always sensed the distance she kept between them, even as a small child.

I hurried up the steps remembering scenes from my childhood here. Our house, Helen's house, is an old Victorian from a time when ostentatiousness among early-day Texas oilmen moved our father to build a mansion in the middle of a cow pasture where no one could see it unless they were invited guests. A gravel road from the highway to our house is more than a mile long, making even a three-story home with gabled roof invisible from the Brady highway. And as I always did, I'd stopped by Tom's house just inside the front gates to say hello to the man I credit for my sanity, if I am indeed sane. I never told Helen I dropped by to see Tom first every time I visited the ranch . . . she wouldn't have understood how I could feel closer to her ranch foreman than I did to my own mother. An old cowboy with virtually no formal education taught me values neither of my parents took the time or had the inclination to show me: how to love the land for the land itself, not for the oil underneath it and the money our oil wells produced, the beauty of a clear west Texas sunrise, the importance of keeping your word when a promise is made no matter what the personal cost, and countless other things. He had answers to my questions and took the time to give them to me. I remember wishing Tom had been my father from time to time and those thoughts made me wonder who I was, if there might be something wrong with me.

When I put my arms around Helen I felt how truly thin she was, though her loose-fitting blouse and long skirt hid the fact well enough from a distance.

"How are you, my darling?" she asked, looking up at me with what might have been a trace of a tear in each eye. Her throaty voice, deep for a woman, often had a calming effect on me, like listening to the sound of the ocean. As a child, that voice and the approval it sometimes conveyed became the center of my universe and even now, when we spoke on the phone, the tone of Helen's voice when she praised me for something calmed the tiny tremors in my fingers in a way no amount of Scotch ever could.

"I'm fine, Mother. We're all fine," I added, turning my head so I could include Cathy and David in my wellness report.

On cue, Cathy started across the driveway and I saw in her eyes how much she dreaded a stiff, formal embrace with Helen. I beckoned to David because he appeared to be daydreaming, leaning against the front fender of our Mercedes with his hands stuffed into the pockets of his shorts, watching a vulture circle in the sky with a half smirk on his face.

Cathy came up the steps forcing a smile. Helen glanced down at her bare legs, showing as much disapproval for summer shorts on a woman Cathy's age as she could with nothing more than a look and a slight frown. Cathy won't be thirty-six until September, but Helen is from another generation.

"It's so good to see you, Cathrine," Helen said, giving her own unique version of a formal smile, the kind you see at parties where you hardly know anyone and everyone seems to wish they were someplace else as they shake your hand.

"It's good to see you, Helen," Cathy said, pushing a lilting quality into her voice that was so unnatural I almost shuddered. She put her arms around Helen's shoulders with enough distance between them to allow the *Queen Mary* passage.

David plodded up the steps like a doomed man on his way to the gallows. "Hi, Grandma. What's up?" He stepped forward for his embrace, pulling his hands from his pockets with a show of reluctance, giving Cathy a chance to end her stay in Helen's arms even earlier than she'd hoped. "Somethin's dead around here," he added, looking beyond the porch roof to the vulture before he folded his slender arms around Helen's waist, closing his eyes as she gave him a peck on the cheek, wincing slightly when he heard her lips smack against his skin.

"You've grown so much, David dear. You'll be taller than your father." Helen patted his neck and immediately turned her attention back to me. "Did you notice how dry the ranch is on your way in, Matthew? It hasn't rained since April. I told Tom to take all the calves and half the cow herd to the auction last month. There just isn't any grass to speak of."

Tom Walters had been Mother's ranch foreman for thirty years and everyone in the family trusted him, although none more than me. He knew the cow business inside out and saw to Helen's other needs, hiring gardeners and seasonal ranch hands, repairing fences and water wells himself in the absence of hired help. He lived in a three-bedroom house not far from the front gates that Helen built especially for him and his family, sometimes serving as a security guard should uninvited cars attempt to drive toward the main house when the gates were left open for oil well service trucks.

"You don't need cows anyway, Mother. They're nothing more than a nuisance."

"They keep the grass eaten down. And a ranch isn't a ranch without cattle. Your father always kept good Angus cattle."

"They always take a big wet dump in your front yard, Grandma," David said. "It gets all over your shoes."

"But you said there wasn't any grass this year," I offered quickly, to prevent David from any further descriptions of cow dung.

She gave me a mildly irritated look. "I'm keeping some, the best mother cows. Tom wouldn't have anything to do if I got rid of them. Let's go inside. It's dreadfully hot out here."

"You oughta try wearin' shorts, Grandma," David said as he gave his mother a glance Helen couldn't see. "You'd be a whole lot cooler if you wore shorts."

Helen reached for one of the front doors. "It isn't proper for an older woman to show her legs, David." Her tone became slightly cooler when she added, "Your mother should know that."

"But Mom's not near as old as you, Grandma. Besides, ain't nobody lookin' out here."

Now Helen directed her chill toward me. "You send David to the very best private schools in Austin and he has not yet learned to speak without using the word 'ain't.' Surely he's been taught the correct use of the English language." She opened one heavy oak door and stood there, staring at me, awaiting my explanation for David's language.

"It's his group of friends, Mother. They talk that way to be cool, I think. He knows better. His age has a lot to do with it."

"Nothin' wrong with bein' my age," David complained quietly to his mother. "I don't ever wanna get old."

"Hush," Cathy whispered, ushering David inside.

We entered a spacious hallway with a chandelier hanging from a brass chain above our heads, crystal ornaments flashing brilliantly. Through a door to the left was a formal sitting room, to the right a library where old photographs of Lee King's first oil derricks and the ranch were displayed among shelves lined with dusty books and memorabilia . . . the first ranch branding iron, a Rafter K, and an old pair of leather chaps my father wore working cattle. A faintly musty smell prevailed in the library no matter how much dusting and waxing Helen's housekeepers did, as though the room itself required a scent befitting its aging keepsakes.

"Let's go to the den," Helen said. "I had Maria prepare all your favorite snacks, Matthew. She made her special quacamole dip, the one you like. Howard refuses to touch it, so you'll have the bowl all to yourself."

"Howard never did like avocados," I remembered, following Helen down the hall. "Come to think of it, he never liked anything green. Except money."

David chuckled. He didn't like his Uncle Howard's bookishness. Howard became a very successful investment banker because he studied markets voraciously, reading everything in print about companies and corporations—even the most obscure ones—and he could recite the most minute details having to do with the bond market. It also helped that he managed large sums for our mother in banks across the country.

Helen spoke to me over her shoulder. "Howard was never as healthy as the rest of you. He ate like a sparrow and did not like going out in the sun. It always disappointed your father when he wouldn't ride over the ranch with him. Howard had other interests Lee didn't understand."

I don't remember much about my father. He was away making oil deals most of the time when I was young, and he died suddenly of heart failure right after Suzan was born. "I'm sure Father would be proud of him now," I said, hoping to assuage Helen's need to ramble on about our father's disappointments with Howard and me, or Tommy Lee, a topic she could discuss for hours. I never knew what she said about me to them, or to my sisters. We had an unofficial code of silence when it came to discussing other family members with Helen. She decided who would be talked about, and when.

We were shown into the den, my favorite room in the house because of its windows. The rest of the house is usually dark and dreary, curtained windows keeping out the sun and in some ways the outside world too. When we were young we stayed behind our shuttered windows, leaving rarely except for school and only when it suited our mother. At least those are some of my early recollections of the time right after my father died.

The den was just as I remembered it, although the quiet hum of air-conditioning seemed out of place with my oldest memories. Overstuffed leather furniture of soft split cowhide, sofas and chairs and ottomans, the best money could buy thirty or forty years ago, were arranged in a semicircle around a massive stone fireplace. Oil paintings of western scenes hung on walls paneled with knotty pine. And the picture windows showed distant rolling hills covered with oil pumpjacks. Only now, with crude oil prices at rock bottom, the pumpjacks were still, looking a bit like faraway whooping cranes frozen atop the grassy crest of a slope, awaiting some signal to begin raising and lowering their steel heads again.

Helen showed us to a table laden with food: chili dips and hot sauces and guacamole amid bowls of tortilla chips and potato chips and sliced vegetables. I needed a Scotch on ice desperately before I ate, after a long drive filled with anxieties over our annual get-together at Eden.

"So how is the legal profession?" Helen asked, stepping off to one side when David began filling a plate with chips. Cathy pretended to be interested in a painting across the room, one she'd seen dozens of times before.

"About the same. Several big negligence cases on referral from those Houston insurance companies again. The phone call you made has sent us a lot of business." Mother wielded her financial power sparingly, preferring to stay out at the ranch rather than travel. But when she made a telephone call to the right men in the right places, things happened. I had become, in a relatively short time, a hired legal gun for several large workers' compensation insurance companies, thanks to calls Helen made to a few high-placed executives with corporations she invested in.

"You're a good lawyer," she said, watching me head over to the bar. "You deserve every cent."

Until we were alone, she wouldn't talk about how close I'd come to failing as a lawyer, how many times she sent me money to keep going when it appeared I would have to close my doors. Helen would, however, talk freely about how Tommy Lee's Buick dealership was losing money, or recall a time when Howard almost lost his job at Texas Bank and Trust, until she moved over two million dollars into the bank's depositories. But she wouldn't mention any of this in front of Cathy or any other outsider. Our failures were always private discussions within the immediate family—discussions that were never reproachful, simply a subtle reminder that we owed our success to Helen. To her power and money.

I poured a healthy Scotch on ice, deciding I'd ask her about the weight she'd lost. If anything were wrong, Helen wouldn't discuss it here, in front of Cathy and David. "Let's go out on the back porch, Mother," I suggested casually.

She looked directly at me, and I knew she had guessed what I wanted to ask.

"Not now, darling. We'll wait until the others arrive."

From that moment on I felt certain Mother was seriously ill.

I went out on the patio alone, gazing across a sea of grass that stretched for miles in every direction, undulating in gusts of hot summer wind and browned by lack of rain. And beyond that, distant flat-topped mesas, the result of prehistoric disturbances in the earth's crust, which belonged to us, to me. Unlike my mother, or what I remember of my father, I took no personal satisfaction in this feeling of ownership. I merely felt a sense of awe every time I saw the vastness of it. It made me feel small, unimportant on a scale not related to amounts of money. I truly believe I was the only member of the family who felt this way.

2

"**I**'M GOIN' SWIMMIN'," DAVID ANNOUNCED, peering through the glass patio doors at the kidney-shaped pool encircled by a limestone wall. He chewed a final mouthful of tortilla chips and cheese dip.

Helen's frown drew my immediate attention and I knew exactly what she would say. "You'll get the cramps so soon after you've eaten." She directed her stare at me. "Surely your father has better sense than to allow you to swim until your food is properly digested."

"Wait a few minutes, David," I said obediently.

David's downcast look reminded me of my own years ago when I wanted to swim and was told I couldn't, not for at least forty-five minutes after a meal, something Helen read in a magazine in a doctor's office.

"Dad lets me swim at home after I eat," David said under his breath, robbing Helen of outright victory, "and our pool's deeper than yours, Grandma."

Cathy intervened. "Respect your grandmother's wishes, David. It isn't too much to ask. Find something else to do."

"There's nothin' to do out here besides swim, or look at a bunch of stupid cows. It's boring."

"David!" Cathy snapped, saving me from having to scold him myself.

David bowed meekly and went outside—he recognized the tone of genuine anger in Cathy's voice.

"He's at a difficult age," Cathy explained, pouring

herself a second Wild Turkey and water. "He's become interested in girls all of a sudden."

"His friends are rebellious," I added. "He comes home from school with all kinds of new things. I talked to his counselor at St. Stephens. She says it's a stage he's going through."

Helen was watching me. "You were always strong-willed like your father. Tommy Lee was my problem child. Lee flatly refused to whip him and it shows in everything he does to this day. He should have been spanked more often. Howard, on the other hand, was always a gentle person. Intelligent, and gentle as a lamb."

Cathy gave me a furtive glance. My wife despised it when Helen talked about what she believed was Howard's superior intellect in front of me, and Cathy showed it by taking a healthy swallow of her drink. I was certain now it was going to be a very long Fourth of July at the ranch, longer and more difficult than usual.

"What time is Martha coming?" I asked, changing the subject to a topic with fewer possibilities for unpleasant comparisons. My sister's divorce was an event Helen had greeted with outright joy. "I hope she isn't late. I rarely get to talk to her. She's so busy with the museum and her art gallery."

"She promised to arrive early this year," Helen said. "But you know how dedicated she is to her work with the foundation. Since her divorce she finds happiness in the collections and the exhibits and meeting with benefactors. Ray was such an awful bore, always talking about his practice as though medicine were the only field worth discussing. Martha stood it as long as she could, I suppose. How she endured so many endless descriptions of heart surgery is totally beyond me. He was an egotist. Thank God there were no children in that dreadful marriage. Think how awful that would be, if she were burdened with raising his offspring.''

Realizing I'd opened another old wound, I asked, ''What about Howard? His drive is the longest.''

''He called last night to say they'd be leaving early,'' Helen replied, ''although I must say I'm not looking forward to the wild behavior of his children. David can be so well behaved, but the same can't be said for Timmy or Becky. It's Diane's fault. She never disciplines them. And she married Howard for his money. I was against it from the very beginning; however, Howard insisted he loved her. He told me she would make a good mother, and that she kept a spotless house. But she knows nothing about raising children, it would seem, and poor Howard is much too busy at the bank to do everything by himself.''

I should have known not to discuss it. I left the window and poured myself another big Scotch as Cathy was refilling her glass. We shared a look. We had talked about what to expect, though it already seemed worse this year. I told myself this day would eventually pass.

''Suzan and Carl are always running late,'' I said. Suzan and I had never gotten along, thus I didn't mind when Helen took potshots at her, or her architect husband. If anyone had married a member of the King family for money, it was Carl Westerman. His architectural firm in Midland was mediocre, failing miserably in a boom period, until Helen made a few of her pointed telephone calls. Now Carl was prospering, and he believed it was due to his own efforts. Suzan had been blessed with good looks, blond hair and bright blue eyes, a full figure and perfect teeth. Every boy in high school wanted Suzan and as she grew older, her vanity made her virtually intolerable to the rest of us. Carl had been a top-notch college football player at the University of Texas, widely considered a ''catch'' because of his good looks. But now his hair was falling out and his potbelly belied his former glory as a campus athletic hero. I never liked him much and neither did Helen, a fact she would make plain as soon as they arrived for our annual gathering. I felt Suzan deserved exactly what she got.

I settled into a soft leather chair with a view of the hills while nursing my drink. Cathy stayed near the wet bar as though she feared being too far away from the bottle of Wild Turkey, in case things deteriorated further. Which we both knew they would.

"No change in crude oil prices, I hear," I said. "I've read they may go even lower."

Helen sat in her favorite chair near the fireplace watching Cathy consume large swallows of whiskey and water. I knew the look she was giving Cathy all too well. Disapproval came in many forms from my mother. A certain kind of obtuse glance conveying irritation, disappointment, or outright disdain. But I knew Cathy had to fortify herself and thus I said nothing. My wife's nerves aren't built for the kind of tension present at our family gatherings.

Helen looked at me, fully expecting I'd read her mind and say something to Cathy about her drinking. "I've talked to Howard about it. He believes oil prices will rise in the coming months. He's quite optimistic, really, and you know how carefully he studies the markets. America will always need oil and beef. That's what your father used to say."

I sipped Scotch, unable to recall my father saying that, or much of anything else. My memories of my dad were dim, hazy. I remember wanting desperately to have his approval. But I couldn't master riding horses to suit him, nor did I ever truly have a feel or a fondness for ranching. He criticized almost everything I did and I continually had to listen to how much he wished Howard took an interest in the ranch. Tommy Lee, on the other hand, was born a horseman. He had natural balance, our father sometimes said at the dinner table—on those few occasions when we ate supper as a family. But Tommy Lee's heart was never into ranching or horses or anything of the kind. He was twelve when our father died and from then on he spent as much time away from Eden as possible, visiting friends, going to movies, anything that would keep him away from home.

I heard Cathy adding more ice to her glass. Mixing another drink was certain to evoke a response from Helen unless I could head it off.

"Howard told me you've done very well in tax-free municipal bonds, Mother," I said. Howard and her money were her favorite topics, although talking about the ranch and its oil was a close second to either one.

Helen, as usual, would not be turned aside from behavior in need of criticism. "Cathrine, dear, it seems you're drinking so much more than I remember. Is something bothering you?"

I feared the worst—this was Cathy's chance to say the wrong thing, about her nerves or how much she hated coming to Eden every Fourth of July, or even worse, how much she dreaded a conversation with Helen. I gritted my teeth and then took a substantial swallow of Scotch, waiting for the bomb to go off.

"Nothing's wrong, Helen. Isn't Diane the one with a drinking problem? You said something about it last year, I believe, or was it the year before? I hardly ever drink except on special occasions, like this."

I had to hand it to Cathy, how she skillfully deflected Helen's accusation onto Howard's wife. Diane had been a thorn in Helen's side from the beginning, with her low breeding and refusal to discipline her children. But at the top of her list of irritants was Diane's consumption of alcohol. I often wondered if getting drunk was simply Diane's way of getting through our Fourth of July celebration in one piece.

"Diane has been having a few emotional problems," Helen said quietly. "Howard is sending her to the very best psychiatrist in Dallas. It is small wonder she drinks too much, with Timothy and Rebecca to raise. I have spoken with Howard about it. He says she's getting much better, although I have my doubts. The woman comes from a drinking background. If she only disciplined those children, perhaps her nerves would settle down somewhat."

I took my shot at Howard, albeit an indirect blow. "Howard could help with that," I said. "It shouldn't be solely Diane's responsibility to raise their kids."

"He's very busy at the bank these days," Helen said. "Bank failures have become so common in Texas it frightens everyone with good sense. Howard devotes a tremendous amount of time to the bank's investments. He can hardly be expected to hurry home every time Diane has a crisis with the children. The woman has a full-time housekeeper and a gardener. If she didn't spend so much time playing backgammon at the country club . . . it seems to me their children are left to raise themselves too much of the time. A housekeeper is a poor substitute for a mother."

I got up and made myself another drink. I needed a cigarette. No one was permitted to smoke in the house and I would have to suffer or step outside, a dangerous undertaking as it would leave Cathy alone with Helen to answer probing questions about our marriage, my drinking, or any number of other private matters.

David poked his head through a patio door. "Can I go in the pool *now?*" he asked.

I took charge before Helen could. "Of course. It's been at least forty-five minutes." I avoided Mother's icy stare, awaiting some remark to the effect that I couldn't tell time.

"I hope he doesn't drown," Helen said.

"I'll accept full responsibility if he does," I replied. "He's really a good swimmer."

I noticed Cathy's hand shaking as she brought her glass to her lips.

I tried some of the guacamole dip. "This is delicious," I said. "Tell Maria I'm really enjoying it."

Helen was watching David undress with his back to the patio doors. "He has no modesty whatsoever, Matthew. A young man his age shouldn't go swimming in his underwear."

Cathy looked at me as if it were all she could do to keep from making some remark. I wagged my head against it, knowing it would be fruitless to argue over anything with Helen.

Martha's dark blue Mercedes looked like a twin to ours, and when she got out in the driveway I saw more of the family resemblance than I had ever noticed before. Her blue eyes were like mine and Howard's. For a woman of forty she was remarkably fit and I thought she looked thinner than last year. I crossed the drive to give her a hug, most likely the only genuine show of affection that would take place at the ranch all day. She smiled, and when my arms were around her she whispered in my ear, "How is it going so far?"

"A typical King family disaster," I whispered back. "Thus far, you've escaped being roasted."

"What wonderful news, Matt. I've been dreading this for a whole week."

"So has Cathy. And so have I. If you drink enough it may take some of the sting out," I said, taking her hand.

"They don't sell enough booze in Texas to do that."

Martha glanced toward the porch. "She doesn't look good, Matt. Is anything wrong with her?"

"She won't talk about it until everyone gets here. I tried to ask her about it. She's lost a lot of weight."

Martha let go of my hand when we reached the steps. As I watched her prepare for her embrace with Helen, I noticed that Martha was wearing denim shorts. Another thing for Helen to comment on.

3

MARTHA GAVE HELEN A GENTLE HUG, SMILING her well-practiced smile. Helen kissed her cheek and once again I had the impression Mother was on the verge of crying. To an outsider it might appear we were having a warm family reunion, with embraces and kisses and tears of happiness shed over seeing each other again.

"You look so well, dear," Helen said. Before the last word left her lips her eyes strayed down to Martha's legs. "Where in the world did you buy those dreadful shorts?"

"At Foleys, Mother. I'm glad you like them." Martha was in no mood to be pushed, it seemed. "The ranch looks so dry. Does it ever rain here?" She also knew how to change a subject.

Helen was torn between continuing her discussion of Martha's bare legs and talking about the ranch. She hesitated. "Not since April. Tom took the calves and half the cow herd to the auction. There simply is no grass. I'm keeping the best mother cows and several good bull calves. Do come inside out of the heat. Maria has prepared some of your favorites and Tom smoked delicious ribs for us. The meat is so tender it falls off the bone."

We followed Helen toward the den. I brought up the rear, feeling quiet pride at my sister's courage. As we entered the den Helen turned, pointing through the windows to the pool.

"Matthew David is swimming in his underwear," she

said with as much disgust as she could show with simple words.

"He's just a boy, Mother," Martha said, smiling when she saw Cathy at the bar ignoring both David and Helen's chilly remark. "Hi, Cath. Good to see you again. It seems like such a very long time." She went over and hugged Cathy briefly, then took a glass and began filling it with ice.

"It's been a year," Cathy replied, a slight flush brightening her cheeks. "It was the Fourth of July last year, in fact."

I sensed Cathy was dangerously close to antagonizing Helen, a result of large doses of Wild Turkey and tension. And Martha was filling her glass with straight Scotch.

"So tell me, Mother," Martha said, looking at Helen as she raised her glass to her mouth, "have you been feeling well? You look like you've lost some weight."

Helen sat back down in her chair, smoothing her skirt across her lap. "I don't have much appetite lately. It's the heat, I'm quite sure. I never eat much in the summertime."

Martha gave me a glance. "Have you been to see your doctors?"

"I have regular checkups." Her gaze fell to Martha's legs again when Martha left the bar. "Those short pants look dreadful on you. A skirt would have been far more appropriate, my dear."

"I didn't realize we had a dress code for family gettogethers, Mother."

Helen closed her eyes as if to dismiss the subject for now, a signal we all understood after years of conditioning to Helen's mannerisms.

Cathy seized the opportunity to salute Martha with her glass even though Martha's back was turned. I went behind the bar.

"That wasn't nice," I muttered near Cathy's ear while

I took more ice from an ice bucket, freshening my drink, certain we would all be drunk by the time dinner was served.

"How are things at the foundation?" Helen asked as Martha took a handful of corn chips from Maria's neatly arranged snack table.

"Contributions are down considerably," Martha replied with a note of resignation. "It's this oil thing. So many of our big benefactors are in the oil business. Everything is suffering to some extent. The museum just received the loan of a wonderful antique firearms exhibit from a private collector in San Antonio. We'll have it until school starts. It has given us quite a few visitors, although donations are still down. We are struggling just to make it, I'm afraid." She sat in a chair across from Helen. "Without your generous contributions we would have to close our doors. It seems not enough people care about the arts or history anymore. I get so frustrated when no one appears to care about preserving fine art or important historical artifacts. The general public is so damn indifferent these days."

Helen averted her eyes briefly to a window facing the hills. Martha took a big gulp of Scotch.

"What's wrong, Mother?" Martha asked.

Helen waved it away with a liver-spotted hand. "It's really nothing, dear. We'll talk after supper."

Martha looked over her shoulder at me. We both knew there was a problem Helen wouldn't talk about until she was ready.

David ended an uneasy silence when he did a cannonball off the diving board, splashing water on the glass of the patio doors. I headed for the pool to bring an end to his antics before everyone's nerves were further frayed. Clutching my drink, I aimed a finger at him after he sputtered to the surface.

"Don't do that again!" I warned. "If you can't swim without splashing like that, then find something else to do."

"There ain't anything else to do around this ol' dump, Dad. I hate comin' here. Why do I always have to come to this stupid party? Nobody ever has any fun an' Grandma's actin' like a real bitch this year. Mom's gonna get drunk like she did last year an' she'll cry all the way home."

"Be quiet!" I snapped, before I realized I could be heard by everyone inside. I lowered my voice. "Don't do any more cannonballs and stop saying 'ain't.' Your grandmother isn't well. We don't know what it is yet, so please show a bit of understanding. Your mother is only having a couple of drinks, that's all. It's disrespectful to say your grandmother is acting like a bitch when she isn't feeling well."

David crawlstroked over to the edge of the pool. "What's wrong with her? She's skinny as a rail."

"I have no idea. So please keep a civil tongue in your head while we're here and stop knocking water out of the pool. That's not too much to ask of a fourteen-year-old."

David glanced at the patio doors. "Everybody's always nice to her just because she's rich," he said softly.

"That's enough from you," I said. "Be quiet or get out of the pool."

Martha met me outside the glass doors with worry on her face. I also noticed streaks of gray in her dark brown hair that I hadn't seen before.

"She's seriously ill, isn't she?" Martha whispered.

"I think so. She'll tell us what it is when she's good and ready, after everyone gets here."

"It's cancer. It must be."

"Don't let her see us talking behind her back. Let's go in before she gets suspicious."

•   •   •

Tommy Lee's Riviera sparkled like a giant white pearl with wheels when he parked it in the driveway. He got out wearing a pair of skintight bicycle shorts and a pink floral shirt open at the neck to show off loops of heavy gold chain. A Rolex watch with a nugget band adorned his wrist. A pinkie ring flashed an assortment of big diamonds in direct sunlight. His wavy blond hair was like Suzan's, a natural golden color he emphasized with highlights added at a San Antonio hair salon. He was thirty-eight years old, but trying to look much younger. Divorced twice in the last fifteen years, he had a child by each wife costing him thousands in court-ordered support each month: a son and a daughter he saw on Christmas and Easter for a few hours. He owned King Buick on San Pedro Avenue in San Antonio, but he was rarely there, preferring the sights of Las Vegas and Reno to the mundane day-to-day operation of an automobile dealership. Helen loaned money generously to Tommy Lee's car enterprise when he needed operating capital, which happened more frequently of late. Only Howard knew exactly how much Tommy Lee was losing annually—Howard wrote checks to bail Tommy Lee out when Helen told him to give yet another "loan."

"Howdy, Matt," Tommy Lee said, grinning as I met him in the driveway to shake hands. We never embraced like some brothers do. Our family has always had trouble showing emotion and in truth, there was very little real feeling between most of us. I suppose feelings between Martha and me were a singular exception, although we upheld family tradition by disagreeing over as many trivial things as we could.

"Good to see you, Tommy," I said, smelling a heavy dose of aftershave. "How have things been?"

Tommy Lee winked. "I just got this great blow job from my new secretary before I left. That bitch can suck hard enough to take the chrome off a bumper. She's fuckin' gorgeous. Big tits an' the whole works. Wait'll you see her. She gives the best head I ever had. It's better'n pussy. I want you to meet her."

"I can't wait," I replied as we heard Martha's footsteps behind us. I wondered if Helen would be grateful to learn her youngest son now had a preference for blow jobs over intercourse. It should cut down on future burdens of further child support.

Tommy Lee and Martha embraced in a detached way, a formality. They had never been close, as different in their interests as night and day.

"Hello, Tommy Lee," Martha said. "You're looking well. How is the Buick business?" Martha knew perfectly well the car business was a financial disaster, but her barbs were often disguised as genuine interest.

"Great! Never been better. We're sellin' 'em like hot-cakes this year. The dealership is crawlin' with customers and I can't hire enough salesmen to handle 'em all."

"That's wonderful news," Martha said coolly. "Mother can't wait to see you and I'm sure she'll be delighted to hear about how well your business is doing."

Tommy Lee saw Helen standing on the front porch and his grin faded. "I'll be sure an' tell her," he said, trudging off to get his Fourth of July greeting from our mother, his demeanor suddenly changed.

"He's wearing shorts," Martha observed while we were standing in front of his Buick. "If you'd had a drop of courage *you* would have worn short pants to this gala event."

"Howard won't be wearing them," I assured her. "Besides, I have knobby knees. It was ridicule over my anatomy I feared and not Helen's scorn."

"Bullshit, Matt. You're a conformist. All lawyers are. By the way, in case you haven't noticed, Cathy is getting slightly tipsy."

I watched Tommy Lee climb the steps to give Helen a hug. "I am well aware of Cathy's condition. It's an annual thing for her when she visits Mother. It's the only way she can deal with it."

Martha looked down at her tennis shoes. "She has my sympathy and my full understanding. Howard has been making noises that Helen wants to stop making her contributions to the foundation. He says he doesn't know why. I know she isn't broke. I suppose it must be personal. She never did love me as much as she did the rest of you."

"I'm sure she loves all of us, but in her own way. We've talked about this before." I noticed Helen watching us now. "Let's go inside. She's waiting for us."

I walked beside Martha to the porch. Tommy Lee was saying how dry the ranch looked. Everyone had said the same thing and we all knew why. Helen loved the ranch, all sixty thousand acres of it, its oil wells and rock hills and secret springs and the old rock house that was built by settlers in the 1800s. Helen loved this land because Lee had loved it so much—not to mention the oil it produced. There was hardly a corner of the ranch that wasn't full of memories, according to her. She said she wanted us to appreciate this land and what it had done for us. She wanted us to *notice* what was going on here.

What she noticed now as we climbed the steps was Tommy Lee's tight shorts. "I do declare, Tommy Lee," she said, shaking her head as though in deep sorrow. "If you must wear a pair of little boy's knickers, please buy the proper size. It's almost as if you were naked."

"These are bicyclin' shorts, Mother. They're in style these days, an' I'm ridin' a bike nearly three times a week to improve my heart muscles, so I'll live longer."

As she was showing us in, Helen gave Tommy Lee's Riviera a passing glance. "Unless my eyes are failing me that is not a bicycle parked in my driveway. It looks to me like you could have worn a decent pair of slacks out of respect for your mother.''

We followed Helen down the hall in silence.

''I'll have a beer,'' Tommy Lee said when we got to the den, before he saw Cathy standing behind the bar. ''Hello, Cathy,'' he said cheerfully. ''Long time no see.''

He embraced Cathy as David was doing another cannonball off the diving board.

''It's been a year,'' Cathy said dryly.

''So it has,'' he agreed, moving around her to open an icebox under the bar. He twisted the cap off a beer and downed a long, bubbling swallow before he spoke again. ''We keep meetin' in the strangest places, don't we?''

Cathy almost made a cutting remark until the look I gave her stopped it cold. Our ranch at Eden was indeed a strange place full of strange people—it didn't need to be said in front of our mother. She knew who we were, her odd collection of children without the expected emotional ties to each other. We were like strangers, or at most passing acquaintances, meeting once a year to practice a ritual for Helen's sake.

I hurried out to the pool, hell-bent on drowning my only son if one more drop of water struck the patio doors or windows. My nerves couldn't take much more and the day was still young.

4

TOM WALTERS STOPPED BY IN HIS CHEVROLET pickup to deliver several steaming pans of smoked beef and pork ribs. He is a typical lanky Texas cowboy of yesteryear, slightly bowlegged after too many years in a saddle, approaching sixty with skin like leather from days spent in the sun. He said "Howdy" to each of us and shook our hands after placing the ribs on a butcher block in the kitchen. Tom greeted me as if we hadn't seen each other since last year—I'm sure he knew it would anger Helen if she learned I'd stopped at Tom's house first. He was accustomed to our annual celebration and its regular agenda when he spoke, asking the same question he was expected to ask every year.

"How many of you folks want a drive 'round the ranch?" he asked. "Got room for six. It's real dry this year so it ain't as pretty as usual."

"I'd rather see the pyramids," David mumbled, seething over being forcibly removed from the swimming pool, "or go to a movie."

"I'd like to go," I said, saving everyone—including Tom—any further embarrassment when no one else spoke. "Cathy, wouldn't you like to go too?"

Cathy kept her voice low when she said, "I'd rather have a root canal, but if you insist . . ."

"That's the spirit, Cath," Martha said, finishing her drink. "There's nothing like a tour of a bone-dry ranch to work up a powerful thirst. We can count cows. It'll be fun.''

Tom missed her sarcasm completely. "There ain't but half as many cows as there was in the spring," he said. "We had to sell off a bunch on account of this drought. No grass.''

Martha began pouring another Scotch. Cathy walked away from the bar and for that I was thankful, although I knew it was temporary.

David turned to his mother. "If he can say 'ain't,' then how come I can't?''

"You can say whatever you want today as far as I'm concerned, David. After all, this is a special occasion," Cathy said icily.

Tommy Lee opened another beer. "We'll hunt jack-rabbits from the back of the truck, David. I've got a twenty-two rifle in the trunk of my car you can use an' I'll hunt 'em with a pistol. It takes a real marksman to hit a jackrabbit with a handgun.''

David's face brightened immediately. "Can I, Dad?" he asked in his best begging voice. "Please?''

"We've never allowed David to use any firearms, Tommy," I said. "He's never fired a gun.''

"I'll teach him. There's nothin' to it. C'mon, David. We can fire a few practice rounds before everybody's ready to go.''

Neither Cathy nor I believed in having a gun around the house, or guns in general. "What a great idea," she said tonelessly, watching David's eager face. "You can learn how to kill the Easter Bunny while we're here. It seems fitting somehow that we should begin this celebration by shooting harmless little rabbits." She looked at me. "Why don't you see if Tommy Lee has another gun for you, a really big one? This might become known as the Great Eden Bunny Slaughter of 1992."

"C'mon, David," Tommy Lee said. "You're old enough to learn a few manly arts."

I nodded my silent permission to David. He leapt from the sofa grinning and followed Tommy Lee into the hallway. I was glad Helen was still in the kitchen.

"A manly art?" Cathy asked me, arching an eyebrow. "Killing furry little rabbits is something manly?"

"It's a chromosomal thing," Martha offered. "It puts more hair on their chests. It's unimportant what they kill. Killing is the only objective."

Tom Walters headed for the side door. "I'll start the truck an' get the air conditioner goin'," he said as he walked out of the room.

Cathy gave me a hurt look. "You *could* have put your foot down, Matt. 'No' isn't a difficult word . . . not too many syllables for you to manage."

"He's fourteen," I argued feebly, downing more Scotch after I said it. "I suppose I could have told him he couldn't."

"You're being an old fuddy-duddy, Matt," Martha said. "Let the boy experience the thrill of blasting tiny rabbits to pieces once in his life. It's an important part of growing up. By now he should know the Easter Bunny is a folktale. He has to grow up sometime."

"I feel like *throwing* up," Cathy said.

Martha took a full bottle of Scotch from the bar for herself, then the ice bucket. She smiled at me. "I'm taking along a care package. You may need a drink before this is over."

I would probably need several.

Cathy said, "I wish I could drink enough so I didn't care about any of this."

"I'll tell Mother where we're going," I said. "It'll make her happy that we're going on a tour of the ranch."

"A killing tour," Cathy reminded me, and now I regretted more than ever allowing David to go hunting.

"You worry too much, Cath," Martha said as I was going into the kitchen. "They probably can't shoot straight enough to hit anything in the first place."

Driving down a gentle slope along a two-rut lane crossing a dry pasture, a jackrabbit bounded from its hiding place behind a clump of gamma grass. A series of thundering explosions made me wince. Tommy Lee was shouting, "Shoot that one, David!" from the jostling bed of the pickup.

Cathy's eyes were tightly closed. She sat beside Martha in the backseat of the truck holding her empty glass so firmly her knuckles turned white. She'd given up on drinking half an hour ago when too much precious whiskey was spilled crossing bumps.

I heard a small-caliber rifle crack once.

"You missed him!" Tommy Lee cried.

"Thank God," Cathy whispered, her eyes remaining shut.

"That's an awfully big gun Tommy Lee is shooting," I said to Tom as the rabbit in question darted over the top of a hill and out of sight—unharmed. "It's so loud."

"A forty-five automatic," Tom replied disinterestedly, after a passing glance across empty hills to his left. "It fires seven great big bullets as fast as you can pull the trigger. If Tommy Lee does happen to hit a rabbit there won't be much left of it. Might as well use a machine gun on 'em."

"Wonderful," Cathy sighed. "Just wonderful. I can't watch this."

"My money's on the rabbits," Martha said. "Tommy Lee can't hit the side of a barn."

"You aimed too high," Tommy Lee said over the rattle of the truck's springs. "Shoot lower next time." He

loaded a new clip in the butt of his pistol and opened
another beer.

"I've never seen this place so dry," I told Tom.
"There are big cracks in the ground everywhere."

"Worst I've ever seen it myself," he replied. "If it
don't rain real soon Miz King's gonna have to sell off more
cows an' she sure don't want to do it. She nearly cried
when I hauled off that first bunch."

"I've never seen Mother cry," Martha said in a flat
voice.

Another sudden burst of earsplitting gunfire erupted
from the bed of the truck. I watched a rabbit leap into the
air near a cactus plant and then do a curious flip, tumbling
in midflight with fur flying from its back, legs kicking.

"Got the son of a bitch!" Tommy Lee shouted. "I
blew his ass off, Davey! Did you see that? See how much
fun this is?"

The mangled rabbit tumbled to the earth. David hated
being called Davey, although he didn't seem to mind just
now.

"Wow, Uncle Tommy Lee! You shot him all seven
times!" David exclaimed. "I've just gotta kill one myself
so I can tell Bobby about it when we get home!"

I couldn't look at Cathy—I knew what I would see
written on her face.

"Rabbit stew for supper," Martha muttered. "I wonder how it tastes with beef and pork ribs."

"I can't take any more of this," Cathy whispered.
"Please take me back to the house."

Tom gave me a questioning look. I nodded and turned
to the passenger window without saying a word, certain no
explanation was needed.

We drove back through sun-browned fields, past mo-
tionless pumpjacks and dry saltwater runoff hollows.
Rusted oil tanks sat in mute testimony to the decline in

crude prices. This wasn't at all what I remembered about the ranch. It had been a beehive of activity when I was young. Gazing across it now, I thought about what this sixty thousand acres of land had done for all of us. We had wealth beyond the average man's wildest dreams, insulating us: a wall around us made of money. But what few understood was what went on inside our protective wall.

We were, by any measure, a dysfunctional family. There were times when we didn't behave like a family at all. We, the five children of Lee and Helen King, simply bought what we wanted. I never remembered earning anything myself besides a law degree. Helen loved us too much to allow us to work for things. It was like waving a magic wand, and it was all possible because of this ranch and the oil beneath it. Despite the fact I was a beneficiary of its bounty, it seemed unfair that one piece of land could be so rich while most others gave their owners little or nothing but a place to call home. Our father had both blessed us and cursed us with his legacy, and there were times when I believed I would have much preferred to have been born poor.

I remembered Tom telling me when I was growing up that we all took the ranch for granted and whenever he could, he tried to teach me to appreciate the hills, the grasses, or the beauty of the trees and their rich colors in autumn. Tom, for all his outward toughness, became nostalgic at times, telling me he could feel a shift in the earth's rhythms with a change of seasons. When we were alone together he would stop and point to something, perhaps an oak tree silhouetted by a brilliant sunset or a cow with a newborn calf nudging her underbelly for a taste of milk, and he would say odd things like, "The earth is 'bout all we have in common, Matt. I hope you don't ever forget that. Some folks got more of it than others, but it's damn near the only thing everybody shares. Back before the white man came, Injuns understood this. They moved from place to place without diggin' holes in the ground to pump oil an' they left a spot just like they found it. They didn't need a deed to claim ownership of a piece of ground. They showed respect for it. Your pa don't understand none of this. He digs holes to pump oil wherever the hell it suits him because he's got a piece of paper sayin' he can. He loves money, son, an' there's things a hell of a lot more important than money."

While I didn't fully grasp what Tom was trying to tell me back then, I never once doubted he loved land more than money. As we headed back toward the house I let my gaze wander from hilltop to hilltop, ignoring dozens of oil tanks and pumpjacks, looking for what Tom saw when he traveled the ranch—ravines and arroyos winding like errant pathways through prehistoric limestone beds, gullies slicing into sedimentary rock where millions of years ago this desert had been an ocean. Gnarled live oaks clinging to thin topsoil, surviving the extremes of Texas heat on less than ten inches of annual rainfall, and the ever-present mesquites, hardiest of all desert trees, competing with cactus for deep moisture with root systems extending like subterranean spiderwebs for yards in all directions. And beneath it all was "Black Gold," a tarlike, sulfurous substance that turned men into giants . . . if they knew where to look and where to dig, as my father had.

Howard looked pale to me, as if he were bordering on illness. We shook hands in the den and I gave Diane a tentative embrace, thinking she looked older, tired. Howard's hair was so thin on top his skin showed through. I noticed it right away. Diane had crow's-feet around her eyes and so did he. I stepped aside so the others could take turns exchanging their greetings. I excused myself and went to a downstairs bathroom to wash my hands, and relieve the pressure in my bladder from too many glasses of Scotch.

When I looked in the mirror I didn't like what I saw. My eyes seemed the same, but my brown hair was turning gray above my temples and I had wrinkles where I hadn't noticed them before. I was forty-two and looked fifty, I decided, although I was still reasonably fit. I wondered if the signs of rapid aging in Howard were making me more conscious of my own physical changes.

I dried my hands and steeled myself for a long afternoon. With Howard's arrival, his kids and his wife's drinking would irritate Helen as they always did. And we were assured a higher level of anxiety as soon as Carl and Suzan arrived with their two children. By then, the bickering between us would be in full swing, sisters and brothers reunited long enough to be reminded why we didn't like each other. We would eat ribs and potato salad and beans while we took sides as if we were playing some form of human chess. And presiding over this, our mother would listen and make comments on occasion, reminders that we owed her for everything we had and everything we were, or ever would be. After we ate, her five children would be summoned upstairs to a discussion held in what was once our father's study. A business meeting of sorts, during which she would tell us what to expect next year in the way of financial support.

I turned out the bathroom light and went for a drink. I saw Howard at the bar fixing Diane her usual vodka and tonic and one glass of Crown Royal over ice for himself. Martha was with Helen in the kitchen. Tommy Lee was outside with David giving him more shooting lessons—I'd heard the crack of a rifle several times while I was in the bathroom. Diane was out by the pool supervising her children's swimming. My wife was at the pool reclining in a chaise lounge, a fresh drink beside her.

"How's banking, Howard?" I asked.

"A continual struggle. My big ulcers are eating my smaller ones." He fingered his glasses higher on his nose and stared at me. "Mother looks bad," he said, almost in a whisper. "She won't tell me what's wrong, however I suspect something may have been discovered by her doctor in Houston last month. She seems very irritable lately."

"No more than usual," I said, which was the truth as I saw it.

Howard scowled. "What a terrible thing to say, Matt. I do hope you've been civil to her. She loves us all and you should know it as well as the rest of us."

"I believe she loves us as much as she can. I would gladly have traded some show of genuine affection from her for checks from her trust fund once in a while."

"You'd have gone broke opening your practice if it hadn't been for her generosity. Where's your sense of gratitude?"

"I'm grateful. We were talking about love," I replied.

"You're impossible, Matthew. She gave us a great deal of love, and she still does."

I took a sip of my drink, watching Diane and Cathy and the children through a patio window. "What she gave us a great deal of, Howard, was money. The two aren't the same."

5

DIANE'S PUPILS WERE SLIGHTLY DILATED WHEN she took off her sunglasses and accepted the drink Howard made. "Thank you, dear," she said, glancing up at me from her lawn chair. Her hand was trembling as she brought the glass to her lips. Timothy pushed Rebecca into the pool when he thought no one was looking, pretending not to notice her screams or the splash as he strolled casually toward the diving board.

"So how have you been, Matt?" Diane asked. "We haven't seen you since . . ."

"Last year," Cathy said. She had never liked Diane or Howard.

I noticed Diane was wearing slacks, not shorts. "We've been fine," I replied, wondering how long it would be before Cathy and Diane got in an argument over something.

"Isn't this a beautiful place?" Diane asked, like she hadn't seen the ranch before, a diamond sparkling in her wedding ring as she pointed to the hills. The ring cost Howard a little more than ninety thousand dollars fourteen years ago. At thirty-one, he'd married relatively late in life, and I've always believed he finally gave up trying to find a woman Helen would accept. So he married Diane.

"It takes your breath away," Cathy replied, even though the question was not directed at her. A gunshot from the far side of the house startled her. "Did Matthew tell you we've been rabbit hunting? Tommy Lee killed several and now he's teaching David how to do it. I'd planned to have one stuffed and mounted on the wall of our living room above our sofa, only there wasn't enough left over after Tommy Lee shot each one seven times. Tom Walters said the gun was a forty-five or something like that. It's big enough to kill an elephant, only we didn't see any elephants today so Tommy Lee used it on the next best thing.''

"How disgusting," Diane agreed. "Timmy wants a gun for his birthday, a real gun. I'm against it. I'm afraid he'll shoot someone. He has such a terrible temper."

I wanted to say he was simply spoiled, but I held my tongue.

"I'm against guns," Howard said, ignoring Becky's complaints about Timmy pushing her into the pool. He rattled the ice in his glass and looked across at the patio wall as though his mind was on something else.

Cathy gave me one of her looks. "We *were* against guns until today. Matt and I agreed we wouldn't allow David to have one. I thought we had an understanding. I was wrong, apparently."

Howard wanted to change the subject. "Those shorts Tommy Lee is wearing look ridiculous on him, and with that pink shirt he has on, someone might suspect he's a homosexual."

"I'm sure he's not gay," I said, thinking of his story about the wonderful blow job from his secretary. "He has two children."

"By two different wives," Howard said. "It has always broken Mother's heart that Tommy Lee will not bring them to visit her."

The rifle cracked again, sounding louder than before, which prompted Cathy to remark, "They're missing out on a lot of really good rabbit killing too. I think I'm ready for another drink."

"Me too," Diane said. "This heat is making me thirsty."

Howard dutifully took Diane's empty glass and I reached for Cathy's. "Should I bother adding any water to this one?" I asked politely as Timmy jumped off the diving board, landing near his shrieking sister and splashing water in her face.

"I'll take it straight," she replied, looking away.

Diane told Howard, "Don't put so much tonic in mine either, dear. Too much tonic ruins the taste."

It was a remark I couldn't pass up. "I didn't know vodka had much taste," I said to no one in particular as I followed Howard to the patio doors.

Helen and Martha were waiting for us in the den.

"Those children, Howard," Helen said in her throaty voice, a clear note of irritation in it. "Can't Diane control them? They are making so much noise I can't hear myself think. Ask her to quiet them down. Rebecca hasn't stopped screaming since she got here."

Howard turned on his heel carrying the two empty glasses. We were all trained to respond to that tone of voice—we knew what it meant if we dared question our mother.

As I was walking to the bar I noticed Martha sitting in a chair staring vacantly out a window. "Can I fix you a drink, Martha?" I asked, trying to read her expression.

For a moment I didn't think she heard me.

"Of course," she replied softly. "I can always use a drink when I'm visiting Eden. It must be the heat." She got up and brought her empty glass to the bar, some of the usual color missing from her cheeks. "Don't bother adding water to mine," she said.

"Water's very unpopular today," I remarked, putting Cathy's glass beside mine. "Nobody wants any water or tonic. Diane says too much tonic ruins the taste of vodka. She blamed Howard for using too much the last time.''

Helen was standing by the window, listening. ''I've raised a family of alcoholics,'' she said. ''It must be those children screaming all the time making everyone nervous. I do wish Diane would learn to control them. She's an unfit mother to let them shriek like that all the time.''

''I'm not an alcoholic, Helen,'' Martha said. ''I only drink on special occasions, like this. It's a holiday.''

I poured Scotch into both our glasses and added ice. When I fixed Cathy's I put extra ice in her glass to cut down on the amount of whiskey. And I was sure something was wrong with Martha, but I couldn't ask her in front of Helen. She and Helen had been talking before Howard and I came in.

''A stable person doesn't need to drink so much,'' Helen said as Howard began yelling at Timmy and Becky to quiet down.

Martha was looking at me when she said, ''I guess that means we're all unstable.'' She took a deep swallow of Scotch and for added emphasis rattled the ice in her glass.

''You each have your own peculiarities,'' Helen said with a touch of regret while she watched Howard through a patio door. ''I loved you in spite of them and did what I could to help you change for the better.''

Martha was biting her lip, her back turned to Helen. ''Are you saying we're unstable, peculiar drunks?'' she asked as she turned around.

Helen glared at her. ''Don't use that tone of voice with me, Martha Elizabeth. That isn't what I said and you know it, but if the shoe fits, then by all means wear it.'' She got up then and walked down the short hallway to the kitchen.

''So, I'm in trouble,'' Martha said to me quietly. ''I'm

used to it. I was always in more trouble here than the rest of you. That's why I hate coming back. It's an ugly reminder of my unhappy childhood. You may be the only member of this entire family who understands.''

"You pushed her," I said as Howard came back inside.

"Kids," Howard muttered unhappily, crossing over to the bar with a scowl on his face. "There are times when I wish we hadn't had children."

"Mother's feeling the same way today," Martha said. "She said we were all unstable drunks. Peculiar, unstable drunks."

Howard gave her a quizzical look. "I doubt that. What did she actually say, Matt?"

"That we were peculiar, unstable drunks."

"She isn't feeling well," Howard said, adding ice and then a generous portion of vodka to Diane's glass. "Where is she?"

"In the kitchen pouting," Martha said.

"She doesn't pout," Howard argued, splashing a small amount of tonic into the drink. "I'll talk to her as soon as I've given this to my wife."

"You're only contributing to Diane's instability by giving her booze," Martha said, "although she's not really a blood relative, so quite possibly she's simply a drunk."

"Don't talk about her like that!" Howard snapped. "She's only having a couple of drinks so she can relax and enjoy herself today."

"No one ever enjoys themselves here," Martha said coldly.

Howard's pale face was now a bright pink. He quickly poured a Crown Royal for himself and headed for the pool.

"Before the day's over everyone will be pissed off," Martha promised. "Are you mad at me, Matt? Or will that come later?"

I noticed Cathy glaring at me through the patio doors when Diane's drink arrived before hers.

"Excuse me, dear sister, but my wife needs a drink. If she is to hold fast to our family's tradition she'll need to be dead drunk before we eat. It's the only way Cathy's digestion works properly while we're in Eden. Three years ago she passed out on the way home. David kept asking why he couldn't wake his mother up."

"Why do we have to go through this every year?" Martha asked as she touched my hand gently. It sounded as if she were about to cry. "It's not as though we need any more emotional flogging at this point in our miserable lives."

"I'm not miserable," I said. "I have Cathy and David and a life of my own. I'm only miserable on the Fourth of July. That leaves me three hundred and sixty-four days to be happy."

"I envy you," Martha replied. "I wanted to be happy. I used to dream about what it would be like to be really, really happy. Somehow, you escaped the King curse. But then you were always different, gentler, going off with Tom Walters all the time to get away from the insanity under this roof."

I thought about what she said. "Tom had time for me when our father didn't. He answered all my questions and showed me things when no one else would. I felt close to him then and I still do. In some ways I suppose he was more like a father to me than my real father."

"You were lucky," Martha whispered, gazing out a window. "I never felt like I had anyone. You were the only one who listened to me . . . when you weren't off with Tom."

Cathy was still staring at me from outside. "I have to take this nerve tonic to my wife," I said. "We'll talk later."

"There's no need," she said. "The damage is already done."

I hurried outside just as Howard was coming in. He stopped me near the patio doors and lowered his voice.

"What the hell did Martha say to Mother?" he asked.

"I didn't hear what was said before I went in. They must have had some kind of argument."

"Martha's always the one to start trouble."

"Not necessarily. Suzan is really good at it and so are you, I might add."

A gunshot echoed off the patio walls. I felt like shoving a .22 rifle up Tommy Lee's ass when I heard it.

"Helen is sick," Howard whispered. "Martha should be more considerate. I'll talk to Mother and find out what's going on." He went past me into the den.

"Here's your nerve medicine," I said to Cathy as I handed her the glass. "No water, just the way you wanted it."

"Isn't this fun?" she asked me, swilling almost half of the contents in a single swallow. "I can hardly wait until Suzan and Carl get here. He's such a bore. Maybe Tommy Lee will shoot him accidentally as they're coming in the driveway. We can have Carl stuffed and mounted to go with what's left of the rabbits. I do hope David doesn't shoot anyone. He's so very young to be sent to reform school, or to prison."

I decided it was easier to play along. "Shooting Carl would be called justifiable homicide. I could get the case dismissed."

Suzan was fatter than she was last year. Having two children had been hard on her figure. Jody, her eight-year-old, got out of Carl's Cadillac first and immediately became interested in all the shooting in Helen's front yard.

Regina, at six, showed less enthusiasm for gunfire. She carried an inflatable pool toy shaped like a duck under her arm.

"Blow it up, Daddy, so I can swim," she pleaded.

Carl locked his car like he expected someone to steal it as we were coming off the porch to greet them.

"Not now, Gina," Carl said. "Wait 'til we say hello to everybody."

Both Carl and Suzan were wearing shorts. Carl's legs were still muscular while the rest of his twenty-nine-year-old body had become soft and flabby. His bald spot was larger. Suzan had rounded hips and a belly she couldn't hide inside loose-fitting yellow shorts. Her blouse strained at the buttons to cover her pendulous breasts. It was easy to see she didn't care about her appearance anymore. Her hair had been cut short, almost boyishly short, and her bloated face looked nothing like it did when she was in school.

"Hi, Matt," she said, since I was first to greet her in front of the car. She smiled.

"Hello, Suzan," I said, putting my arms around her shoulders briefly, a King family embrace lacking any real feeling. "Good to see you again." I let go of her and shook hands with Carl. "Good to see you too, Carl."

"Nice to see you again, Matt." He glanced at the house for a moment. "This is a great place, ain't it? One of these days me an' Suzan are gonna own us a ranch like this."

"It's a wonderful place," I said, trying to sound genuine about it.

Howard and Martha lined up to hug Suzan and shake hands with Carl. Tommy Lee was showing David how to load the rifle near one of the live oak trees. Helen, as always, stood on her front porch while we exchanged feigned pleasantries. I think she knew we weren't happy to be there, or to see each other. Over the years we've had our minor squabbles and a few serious difficulties. But this year, I felt a change in the wind. A little voice inside my head told me this would be our last family reunion.

6

CATHY WAS WEEPING. I FOUND HER OUTSIDE the patio's stone wall, looking at Helen's flower beds. With four children yelling and splashing in the pool I understood why Cathy needed to get away from the noise, though I couldn't guess what was making her cry.

"What's wrong, honey?" I asked, taking her hand, the one not holding her empty glass. Cathy rarely consumed alcohol and the drinks she'd had today might have been the explanation for her tears. "Is it the whiskey?"

"I'm miserable," she sobbed, allowing tears to run freely down her cheeks. She looked up from a row of manicured plants bearing hundreds of pink blossoms I couldn't identify. "This family of yours is so weird I can't stand being here. I'm never coming back, Matt. I can't do this again. Maybe I've had too much to drink, but no one has to be sober to see that you hate each other." She took her hand from mine and dried her eyes. The six-foot limestone and masonry wall around Helen's pool kept the others from seeing us.

"I wouldn't call it hate. We just don't like each other." I could hear Carl rambling on about architecture above Rebecca's incessant screams and Regina's sobs that her inflatable duck was losing air.

"You don't act like brothers and sisters," she said.

"We're not like most brothers and sisters." I heard Tommy Lee telling Howard about the rabbits he killed. "We were never close. I know how much you hate this every year. I'm sorry to put you through it. It'll be over in a few hours and then we can leave.''

"You aren't like them," Cathy said, looking me in the eye.

"No. I don't think so. At least I hope I'm not."

"I wish we could go home right now."

"We can't. I couldn't do it to Mother. I have this feeling she's seriously ill. You've seen how thin she is."

Cathy looked at the flowers again. "She's the coldest woman I've ever known. She lacks the capacity for real affection. She goes through the motions but there's no feeling. You *aren't* like her, Matt. When we first met I thought you were the most gentle, the most considerate, the kindest man in the whole world. You aren't like your brothers or sisters or your mother at all."

I met Cathy at Baylor. I was a first-year law student and she was majoring in biology, a homecoming queen candidate, one of the prettiest girls on campus. Her sandy hair and emerald eyes captivated me the moment we were introduced to each other by a mutual friend. She came from a solid southern background, the daughter of a Baptist minister in Tyler, and so naive she had never touched a drop of alcohol or been to a school dance. She was the most sincere person I ever met and she cared nothing for the fact I was from one of the richest oil families in Texas in 1977. Happiness meant more to her than money. We married three months after we met. I'd tried my hand at the oil business after I got my business degree, and hated it. I've always been thankful I went back to Baylor for law school. Otherwise, I'd have never known Cathy Baker, or what real love was about. A year after we were married I discovered something else about myself—our son was born and I found out I could love a child the way I'd always wished my mother and father could have loved me—without restraint. Although in a strange way I felt Tom loved

me like a son. In his own rough, range-cowboy manner
Tom showed me he cared for me and for what happened to
me. He let it show in subtle ways, taking the time to listen
and answer all my adolescent questions when my father
wasn't there or when he was too busy with oil deals to talk
to me. I think because of that, because of him, I was able
to discover a part of myself that I'm not sure my siblings
ever found for themselves, the capacity to feel and listen
and share emotions. Cathy nurtured this as our marriage
grew, enabling me to give love back without fear that
expressing emotion was somehow wrong.

"My brothers and sisters never met anyone like you,"
I said, reaching for her hand again. "The kind of affection
Helen gave us was all we'd ever experienced. It's wrong to
say she doesn't love us, or show it. She shows it in her own
way. I think she has always believed she could buy our
affection. It may not be her fault that she isn't capable of
anything else. At times, I wonder if she loved us too much,
trying to shield us from reality by giving us everything we
ever wanted. She listened when we told her about our
failures. Her solution was to give us more money. We
bought our success."

"But you're a good lawyer?"

"I'm successful. There's a difference. Having the right
clients makes any lawyer look good. I have big clients because Helen made phone calls to the right people."

"You would have made it anyway, sooner or later."

I wasn't so sure, though I didn't tell Cathy about my
doubts. She knew nothing of the cutthroat games played by
big-time civil attorneys. "Maybe. I have a good practice
now. I don't suppose it matters in the long run how it
came to me."

"I wish we could go home," she said.

I squeezed her palm. "We can't. Please try to understand."

• • •

"You're a fat slob," Tommy Lee said to Carl, during a lull in conversation and children's screams around the pool. "If you rode a bicycle you'd get rid of some of that belly." Tommy Lee was drunk and he resented a remark Carl made about his bicycle shorts.

Carl grinned, but there was no humor behind it. "At least I don't dress up like some fuckin' fag. That's a fag's pink shirt if I ever saw one. I can see your balls an' your dick under your shorts. Only a queer would dress like that."

I looked over at Cathy. Her eyes were closed again just as they were during the rabbit hunt. We were seated around the pool in lounge chairs. Howard was missing; he was in the kitchen talking to Helen.

"Watch your language in front of the children, Carl," Suzan said, nibbling on her second helping of tortilla chips and cheese dip. "Tommy Lee isn't a queer anyway. He knocked up two wives. A real queer can't do that. They like little boys."

"Isn't this pleasant holiday conversation?" Martha asked as she settled into a chaise lounge with a new drink. "We've been reduced to calling each other names and it's so early. I fully expected this to happen later, while we're trying to digest Tom's smoked ribs. Nothing like a spirited name-calling contest to whip up an appetite for spicy barbecue. As soon as Howard gets back from his ass-kissing mission I'll call him something, some awful name, like cocksucker."

From the corner of my eye I saw Cathy flinch.

Diane took immediate offense. "Howard isn't a cocksucker."

"How would you know?" Martha persisted. "You're too drunk most of the time to know what he does."

"I resent that remark," Diane said, looking at the

empty glass in her hand. "You're the one with the drinking problem."

"My drinking isn't a problem. I do it as a means of escape from this madness." Martha cast a steely glare around the group at the pool, I suppose as a way of including all of us in her decree that we were mad as hatters.

"Amen," Cathy whispered in the chair beside me, squeezing my hand as though touching me might get her through the rest of this long afternoon. Her staunch Baptist upbringing hadn't prepared her for intellectual duels like the ones we fought where no language was too foul, no insult too deep to be declared off-limits.

"I still say he looks like a fuckin' fag in those shorts an' a pink shirt," Carl muttered to Suzan, although everyone could hear. Carl is what most people call a cheap drunk. Two drinks and his words became noticeably slurred.

"Shut up, Carl," Suzan said around a mouthful of chips and dip, wiping a spot of melted cheese off the front of her blouse.

Rebecca screamed at the top of her lungs when Timmy pushed her into the pool again.

"Be quiet, Becky," Diane said, having some difficulty rising from her chair to make a fresh drink. She staggered when she got to her feet and would have lost her balance completely if she hadn't grabbed the handle of a patio door.

"Hell, I'm sorry, Tommy Lee," Carl said. "It was a hell of a long drive out here with those kids yellin' their heads off. Gina had to stop an' pee every fifteen minutes, then she'd want a big Coke so we'd only go another ten or fifteen miles before she had to pee again."

Tommy Lee belched loudly and got up. "It's okay, Carl. If you want another beer I'll get you one. I just want you to know I sure as hell ain't a fag. How 'bout a beer?"

"Sure," Carl replied, paying no attention to Regina's loud requests to have her floating duck blown up again. "A beer does sound mighty damn good."

"Peace at last," Martha said. "A potential for violence has been avoided by means of liquid refreshment."

I looked over at Cathy and I knew I could never ask her to come to another Fourth of July at Eden, not ever again. She was watching the horizon with tears in her eyes.

Howard came out a few minutes later and held up his hands for silence. He told us that Diane was lying down on a sofa in the den with a damp rag over her face. Even the children splashing in the pool sensed something was wrong, quieting, looking at Howard.

"Mother has gone upstairs," he continued gravely. "She's lying down. The strain and the noise have been too much for her. She asked me to offer her apologies. I'm afraid we're in for some bad news. Helen is terminally ill. She'll explain after we have dinner."

The silence lingered. We all looked at Howard, expecting a further explanation, I suppose.

"That's all she would tell me," he said. "She's dying, and she has things she wants to tell us." A tear trickled beside his nose.

I sat up abruptly. I'd known something was different this year, with her weight loss, and her impatience with almost everyone. "What is it, Howard?" I asked.

"I don't know," he replied. "My guess is, it's some form of cancer. She didn't say, and I did not press her. She said she'd tell us about it later. Upstairs."

"What'll happen to the ranch, and our trust funds?" Suzan asked.

"I have no idea," Howard snapped. "It seems to me you should be more concerned with our mother's well-being."

"I am," Suzan explained, looking around as though she owed everyone an apology. "I was just wondering."

Cathy squeezed my hand again. "You were right about Helen," she whispered.

Tommy Lee put down his beer. "I say we sell the ranch," he said. "Divide it up, or sell it just like it is. None of us is a damn bit interested in livin' here."

Howard's expression grew stern. "You sound like you can't wait for Mother to die."

"I never said that. All I said was, we oughta sell this big ranch an' divide up the money 'cause nobody wants to live here."

"This was our home!" Howard said angrily.

"This was never a real home," Martha remarked without a hint of feeling, gazing at the house. "We lived here, but this was never a home."

"What a shitty thing to say," Suzan said, folding her arms across her ample stomach and looking to her husband for support. But Carl was finishing his beer and didn't respond.

"I have nothing but shitty memories of this place," Martha replied.

"You can be such a bitch," Suzan said. "Our mother is up in her bedroom dying, for Christ's sake, and all you can say is this house gave you a bunch of shitty memories."

Martha smiled an empty smile. "You were too busy screwing half the Eden high school football team to have any memories of this house. At least you had the decency to screw them in the backseats of their cars, away from here. I was told the Eden Drive-in Theater paved their entire parking lot with condoms you tossed out car windows."

"That was a lousy thing to say," Carl said, slurring every word.

Suzan's jaw jutted. "That was because you were too

ugly to get laid in high school!'' she cried, pointing an accusing finger at Martha.

"These children are listening to every word you say,'' Howard protested. "We can talk about this some other time, can't we?''

"Why?'' Martha asked bitterly. "They are part of this sick family, aren't they? They should get used to hearing some shitty remarks now and then. It's a King tradition, like observing the Fourth of July being miserable.''

"You've had too much to drink,'' Howard said.

"I haven't had nearly enough to drink. This occasion calls for tremendous amounts of booze,'' Martha answered. "Helen told me earlier we were all unstable drunks in the first place.''

"Peculiar, unstable drunks,'' I reminded her. "I was present when Mother said it.''

Martha nodded. "She did say we were peculiar, but that she tried to help us overcome it. Just looking around, I'd say she failed rather dismally.''

"Mother didn't say that,'' Tommy Lee argued.

"You were outside shooting off your guns,'' Martha said.

"What's gonna happen if we sell this ranch?'' Carl wanted to know. "Will the money be divided in equal shares?''

"Shut up, Carl,'' Suzan said, still glaring at Martha. "You have nothing to say about it anyway. Helen had you excluded from her will because she didn't think you were trustworthy. My share is mine as separate property under Texas law. Isn't that right, Matthew? You're the lawyer.''

"Helen told me she made provisions in her will for separate property for each of us,'' I answered. "She had to consider the possibility of divorce.'' I didn't mention that she didn't trust my legal judgment enough to have me draw or make changes in her will. A firm in Houston handled all her legal affairs.

"How thoughtful of her," Cathy observed while the others were quiet. "It's comforting to know Helen believed in our marriages so strongly."

7

"IS ANYBODY HUNGRY?" CARL ASKED. "THOSE ribs sure smelled great a while ago."

A gloom settled over all of us shortly after Howard made the announcement about Helen's illness—everyone except Carl, who didn't seem to care after consuming four beers. Of course, I'm not sure he cared for Helen before the beer, either. We'd moved into the den to cool off in the air-conditioning, forcing all four of the younger children to get out of the pool. We set them up watching television in a playroom Helen converted behind the garage for just such activities. David was nowhere around but I figured he was old enough to be on his own for a while.

"How can you even think about eating at a time like this?" Howard asked.

"He never stops thinking about eating," Suzan said, filling a corn chip with guacamole dip after preparing a large bourbon and Coke.

Her remark should have evoked some wisecrack from Martha or Tommy Lee. Everyone remained silent. I suppose we were each thinking our own private thoughts about what would happen after Helen died.

"I wonder how long she's got," Tommy Lee said in an offhanded way.

His question offended Howard. "You can't wait, can you? If I were you I'd be ashamed of asking a question like that."

"Fuck you, Howard. I was only wonderin'."

"She didn't say," Howard replied bitterly.

Cathy sat beside me on the love seat holding my hand. Diane appeared to be asleep, or passed out, on a leather sofa in front of the fireplace with the rag covering her eyes. Every now and then Cathy would squeeze my palm. It was her way of staying in contact with reality, the happy reality we shared in Austin. She hadn't said a word since we came inside.

Howard poured himself another Crown on ice. "I had a bad feeling as soon as I saw her. She's lost so much weight and it almost seemed like she was in some sort of pain when I put my arms around her. I hope she isn't suffering too much."

We all heard Suzan munching loudly on her tortilla chip as another quiet moment passed.

"Where's David?" Cathy asked softly.

"I'm sure he's only walking around somewhere. He gets too bored being around the smaller kids."

"He's rabbit huntin'," Tommy Lee said. "I let him take the rifle. He'll be okay. He knows how to load an' shoot it now."

"Oh, dear God," Cathy whispered. "Please go look for him, Matt, and take the gun away. I'm so afraid he'll hurt himself by accident."

"Let the boy grow up, Cathy," Tommy Lee said. "He's damn near fifteen. You want him to be a sissy all his life?"

I intervened. "A man isn't a sissy just because he doesn't own a gun," I said standing up, finding my back muscles stiff from too much sitting. "I'll look for him," I told Cathy as I put down my drink.

"You'd look like a sissy in that pink shirt even if you were *wearin'* a gun an' holster," Carl said to Tommy Lee. Carl became more of a bully when he was drinking—I recalled their altercation from last year when Carl pushed

Tommy Lee into the pool. Tommy Lee had wanted to go after Carl, until the sound of Helen's voice calmed him down. She ordered Suzan to have Carl apologize and Carl did so immediately. Even drunk, Carl knew from whence his bread and butter came.

"Shut up, Carl," Suzan said now as Tommy Lee got to his feet. "Leave Tommy Lee alone about his shirt. I like it on him."

"For Mother's sake let's behave ourselves," Howard suggested in a calm voice. "Surely we can get along peacefully just once."

I started toward the door to look for David. "That'll be one hell of a feat if we can pull it off," I said. "Bickering is an inbred characteristic in this family. None of us ever agree on a single thing."

"I agree," Martha said. "And now we can say we've agreed on something."

I went out the front door to find my son, knowing he was carrying a .22 rifle. In an inexperienced pair of hands it could be dangerous. I also reminded myself I might be the one to get shot accidentally, so I decided to call to him from the porch. I examined scattered groves of live oak trees across the front pasture and saw nothing. David would be too far to hear my voice if he'd crossed over the hills to look for rabbits.

I got in the car and started driving toward rows of rusting pumpjacks searching for David, but my mind was on Helen, on what would happen as soon as she died. Squabbling between the five of us would begin before Mother was in her grave.

Howard would catch the brunt of it until her will was read. He controlled Helen's widely scattered fortune. His signature was required on every check except the ones Helen signed herself for personal and ranch expenses. Howard's phone would be ringing day and night with requests, or demands, for money from the trust funds until the estate was settled. From a purely legal standpoint Howard actually managed every inter-vivos trust with his signature, putting money in or taking it out whenever the need arose, or whenever it suited him. He made investments for Helen at his own discretion, and upon her death he could continue to do so until probate. Helen trusted Howard completely and as her oldest son I suppose it was natural he'd been put in charge of things.

David was nowhere to be found as I drove ranch roads and oil well service truck ruts, and after fifteen minutes I stopped the car on a hilltop, hoping he'd come back to the house while I was gone. I didn't want to think about the possibility that something had happened to him. But as I thought about it I knew I should trust him, and his instincts, the way Tom taught me to trust myself when I was David's age. At that point in my life I'd been unsure of almost everything I did because no one told me when I got things right, only when I got them wrong. Everyone but Tom. Tom taught me to have confidence in my own abilities and judgment without the need for approval I wanted so desperately from my father and mother. But Howard was the only one to earn Lee King's approval and even that came with conditions, because Howard couldn't ride a horse or work out in the heat doing ranch chores. He preferred the solitude of his room and the company of books to outdoor life. And Helen never failed to remind us of our father's disappointments with Howard, or with the rest of us.

I got out of the car and leaned against the fender, gazing across drought-yellowed pastures, thinking it was an odd time to be caught up in those old memories—perhaps it was because David was missing with a gun in his hands and I wanted to believe my son had the same self-reliance Tom taught me. I remembered a time when Tom and I were at one of the creeks on the northwest side of the ranch . . . it was autumn, and Tom stopped the truck to show me a flock of northern geese settling onto the surface of a deep pool where the creek made a bend. I was twelve or thirteen, still playing cowboys and Indians with toy guns and a vivid imagination.

"If I had a rifle like Roy Rogers I bet I could shoot four or five of them," I said, imagining the bang of a rifle thundering in my ears and goose feathers flying everywhere.

Tom wagged his head. "Why in the world would you want to shoot somethin' as beautiful as them?" he asked, squinting in the glare of a red sunset as more geese fluttered gracefully to the mirrorlike surface of the pool, cutting V-shaped ripples across silvery water where they landed. "It'd be different if you was hungry, needin' somethin' to eat. But we ain't hungry, so it don't make a lick of sense to kill somethin' just to watch it die or for the sake of provin' you've got good aim."

I recalled being puzzled by Tom's logic then. "You shoot a gun," I said. "I've seen you kill rattlesnakes with your pistol lots of times, and you shot that skunk that was under the floor of the hay barn."

"There's a difference. Rattlesnakes needed killin' because it was calvin' time an' them baby calves ain't got no sense about snakes 'til they get older. The skunk was sprayin' the hay every time I walked across them boards an' a cow won't eat hay that's all stunk-up with skunk spray. A gun's for killin' things when there's a need. You've been watchin' too many Roy Rogers movies without understandin' they ain't for real. It's pretendin'. A man don't need a gun to be a man, Matthew. See all them geese yonder? What sort of man does it take to put a bullet through a beautiful animal that don't harm nobody? Them birds make this world a prettier place to live, if you take the time to look."

Remembering that long-ago conversation now, I knew that Tom hadn't approved when Tommy Lee and David were in the back of the truck shooting rabbits—and neither had I. So why had I allowed David to do it? I made up my mind to take the rifle away from him the minute he got back to the house.

As I opened the car door I glanced across a bed of prickly pear cactus where a jackrabbit was hunkered down between blades laden with thorns. A few lone cactus blooms had somehow managed to survive the drought, tiny pink blossoms resembling fruit more than flowers. I stood there a moment watching the jackrabbit while it watched me, its instincts keeping it frozen in hiding among the cactus needles—the rabbit's ears lay flat against its neck to keep from being silhouetted above the fan-shaped green blades surrounding it. A hot dry wind was blowing in my face as I stared into the rabbit's liquid brown eyes. "Tom was right," I said softly. "Why kill a beautiful animal that doesn't harm anyone when it only makes the world a prettier place to live."

When I got back to the house I saw everyone gathered outside by the patio gate, everyone except Diane, who was still passed out on the sofa, and Cathy. I hurried toward the group and found David the center of attention.

He was holding the rifle in one hand and a dead jackrabbit in the other, gripping the animal by its ears. Blood dribbled on the concrete patio below and on David's expensive tennis shoes and socks.

Martha spoke to me first. "Your son's a born killer. It's in his genes."

"Where's Cathy?"

"In the bathroom throwing up. She almost fainted. Howard had to help her to the bathroom."

"Look at this, Dad!" David cried, holding his rabbit higher. "I got it with my first shot. Whamo! Right through his head."

"Aren't you proud of him, Matt?" Tommy Lee asked, smiling.

"Immensely. Take it outside the wall, David, and then clean that blood off the cement. You'll have to wipe your shoes before your mother sees them." I was furious yet I wasn't going to let it show, not until later, when David and I were alone.

"She already saw 'em," Carl said, chuckling. "She's in the can right now, pukin' her head off."

"Shut up, Carl," Suzan said. "Some people have weaker stomachs."

"Hell, it's just a dead rabbit."

"Shut *up*, Carl! The kids might hear you and they'll want to see it too."

"I don't see a damn thing wrong with that," Carl argued, his face turning red. "I'm gonna get Jody a gun for Christmas, one like that, a twenty-two rifle. A single shot. Every normal boy in the world wants a gun."

"He's only eight," Suzan replied as David walked through the gate with his prize.

Howard came over to me as I was going in to check on Cathy. "It's barbaric," Howard whispered. "Carl Westerman has to be the crudest man I ever met, wanting to give an eight-year-old a gun. And what's the sense in killing rabbits after all?"

"Tommy Lee loaned David the gun," I said, closing the door behind us, thinking this might be the only thing Howard and I would agree upon the rest of the day. "I wish he hadn't. It's only made a bad day worse."

Howard caught me by the arm. "You and I will need

to talk, after we hear what Mother has to say. I expect
. . . a few problems from some of the others. Helen
doesn't want the ranch sold. I know it will cause some
dissension.''

"I think that's putting it mildly. Why does she want us
to keep it?''

"Sentimental value. This is where she and Lee lived
their entire married lives. She wants it placed in trust. All
income from the property will be divided five ways, after
the expenses, naturally enough.''

"Tommy Lee and Suzan want to sell it. Martha hates
this place, so she'll side with them.''

"It won't come to a vote," Howard confided. "Helen
gave me her instructions. She insists it must be done before
she dies.''

I envisioned all sorts of problems. "If one or two of
them hire lawyers, it might get ugly. Someone could try to
break her will, saying she wasn't of sound mind lately.
Individual testimony as to Helen's mental fitness can weigh
heavily in a judge's decision. If all three of them swear she
was losing her mind it could invalidate everything.''

"She is *not* losing her mind and you know it.''

"I didn't say she was. It's what they might say that
stands a chance of changing her plans.''

"Surely none of them would be so selfish, so inconsid-
erate.''

"It's because they are selfish that the possibility exists,
Howard.''

"But there is more than enough money in her investments and certificates of deposit to last everyone a lifetime,
and almost an equal amount set aside in trusts for her
grandchildren. How can anyone justify going against
Mother's last wishes?''

"Greed," I said simply. "Tommy Lee has never been
satisfied with what he got, nor has Suzan. Martha believes

strongly in her foundation, and you heard her say she needed more support from contributors.''

"Which presents another potential problem," Howard continued quietly. "Helen has instructed me to stop all charitable donations to the Carter Foundation. She believes it's wasteful when her money could be used for more worthwhile purposes. The futures of her grandchildren, for instance.''

"Did she tell all this to Martha?" I asked.

"Not everything. Only that reduced oil prices were forcing her to cut contributions significantly. She didn't say entirely, which is what she plans to do. Martha's personal income from the trusts will not change, but donations to the foundation are to be eliminated entirely. Helen will tell everyone what she intends to do after dinner, when we have our meeting upstairs.''

"Ah yes, the annual meeting upstairs. There won't be a dry eye in the house this year.''

"I hope you'll agree to accept her position, after all she's done for us. I don't expect some of the others to be reasonable about it.''

Diane sat up unexpectedly and pulled the cloth off her face. "Fix me a drink, darling," she whimpered. "Where is everybody?''

"Outside looking at David's dead rabbit," I said. "It's bleeding all over the concrete. Tommy Lee has proven to be an excellent instructor in the fine art of killing small game. He has good teaching instincts. My son is an accomplished hunter after a single lesson.''

"It's still bleeding?" Diane asked, glancing through a patio door. "How ghastly. Please fix me that drink, Howard. Not too much tonic.''

"I'd better go check on Cathy," I said, heading for the bathroom at the end of the hall.

I saw light coming from a crack below the bathroom door and I knocked gently. "Are you okay?" I asked.

"Hell no, I'm not okay. Did you see David's dead rabbit?" Cathy wouldn't open the door.

"I saw it. I'm sorry I agreed to let him learn to shoot. I know it was a mistake."

Silence.

"Please open the door, Cathy. It's almost time to eat."

More silence.

"I said I was sorry. The day's almost over and then we'll be leaving. I promise I won't ask you to come back here. This will be the last time you'll ever be in Eden. I'll give you my word on it."

"Your word is worthless. You said we would *never* let David have a gun."

"It isn't his gun. It's Tommy Lee's; however I agree I made a terrible mistake letting him learn to shoot it."

"You lied to me."

"I didn't lie to you. I wasn't thinking and it won't happen again."

The door opened a crack. Cathy was wiping her face with a wet washcloth and I could see she'd been crying. "Let's go home right now," she said. "If you love me, we'll leave immediately. I can't take any more of your family, or this madness. This is a loony bin."

"I know," I whispered, putting my arms around her waist even though she tried to pull back. "I grew up in this place. I know my family is crazy. My friends in school used to envy me because we had all this land, all this money. But what they didn't know was how much I envied them, because they led normal lives, lived among normal people who loved each other and showed it in normal ways. Please be patient a few more hours. Mother is dying. This will be our last visit. I promise."

"I should be more understanding," Cathy whispered, resting her head against my shoulder. "I'm sorry."

I held her. "She'll tell us about her plans for the estate after dinner and then we'll be going home. I'll fix you a drink. I need one myself and I suspect I'll need several more before the day is over. It isn't going to be pleasant. The real fighting is about to begin, but after today you won't ever have to listen to it again."

"I don't want another drink," Cathy said, sniffling back a new rush of tears. "I just want to go home . . ."

8

HELEN CAME DOWNSTAIRS AT THREE o'clock, and when we saw her at the bottom of the staircase conversation stopped. She gave us a look, sparkling blue eyes pausing when they fell on each of her children. It was so quiet I could hear the whisper of air coming through vents in the den.

"My, what a cheerful group," she said, her deep voice, one that could reassure as well as cut to the bone, was cold as ice now. "It would appear Howard told you about my condition. Let's not spoil our dinner with somber faces and questions about how long I'm expected to live. We'll talk about it later, just the five of us."

"We're all so sorry to hear about it, Mother," Suzan said as she walked toward the stairs with her arms spread to embrace Helen.

Helen halted her by raising the palm of her hand. "None of that now. We'll say our good-byes upstairs."

Tommy Lee had gotten out of his chair. "Why didn't you tell us sooner?" he asked. "We'd have come to see you, or somethin'."

"Like sending flowers? I didn't want flowers. I wanted all of us to be together again. I don't want your sympathy. I will explain everything after dinner."

I stood up. "You shouldn't expect us to act like nothing is wrong. That's unrealistic. Like everyone else, I'm very sad to learn about your illness."

She looked at me. "Of all my children, Matthew, you

had the most compassion. I fear you've lost some of it while practicing law. I hope not. Compassion is a rare quality. I do not expect any of you to behave as though nothing is wrong, although I hope we can avoid sentimental scenes. I find that sort of thing to be a waste of time and completely unnecessary. I am dying. We all die sooner or later. My time has come and I've accepted it. Now all that remains is to discuss what's to be done with my estate, your father's estate. It has provided well for us. After we eat we'll talk about it. Privately.''

"I'm sorry, Mother," Howard said, "but I felt I had to tell them. We all knew something was wrong."

"We're all real sorry about it," Carl said, leaning against the bar with a beer in his hand.

Diane started to cry. "It's so sad, Helen," she whimpered, wiping her eyes with the rag she had used to cover her face earlier.

"You're simply drunk, Diane," Helen said. "As soon as your head is clear you'll feel better." She looked at the rest of us. "I'll put the food out. Maria set the table last night. Please ask your children to conduct themselves in an appropriate manner while we're eating. It isn't too much to expect good behavior at the dinner table, I should hope."

Helen walked past us toward the kitchen. No one said a word until Helen had left the den.

"Please tell her I'm not drunk, Howard," Diane said. "That isn't fair, to say that in front of everybody."

"She didn't really mean it," Howard assured her, moving over to the sofa and placing his hand on Diane's shoulder.

"Yes she did," Martha said softly, staring out a window at rolling hills baked by summer sun. "Helen King means everything she says. I've never known her to say anything she didn't mean." Martha's face was pale. Ever since I can remember Martha was prone to long periods of depression, staying upstairs in her room for days at a time in the summer when school was out, having meals brought up by our maid. There were times when she wouldn't answer my knock on her bedroom door no matter how hard I pleaded for her to let me in—I'd only wanted to talk, to find out what was wrong. Once, I overheard Helen telling Howard that some doctor in Houston had pronounced Martha a manic depressive. At the time I didn't know what the term meant.

"I'll help her with the food," Suzan offered, heading for the kitchen.

A brief silence followed, until Carl said, "Helen can be a real bitch at times, can't she?"

"Are you speaking of your wife?" Martha asked.

Carl had been drinking too much to follow Martha's sarcasm. "Hell no, I'm talkin' about Helen."

"I'm not drunk," Diane sobbed quietly, looking at Howard with tears brimming in her eyes. "Tell her I'm not drunk."

Cathy reached for my hand, pulling me back down in the loveseat. "I'd better help out in the kitchen too," she said in her softest voice. She patted my knee and got up, disappearing into the hall.

"You're drunker'n shit, Diane," Tommy Lee said. "You damn near always get drunk while you're here."

"Be quiet, Tommy," Howard warned, staring at his brother. "Things are bad enough without you egging them on. Please show a little respect for Mother by keeping your mouth shut about things that don't concern you. My wife is not drunk. Couldn't we have just one Fourth of July without a big quarrel?"

Diane buried her face in the rag and wept.

"See what you've done?" Howard asked heatedly. "You ruined her day with your false accusations."

Martha said, "The day was ruined by coming here, Howard. It isn't possible to ruin something twice, is it? If it's ruined, it's already ruined. Period."

I reminded Howard, "It was Mother who accused Diane of being drunk."

The room was silent now, save for Diane's muffled weeping.

"Let's change the subject," Carl suggested, moving around the bar for another beer. "I can't wait to sink my teeth into those ribs. Ol' Tom makes about the best barbecue sauce I ever tasted."

I sat nursing a Scotch watching my brothers and sister and Carl and Diane, wondering which one would strike the first legal blow when Helen told us about her plans for the ranch. Down in my gut I knew it could never happen peacefully. In the past we took sides during arguments on the Fourth of July, nurturing old jealousies, dislikes, envy. But with millions of dollars hanging in the balance, the value of the ranch boosted by future oil earnings, this would not be merely a name-calling contest ending as soon as we headed home. Far too much was at stake. For the purpose of estimating estate taxes, the ranch and mineral rights had been appraised at forty-seven million dollars, back in the seventies. It was certainly worth less now with oil prices down, but not a hell of a lot less. The land, Helen's house, and the oil reserves were easily worth thirty-five million. During better times those oil wells had generated cash payments sufficient to give Helen King a net worth of roughly one hundred and fifty million dollars in money, stocks, bonds, and land. When our sibling infighting started it wouldn't be over nickels and dimes.

"Why's everybody so goddamn quiet?" Carl asked. "Ain't this supposed to be a party?"

"You have all the sensitivity of a clam, Carl," Howard

said. "We just learned our mother is fatally ill. Have you no feelings whatsoever?"

"I'm feelin' hungry," he replied. "The old woman's gonna die. What's the big deal? Everybody's gotta die sometime. My wife hates comin' here every year. Nobody likes Helen, so why does everybody make such a big deal about it? It's only because she's rich that everybody kisses her ass."

Howard's flush became a crimson shade. "You're an idiot, Carl, a complete idiot. Were it not for Helen's generosity you'd be bankrupt. You can't draw a straight line with a ruler if you had all day to do it and you have no business sense at all."

Carl turned away from the bar doubling up his fists. "If it wasn't for you bein' such a four-eyed sissy I'd bust your fuckin' skull for sayin' that."

"Now now, children," Martha said, getting up to make another drink. "Violence isn't the answer. Let's try to muddle through this awful day without bloodshed. We usually settle our differences with insults, or deeply personal humiliations, reminders of our colorful pasts. We have a tradition to uphold. It's time to eat, the high point of our celebration. I suggest we walk to the dining room and sit down like the cultured people we are, instead of being reduced to throwing punches, bleeding all over Helen's polished floors and expensive rugs like a pack of wild animals."

"Tell Helen I'm not drunk," Diane muttered, holding her face in the rag. "I don't want her thinking less of me."

"It would be almost impossible for her to think any less of you," Martha said, sloshing Scotch into her glass and adding a few small cubes of ice.

"I'll get the children out of the playroom," I said. I'd had enough of Martha's acid rambling. "Their screaming should be sufficient to change everyone's mood."

Howard was still glowering at Carl as I went to the patio door. "He shouldn't have said that about my wife, and Tommy Lee is no better for saying what he did," he mumbled angrily.

"Forget it," I told him. "You can get even with Carl when you forget Suzan's trust fund interest check at the first of the month. The next time Tommy Lee needs a loan you can say you were out of the office and missed his call. You've got the purse strings, Howard, and they are more powerful in this family than a right hook or a stiff left jab."

We sat down at the dinner table, a twenty-foot piece of the world's best mahogany polished to a shine that would be the envy of any mirror. Straight-backed chairs, as uncomfortable as any I'd ever sat upon, held nine adults and five children. We drank from crystal goblets and served ourselves plates of food on china so exquisite and rare that dealers in antiques could only guess at their value. We used silverware polished to a high brilliance and the best linen napkins money could buy.

Helen sat at the head of the table. We assumed our regular places flanking our mother, the chairs in which she asked us to sit having some significance known only to her. Children sat at the far end of the table. David was afforded a special place between me and his mother, I suppose because of his advancing age.

"Pass the ribs," Carl said.

"Women are served first," Suzan declared, taking a rack of ribs for herself. "It's called etiquette."

"He'll never be able to pronounce it," Martha muttered as a plate of ribs was handed to her.

"Like hell I can't," Carl said, grinning. "They're called ribs."

His feeble attempt at humor went unnoticed. Ribs and

bowls of beans and potato salad and cole slaw went back and forth from one family member to the next.

"Gina's chewin' bubble gum," Jody announced as he took a rib and dropped it on his plate. "I told her she had to spit it out an' she won't."

"Spit the gum out!" Suzan snapped, glaring down the table at her daughter.

Regina put a mushy ball of pink gum on the edge of her plate and stuck her tongue out at Jody.

"These ribs are great!" Carl declared, cheeks stuffed with meat, sauce dribbling down his chin. "Tell ol' Tom he did a hell of a good job again this year."

Cathy glanced over to me, taking a small portion of potato salad.

Helen fixed Carl with a steely stare. "Please refrain from using curse words at the dinner table, Carl," she said.

"All I said was, he did a hell of a fine job?"

Martha stirred aimlessly through her beans. "Mr. Westerman is not aware that hell is a cuss word, Mother."

"Timmy knows a new cuss word," Becky said, pushing cole slaw to one side of her plate where the juice wouldn't mingle with the rest of her food. "He yells 'shit' across the fence when nobody is listenin'. Ricky yells it back real loud . . ."

"Be quiet!" Diane snapped. "No one wants to hear that kind of language at the dinner table."

"What does it mean, Mama?" Becky asked. "Timmy won't tell me, but I know it's a bad word."

Howard took control of the situation when Diane hesitated a moment too long. "It isn't a word you need to know, Rebecca, and I shall speak to Timothy privately about it after we eat."

Helen's cold stare reached all of us before she returned to her plate of barbecue.

"I'll tell Becky what it means," David whispered to Cathy as he passed a plate of sourdough bread down the table.

"You'll keep your mouth closed," I said, discovering that I had no appetite.

9

I WAS OUTSIDE SMOKING A CIGARETTE IN THE driveway, dreading our meeting upstairs, when Tom drove by on his way to the front gates. Heading home, I judged. He stopped his truck in a cloud of dust and rolled down the window.

"How was the meat this time?" he asked as I ambled over to talk. After this afternoon's revelation I felt I really needed to talk to him.

"As good as ever," I said, trying to sound cheerful. "Maybe the best you ever cooked."

"What's wrong, Matthew?" he asked, bunching his thick gray eyebrows. Tom always had an uncanny ability to read my moods.

"Helen told us she's dying. She hasn't explained everything yet, but she will after we go upstairs."

"I've been suspectin' somethin' like that," he said. "She ain't been herself lately. She's been real short-tempered with me an' Maria lately. I knowed somethin' was wrong."

"The fighting has already begun between my brothers and sisters over her money, and the ranch. The ranch will be placed in trust so it can't be sold, and that started everybody arguing over who gets what. They sounded like a bunch of hyenas, Tom, picking Helen's bones before she's buried. It makes me sick to listen to it."

Tom's expression softened. "You ain't like them, son. You never was. You've got a real good head on your shoul-

ders an' you never let your family's money change you. I
was always proud of you for that.''

Hearing Tom say he was proud of me came close to
bringing me to tears. I looked into his rheumy brown eyes.
''I owe you for that,'' I said, feeling my throat constrict
with emotion. ''It was you who showed me how to balance
things, how to feel good about myself. I never could work
up the nerve to say thank you for all the times you talked
to me. I suppose it was just as important that you listened
to me too. You gave me confidence in myself I never would
have had. My father and mother were always telling me
what I did wrong. I know this sounds sort of dumb to say it
now, but I'll never forget what you did for me when I was
a kid. I still think about it. There were times when I felt
you were the only real friend I had.''

Tom looked away suddenly, staring through the windshield of his pickup truck like what I'd said embarrassed
him. ''You was always a good boy, Matthew, an' that
comes from inside. Wasn't nothin' I did. It was in you to
start with.''

I felt like we were both a bit embarrassed now, but I'd
said things I needed to say even though they came years too
late to make much of a difference. I heard the front door of
the house close behind me. ''We'll talk some more another
time,'' I said as Tom put the truck in gear. He nodded and
pressed the accelerator.

David came out with a downcast look on his face. I had
excused myself from the table early, as blackberry cobbler
was being passed around. I'd eaten just enough barbecue to
worsen indigestion brought on by too much Scotch and the
same case of jangled nerves I had every year on the Fourth
at Eden.

''What's the matter?'' I asked as Tom drove off.

''Mom's mad at me because of the rabbit. She said she
was gonna kill me when we got home.''

"She doesn't mean it literally."

He watched my cigarette. "I tried smokin' once with Bobby Roberts. It made me sick."

"I'm glad it did. You shouldn't ever develop the habit. I wish I could quit. I've tried a thousand times."

"Mom told me Grandma's dyin'." He said it looking down at his bloodstained shoes as though the subject embarrassed him.

"She told us earlier. When we go upstairs she'll tell us more."

"Nobody acts very sad about it except you an' Uncle Howard. Diane's cryin', but it ain't because of that. She keeps tellin' everybody she ain't drunk. Seems like she's always cryin' over somethin'."

"Please stop saying 'ain't.' It's poor grammar. Your Aunt Diane is having some emotional problems. It's nothing to worry about."

"I feel sorry for Grandma, only I don't know what to say to her. Should I just tell her I'm sorry she's gonna be dead?" He had his hands thrust in his pockets, toeing rocks in the driveway without looking at me.

"You could simply say you're sorry she's ill. That'll be enough."

"Nobody likes her, Dad, not even you. How come you don't like your own mom?"

"It isn't that I don't like her, exactly. We just didn't get along well when I was a boy. We still don't. She can be a cold person at times. She loves us, although she doesn't know how to show it appropriately, I suppose. It's hard to explain."

"She never liked me much. She gives me a hug every year, but it doesn't feel real. It's like . . . she does it because she thinks she has to, or somethin'."

"I think it's because she doesn't know how to hug

someone, or how to let go of her feelings. She keeps them inside.''

"It's like she ain't got any."

I ground out my cigarette. "Stop saying 'ain't.' ''

David squinted in the sun's glare, following the gravel road leading to the highway with his eyes. "After she dies we won't have to come back here anymore," he said quietly. "Mom'll be happy about that. She hates this place, an' she doesn't really like Grandma all that much either.''

"I know. Helen can be very hard on outsiders sometimes. I share Cathy's feelings about this house. I wasn't happy here.''

"She's rich an' everybody acts like they like her because of that. How come you weren't happy livin' in a fancy house with a swimmin' pool an' bein' rich?''

"Money isn't everything. It can't make you happy."

"My friend Bobby says we're rich. Are we really?"

"We're better off than most."

"Are you a millionaire? Bobby's dad says you are."

I wondered briefly if I should tell him the truth, how it might change him, alter his ambitions. Knowing he would inherit huge sums of money, that I was several times a millionaire, might not be good for him. I'd hidden from him that he was already a millionaire himself, a trust fund established in his name by Helen the year he was born. "We have a million dollars, David, but you shouldn't think about that. You'll want to make money yourself one of these days, your own money. Being happy can be worth a great deal more than money.''

David's gaze was fixed on distant oil wells now and his brow was deeply furrowed. "Havin' a bunch of money sure never made Grandma happy, did it? She lives all alone way out here so she can't even go to a movie when she wants. She don't even own a VCR. Looks like she'd have gotten real lonely all by herself.''

"I don't ever remember seeing Helen when she was happy. I hardly ever heard her laugh at anything. Maybe she was happy after all and never showed it."

I heard the front door open. Martha came out on the porch with a drink in her hand.

"It's time," she said. "The queen bee has summoned us to her chambers. I'm sure you'll need a fresh drink before we go upstairs. I'm taking a bottle of Scotch, but it's all mine."

"I'll be right there," I said.

Martha nodded and went back in.

"Aunt Martha doesn't ever act happy either," David said as we turned for the house. "She's always makin' some wisecrack about everybody else. Uncle Tommy Lee's the only one who ever has any fun around here. Boy, he sure can shoot good."

"He shoots well," I reminded. "Does anyone at school speak correct English?"

Our father's study was lined with bookcases. A rolltop desk sat beside a window overlooking hills to the south. A round, clawfoot oak table occupied the middle of the room. Six chairs were set around it, six assigned seats. Howard would be at Helen's right elbow. My chair was to her left. Tommy Lee sat next to me and Martha sat beside Howard, leaving Suzan directly across from her mother.

We filed in one at a time, leaving our spouses and children downstairs. Howard carried his briefcase. A large manila envelope lay in front of Helen's chair.

"Please be seated, everyone," Helen said. Martha and I placed our drinks on the table in plain sight. A bottle of Scotch jutted from Martha's purse beside her feet. Tommy Lee put a beer in front of him and another on the floor. Suzan kept her glass between her thighs. Howard was the only one of Helen's children who came upstairs without liquid fortification.

Helen allowed her gaze to wander slowly around the table as she stood behind her chair. "As usual," she said in a rasping monotone, "Howard has prepared an annual report of our earnings. He'll hand them out now. You will note that oil revenues are down considerably . . ." She waited for Howard to hand us bound copies of the year's financial report. I took mine and left it closed in front of me. Helen and Howard would tell us all we needed to know. Very little changed from year to year, with the exception of oil well earnings. We all knew the price of crude these days.

As though with the intention of adding ceremony this year, Helen drew back her chair and stood in her usual place, resting her hands on the tabletop rather than sitting down. She continued to stare at each of us for an inordinately long period of time.

"This year," she began, "we have important matters to talk about which will bring about significant changes. As Howard has already told you, I am dying. Doctors found an inoperable tumor in my brain and the cancer has spread to my lymph nodes. They tell me I may have six months to live, possibly less."

"Oh, Mother," Suzan whispered, putting a hand over her lips. Tears formed in her eyes.

"Please be quiet, dear," Helen said. "I ask that all of you respect my wishes in this. No slobbering or crying, even if any of you feel moved to tears. Hysterics are for children and those who lack intelligence. We have very important business matters to discuss affecting your futures and the futures of my grandchildren. My illness has forced me to make difficult decisions with regard to my estate. I felt that as long as I was alive I could make individual exceptions. That will change. Howard has been given my written instructions. He will begin at once to see that my wishes are carried out. I've thought things out carefully in each and every case. My mind is made up to go forward with a plan to keep the estate intact. Let's not have any argument over any of the items. I will not be swayed by protests or even the most impassioned pleas. As you know, I've left each of you a substantial fortune in trust, and your children have been equally provided for."

"You've been very generous," Howard said quietly.

It was then I noticed Helen's eyes were dry—she could talk about her own death without shedding a tear and I couldn't begin to imagine it. She knew this was our last family gathering and showed no visible emotion.

"This ranch is being placed in trust," she continued. "It cannot be sold or mortgaged as long as property taxes are paid, which I have provided for with a separate trust fund that will automatically pay whatever is due. The house may be used by any of you, and maintained by funds I've set aside solely for this purpose. Otherwise, it will be locked, never to be rented or leased to anyone besides the immediate family or any of your children. All income from the ranch will be deposited in an account managed by Howard, or his assigns, and divided equally among you at the end of every year."

Tommy Lee was visibly upset. "How come you're doin' this, Mother? Once you're . . . gone, none of us wants to come back to Eden." He glanced around the table. "Am I right?" he asked us.

"Not me," Martha said softly. "Not ever."

Suzan spoke. "But there are a lot of memories here. Maybe Mother's right not to sell it."

"Your memories about Eden all came from the back-seat of a car," Martha said. "What's that got to do with the ranch?"

Before Suzan could respond Helen raised a hand.

"Please be quiet, all of you. I will not change my mind. This house, and the ranch, will be preserved intact as a monument to your father's memory for at least one hundred years. This is a provision of the trust Howard will establish."

"A hundred years?" Tommy Lee asked.

"Shut up, Tommy," Martha snapped. "There's more."

Helen looked at Martha. "Yes, dear, there is more. There will be no more charitable contributions made by the estate, nor will there be any more loans. The future of oil looks uncertain and in order to preserve what has been made from it, the balance of my estate, certificates of deposit, all stocks and bonds and deeded land, will be placed in a permanent trust. All interest earnings and dividends shall be divided among the five of you at the end of the year. The principal will remain intact for as long as any descendant of the King family lives. In the event there are no living heirs, the trust will be donated to Baylor University, Lee's alma mater, with the stipulation that a building be erected in Lee King's name."

I listened, saying nothing, certain that lawsuits to break the trust would be crowding district court civil dockets before the first leaves changed color in the fall. Tommy Lee and Suzan and Martha would be calling the best lawyers money could buy by noon tomorrow. Howard had been right to expect difficulties, but I didn't think he could guess how relentless efforts would be to block Helen's moves.

"The foundation will have to close," Martha said, pouring Scotch to the rim of her glass. "All my work, all my efforts to preserve something important to southwestern history and art over the years will have been for nothing. You said you were cutting contributions. You didn't say you were ending them entirely."

"It was a difficult decision," Helen replied. "I had to put our family's needs first."

"But what about me?" Tommy Lee asked. "The car business has been rocky as hell lately. I need those loans once in a while."

"You never paid any of them back," Howard said.

"You told us the car business was great," Martha remembered in a decidedly sour voice. "Was that all a crock of shit?"

It was as if Helen had been expecting this. She sat down, folding her arms across her chest.

Before Tommy Lee could respond, Suzan said, "Carl's going to be so disappointed, Mother. We were wanting to buy this ranch at Alpine, twenty thousand acres. We'd planned to talk to you after everyone left about loaning us the money."

"No more loans," Helen said quietly. "Banks make loans for real estate all the time."

"But Carl said we'd have to pay real high interest. If we got it from you, it wouldn't be so high."

Howard cleared his throat. "He hasn't repaid a dime on the loan Mother made him six years ago. No principal, no interest."

Tommy Lee came to his feet, muscles working in his clenched jaw. "This is your doin', Howard, you wimpy son of a bitch! You want control of the whole goddamn thing, don't you?"

"This was not Howard's idea," Helen said, giving Tommy Lee a stony look he should have recognized, and feared.

Tommy Lee pointed an accusing finger at Howard. "I know it was your idea!" he cried. "You're gonna regret this. The rest of us won't let you get away with it!" He gave Helen a glare as he picked up his beer. "To hell with this!" he shouted. "We all should have known Howard

would try an' screw us out of what's rightfully ours. To
hell with this an' to hell with you, Howard."

Tommy Lee stormed out, slamming the door behind
him. We heard his footsteps in the hall.

"I think it's safe to say he isn't too happy with your
plans for our future, Mother," Martha said.

"Carl isn't gonna like 'em either," Suzan sniffled. "I
told him for sure you'd loan us the money. We already put
some money down on that place to hold it. Escrow, I think
he said. Carl's gonna be mad at me because I nearly promised him you'd loan it to us."

Helen did not lose her composure when she said, "I
felt sure it would not be popular. I'm doing what's best for
all of my children and grandchildren."

"I'd better go downstairs and tell Carl," Suzan said.
"He's gonna throw a fit." She got up and left the room.
Helen did not say another word to her.

Martha picked up her copy of the financial report. "If
we are finished here, I think I'll go home. I need to tell a
few of my employees about closing the foundation, so
they'll have as much time as possible to start looking for
new jobs." She looked across the table at Helen. "I'm so
sorry to learn of your tumor, Mother. I'll be in touch."

As Martha got out of her chair, Helen stood up.

"I too am sorry," Helen remarked, "sorry that you
feel I've slighted you. I know you loved the foundation and
its work. I saw no way to do things differently. I believed
there was a risk draining family resources for the foundation's sake, but you will not starve. You have been well
provided for personally."

Martha walked around the table to Helen. "You've
always been a good provider, Helen." She embraced
Mother stiffly and walked out of the study without saying
good-bye to Howard or to me.

I looked at Howard. His face was unusually pale. He

took off his glasses and wiped them on the front of his shirt
while Helen was sitting down.

I examined Mother's eyes when I thought I saw them
sparkle with moisture. She was staring out at the ranch
through a pane of glass. I was wrong. Her eyes were dry,
expressionless, glinting in the light from the window.

HOWARD AND I SAT BESIDE HELEN FOR AL-
most a full minute in total silence while she stared vacantly
out the window.

"Are you all right, Mother?" Howard asked.

She returned immediately from her distant thoughts.
"I am doing what's best," she said again, no suggestion of
any emotion in her voice. "Tommy Lee is irresponsible, as
you both know. He spends every cent he has on self-indul-
gence without the slightest concern for his financial future,
or his children's. He gambles heavily. Placing the ranch and
my estate in trust will protect him from himself. He was
irresponsible as a child. Suzan, on the other hand, is easily
influenced by Carl. Neither one has a shred of business
sense. If I loaned them the money to buy this ranch in
Alpine, half of it would become Carl's under community
property laws in Texas. Should he divorce her, or should
she divorce him, half of the investment would be lost. I
don't see how their marriage can last. He's an ignorant
dolt who cannot function on his own. I was sorry to disap-
point Suzan, but I'm doing it for her own good."

"You could record a lien against the property," I said,
trying not to sound like I was for or against it. "I could
foreclose on behalf of the estate in the event he misses a
scheduled payment, or if they divorce. Or you could pur-
chase the land in Suzan's name and have it declared separate property. That way, Carl couldn't get his hands on any

of it if either one files for divorce. I could do the paper-work . . ."

Helen shook her head. "It would only cause further difficulties between you and your sister. There is quite enough of that the way things are. Let their anger be directed at me for denying the loan. I won't be here much longer to experience it and nothing will have been done to widen a gap between you and Suzan."

"They are blaming me for this," Howard said, sweating in spite of the air-conditioning.

Helen turned to him. "As the firstborn son of Lee King you have a duty to your family after I'm gone. It isn't a popular position to be in . . . I'm well aware of that. As best I could I've been grooming you, so to speak, to handle this tremendous responsibility. You must not let feelings or sentiment get in the way of sound business decisions. There will be times, I'm sure, when you'll be sorely tempted to make exceptions. But you mustn't be swayed by emotion. Your father devoted his life to making this fortune so that each of you would be spared the hardships he knew as a boy. Your father was very poor. He applied himself, and took frightful risks to acquire this land, borrowing money to buy acreage a small piece at a time without any guarantee the oil he believed was here actually existed. He worked day and night to develop new wells and invest his earnings wisely. By virtue of his hard work he amassed a fortune, and you have been entrusted with it now. I do hope you'll manage it wisely."

I thought, but did not say aloud, that managing the estate required very little know-how or decision-making if it were set up the way Helen wanted. Howard would be reduced to writing a few checks and making deposits, hardly more than a clerk, unless you counted making decisions on which bonds or stocks to buy or sell, and where to invest in certificates of deposit.

Helen was looking at me now. She picked up the envelope in front of her and handed it to me. "As always, we must be practical. In the event of Howard's untimely death, you will become administrator of the estate. The necessary documents have been prepared by Fullerton and Haynes. Your copy is in the envelope. Mr. Fullerton will file them, should they ever be needed."

"I'm in good health, Mother," Howard said. "You shouldn't be worrying yourself with those kinds of details when you aren't feeling well."

I put the envelope aside with my annual report.

"I'm feeling well enough," she said. "Every detail must be attended to now. I'm told I'll be bedridden within a few months and given painkillers which will impair my thought processes to a degree. The trust documents are being drawn by Mr. Fullerton for my signature. As soon as I have signed everything they will be forwarded to you at the bank. Ownership of all certificates of deposit and my stocks and bonds must be transferred immediately. Deeds will take longer; however I will sign a power of attorney so you may execute them for me."

"I'm curious, Mother," I said. "Why didn't you trust me to prepare these legal documents for you?"

She gazed into my eyes. "It was never a question of trust, Matthew. Other members of the family might have doubts about how they were treated if you handled any of this. I wanted to spare you that. As you've seen today, Tommy Lee is blaming Howard for what I'm doing. Martha hasn't said so, but she feels the same way, and Carl will convince Suzan it is Howard's fault when they don't get the loan they wanted. You're a good lawyer and I never doubted your judgment in legal matters. Howard alone is the one who must face accusations as administrator of my estate and he knows it. We have discussed it briefly today and he is willing to accept the responsibility. As you already know, he has been performing virtually the same duties anyway, handling investments and writing checks for interest and dividend payments to each of you."

More than willing, I thought. Holding our purse strings was terribly important to Howard. If any one of us loved the power of money as much as Helen did, it was Howard. And at times, he could wield it like a sword.

"I have the experience to handle it," Howard said, almost a boast, "and I don't mind telling the others 'no' when they ask for special consideration. I can be firm about it."

I spoke to Helen. "I hope you'll understand if we have some differences of opinion. It seems to me that Martha's request is the most unselfish. She isn't profiting from the Carter Foundation. I'm quite sure her motives are purely altruistic and for the sake of preserving art and history. Perhaps, if she were to consider changing its name to the Lee King Foundation, it would better serve our father's memory than a building at Baylor. As I am sure Howard knows, there are tax benefits from donating to a nonprofit entity. Why pay taxes to the IRS when we could make donations to a tax-exempt foundation dedicated to the preservation of something worthwhile?"

Helen's eyelids became hooded, a way of showing anger we'd all grown acutely accustomed to over the years. "I asked her to do that from the beginning and she denied me. She made dreadful statements, disrespectful remarks, about wanting to be rid of the King family name forever. Even when she divorced Ray she refused to have her maiden name restored. Why should I make donations to a foundation named after Dr. Raymond Carter? He was an egotistical bore who turned Martha against me with rhetoric and lies."

We'd come to the truth of the matter. Helen was ending all contributions to Martha's foundation because of

its name, not in the interests of preserving her estate. A
vendetta of sorts, to remind Martha that her foundation
had always depended upon Helen for its existence. Mother
was flexing her financial muscle even now, facing death.

"The tax advantages aren't all that good," Howard
said. "We have sheltered investments and tax-free bonds."

I thought I heard a distant commotion downstairs.
"Whatever you think, Howard," I said. "You're the investment specialist." I took a swallow of my drink. For
some reason I knew this wasn't the end of Helen's revela-
tions nor would it be the last we heard from Martha. I
expected a suit to block the trust would be filed in Bexar
County in San Antonio by week's end, maintaining Helen
King was not of sound mind. And if Tommy Lee joined
Martha in such a suit, Howard might soon regret his earlier
statement to the effect he could handle things. With pending litigation, Howard would be up to his ass in alligators
while Helen suffered the humiliation of examinations by
psychiatrists and psychologists, probably while lying on her
deathbed.

We heard footsteps moving quickly up the hallway.
Suzan burst in the study and motioned to Howard. "You'd
better come downstairs," she said, out of breath. "Diane
passed out and we can't wake her up. She's lying in the
middle of the floor and the kids are scared to death. She
just sort of fell over all of a sudden. Cathy's with her
now."

Howard bolted out of his chair. "She has this blood
sugar problem," he said, rushing down the hall with Suzan
close on his heels.

"She has a drinking problem," Helen said to me
coldly. "I'm quite sure it has nothing to do with her blood
sugar. The woman is an alcoholic and Howard won't admit
it."

I was suddenly uncomfortable sitting alone in this

room with my mother. "I should go down and offer my
help," I said, standing up. "We'll be back as soon as Diane
is attended to." I walked out of the study before my embarrassment showed too plainly. How could I explain the
way she made me feel to her?

I took my time going downstairs. I really didn't want
to help with putting Diane to bed or much of anything
else. Right now all I wanted was to go back to Austin, to
forget about today and all the Fourth of Julys we'd spent
here.

What I found in the den wasn't what I expected. Howard was sitting on the floor with blood running from his
nose. Tommy Lee stood over him with doubled fists. Howard's glasses lay smashed on a throw rug beside him. Cathy
had her back to the wall near the fireplace, her skin the
color of milk. Diane lay on the sofa with the cloth over her
eyes and forehead. Suzan had her hand over her mouth, her
eyes wide, standing near the bar with an ice pack. The
smaller children, Timmy and Becky and Jody and Regina,
stood outside with their faces pressed to the patio glass
doors watching what had happened in the den. Carl was
sitting by the pool drinking a beer as though he hadn't
noticed what was going on. David stood behind Carl's
chair, some of the pink missing in his cheeks.

Cathy spoke to me in a strangled voice. "He hit him,"
she said, pointing to Tommy Lee. "He hit Howard in the
face."

"Goddamn right I did," Tommy Lee snarled, glancing
over his shoulder at me. "I'll hit you too, Matt, if you try
an' stop me from whippin' Howard's ass. He's got one
comin' for what he did to us."

I walked over cautiously, staying just out of Tommy
Lee's reach. "It appears you've already done it, Tommy.
This is no way to settle our differences. Let him up. You've
broken his glasses."

"That ain't all I'm gonna break," Tommy Lee said, staying right where he was. "If he tries to get up I'm gonna break his fuckin' jaw."

"Leave him alone," I said, summoning more courage than I truly had, stepping between them to help Howard to his feet. "I think you made your point." I didn't believe Tommy Lee would hit me from behind so I kept my back to him as I pulled Howard up by the hand.

"I think my nose is broken," Howard said quietly, touching it with his fingers while blood streamed down the front of his shirt.

"This is barbaric," Cathy whisperd.

I asked Suzan to bring me the ice bag.

"It was for Diane," she said in a faraway voice, although she brought it to me, keeping her distance from Tommy Lee.

"Put this over the bridge of your nose and lie down," I told Howard gently. He looked helpless, drenched in blood with his glasses shattered near his feet.

Howard glanced at Tommy Lee and opened his mouth as if he wanted to say something.

"This isn't the time, Howard," I said, taking him by the arm to the love seat.

"He had it comin'," Tommy Lee snapped. "He's a chickenshit. He's always been a chickenshit."

After I helped Howard lie down with his feet elevated I gave Tommy Lee a look. "This won't settle a thing. Go outside before you upset Mother any more than she already is."

"I'm goin' home," he said, lowering his fists. "You can all just kiss my ass. This isn't over by a long shot. I talked to Martha before she left. We're gonna see attorneys first thing on Monday. We'll sue the shit out of Howard. He's tryin' to grab the whole thing for himself. He's got

Mother convinced the rest of us are stupid. You'll wish you hadn't sided with him, Matt, by the time we get done.''

"I'm not siding with anyone. This is no way to resolve an issue.''

Tommy Lee gave Howard a final glare and then turned on his heel, marching to the front door. He slammed it behind him and for a moment there was silence.

"Carl's so mad he won't come back inside,'' Suzan said. "He told me we were never coming back here again, and that he hoped Mother choked on her money . . . he called it her goddamn money.''

At the time I didn't care to comment that Carl was not as inclined to curse Helen's money while she was giving it to him.

"Can we please go home now?'' Cathy asked, her eyes damp.

"I'll tell Helen good-bye for us,'' I replied, taking a last look at Diane, Suzan, and Howard. I said to Howard, "I'll tell Mother you'll be up in a little while.''

He nodded with the ice pack covering his face.

When I entered the study Helen was standing in front of the window. She didn't turn around when I came in. I walked up to her and said, "Cathy and David and I are leaving, Mother. I'm here to say our good-byes, unless you'd like to come downstairs to see them before we go. Howard will be back up shortly. He has a nosebleed.''

"Say good-bye to your family for me, please,'' she said, and there was a strange quality in her voice. "I'm not feeling well.''

"I understand. Good-bye, Mother. I'll keep in touch. Let me know when . . . when you have to go to the hospital. I'll come as often as I can.''

"That won't be necessary, Matthew. I'd rather not have any visitors when it reaches that point. A human being should be allowed the dignity of dying without fanfare or ceremonious shows of emotion. I prefer to face it alone."

"As you wish," I said softly, touching her arm. "I'd like to give you a hug the way I always do, if you're feeling up to it."

She turned away from the window slowly, and I found running down her cheeks the only tears I'd seen her shed since my father died. I put my arms around her and kissed her forehead. "It's okay to cry, Mother," I whispered, but I felt her stiffen when my embrace tightened. "You're facing a terrible ordeal with a great deal of courage."

"It requires no courage to die," she said, her voice firm, unwavering. "Living requires courage, my son, a lesson you will soon learn, if you haven't already. Go now, and give Cathy and David my fondest regards."

11

■ MET SUZAN AT THE TOP OF THE STAIRCASE. "We're leaving," I said quietly.

"So are we," she said, reaching for my arm. "This has been the worst, hasn't it? I thought nothing could top last year, but this beats them all." She glanced down the hallway to make sure the study door was shut and lowered her voice. "Mother isn't acting like herself, is she? Carl and I think she must be losing her mind because of what her doctors told her. After he calmed down, Carl said maybe it was the medicine they're giving her for pain that's making her act crazy like this, putting everything in Howard's name."

I knew at once where Suzan was going with this, although I suspected Carl was behind it. He'd had time to think of another way to get what he wanted. "She doesn't seem any different to me," I said. "Thinner. Howard has always managed her financial dealings. Not much will change, except for the loans and donations to Martha's foundation. We couldn't sell the ranch while Mother was alive, so I don't really see any difference."

"No difference?" Suzan's voice had risen an octave. "How can you say there's no difference? Howard controls every cent, and this big ugly ranch is just gonna sit here. Nobody can sell it for a hundred years."

"It's what Helen wants."

"But what about us? Doesn't it matter what *we* want? I know damn good and well Howard told her to do it this way, and because she's probably half crazy on drugs now, she *listens* to him."

"She isn't crazy. I assure you Mother is in full control of her faculties. She's understandably upset because she knows she is dying. I have no idea what sort of medication she's taking, but it isn't impairing her judgment, in my opinion. Helen has always been like this when it comes to money matters. We aren't exactly broke, Suzan. She gave each of us five million of our own, and we all share equally in earnings off her investments as well. And don't forget she gave her grandchildren a million in trust when they were born."

"But it's *all* in trust funds," Suzan complained. "We can't touch any of the principal."

I nodded. "That's roughly three hundred and fifty thousand a year in interest earnings, not to mention what we get when the stocks and bonds pay a dividend, and from the sale of oil, which is almost twice as much as our interest payments. We're paying taxes on over a million dollars a year in income from the estate alone, and Howard is the one who invested so wisely. I don't see what we have to complain about."

"So you're on Howard's side . . ."

"I'm not on anyone's side. Mother has decided this is the way she wants things done. We all have enough to live comfortably for the rest of our lives."

"I'm disappointed in you, Matt. I thought you'd agree with us," she said stonily. "Good-bye. I'm going to tell Helen we're leaving." She put her arms around me lightly and hurried away, toward the study.

When I reached the den Howard was still lying down with the ice bag on his nose and Diane was still unconscious. Cathy and David were out by the pool saying good-bye to the other children, and to Carl. I walked over to Howard. "We're going. Cathy has asked me to take her home now. She's very upset. Tell Diane good-bye for us as soon as she wakes up.''

"It's her blood sugar, Matt. Sometimes, when she has a few drinks her blood sugar rises suddenly.'' Howard struggled to sit up, wiping blood off his lips with a handkerchief. "I warned you there would be difficulties when Mother explained what she meant to do. Tommy Lee is a spendthrift and irresponsible, but I was totally unprepared for his violent reaction. We were never close due to the difference in our ages, but it's inexcusable that he would resort to punching me. Don't you agree?''

"Hell, Howard,'' I said quietly, ''none of us were ever close. We grew up like strangers. Tommy Lee's behavior doesn't surprise me all that much, and you can bet Carl and Suzan won't take this lying down. Martha is furious. Be prepared for a lawsuit. I'm sure they'll try to have Helen declared incompetent.''

"Do you honestly believe they'll try that?''

"I'd bet heavily on it. It's almost a certainty. They'll be coming after you too, because they believe you're behind it.''

"I had nothing to do with it, Matthew. This was entirely by Mother's design. You heard what she said upstairs, that I'd been groomed for this. I'm certainly the best qualified.''

"Perhaps some of the others believe you enjoy it too much, being in control of everything.''

"That's not true.''

I wondered. When my new practice was failing and Helen gave Howard instructions to loan me money he made quite an issue of my need for Mother's help, complaining that a loan would upset his financial planning for her investments that year. I had, in all honesty, opened a rather lavish office with four junior partners in an expensive bank building in Austin. I paid good salaries to attract the best attorneys without having a clue as to where our first clients would come from. My overhead was staggering and we found no clients to speak of that first year, draining most of my personal resources. I think Helen wanted to watch me flounder in the beginning, knowing I'd have to come to her for assistance at some point. She kept each of us tied to her that way, with an umbilical cord made of money. As Suzan so accurately pointed out, we had millions of dollars we couldn't touch, millions of dollars that kept us bound to our mother.

"Good luck, Howard," I said, sticking out my hand. "I told Helen I'd come to see her whenever I could, although she asked me not to come after she's been hospitalized."

"What a strange request," Howard said, taking my handshake briefly and frowning. "I wonder why?"

I shrugged and moved toward the patio door. "She told me she'd rather face it alone. It really doesn't sound strange, coming from her. Have a safe trip home." I walked out by the pool just in time to hear Carl telling Cathy how weird the King family was, how he was glad they wouldn't be coming back here ever again.

Cathy rolled her eyes at me. "Are we ready?" she asked, sounding hopeful.

"We're ready." I offered my hand to Carl. "Have a safe drive back to Midland."

He ignored my palm. "Listen, Matt, don't you think this whole thing is crazy? I know Howard's your brother, but it sure seems to me like he's screwin' the rest of us out of all Helen's money. Suzan told me what happened upstairs. What the hell's gotten into that old woman anyway, to let Howard get control of everything."

"It's her choice because it's her money, Carl."

He gave me a deeply concerned look. "Maybe she ain't quite right in the head just now, if you know what I mean, after they told her she was dyin'. Maybe she's takin' medicine that won't let her think straight. Suzan an' me were wonderin' about it."

I was sure Suzan hadn't started wondering until Carl helped her. "I'm quite certain a psychiatrist would find her mentally fit. There's nothing wrong with her mind." I turned to Cathy and David and said, "Let's go. We've got a long trip ahead of us."

We left Carl standing by the pool mumbling something I did not hear. It was nothing I cared to hear, I felt sure. As we were walking through the den I saw Howard going upstairs with a bloody handkerchief under his nose and a drink in his hand. It was his turn to say good-bye to Helen.

"Boy, Dad, did you see how Uncle Tommy smacked Uncle Howard in the mouth?" David whispered. "Pow! Right in the kisser . . ."

"I missed it," I replied softly, opening the front doors to let Cathy and David out ahead of me.

For a fleeting moment I was tempted to look back for a final glance at the inside of our house, until I told myself I didn't want to see it again. There was nothing here I wanted to remember. In the beginning this was the only world I knew, and until I was old enough to see and understand how other people lived I didn't realize how out of kilter things were inside our house. Even total strangers make some attempt to establish relations with one another when they live in the same neighborhood. As brothers and sisters we never made any attempt to get to know each other. We existed, with our own private interests and most any expensive plaything we wanted, but we never played *with* each other.

I helped Cathy into the car, remembering one particular spot where I used to go alone. It wasn't far off the road to the gate and I hoped Cathy would indulge me a last visit there.

"I'd like to stop at the old rock house, if you don't mind," I said, starting the Mercedes. "It isn't much out of the way. I went there a lot as a kid."

"Of course, honey," Cathy said, leaning over to kiss me on the cheek as I switched on the air-conditioning. "Just so we're away from *them,* I don't mind what we do."

"If I had a rifle I could hunt rabbits while you were havin' a look around," David said.

The look Cathy gave him made David lean back against the seat again as we wheeled around the circular driveway.

It had been built of native stone right after the Civil War by a German family. Only the walls remained standing, but anyone could see how carefully a stonemason had shaped every rock, every line of mortar. Part of the old chimney had tumbled down a long time ago, probably the result of a tornado or a dust storm with high winds. I came here often, beginning when I was five or six, to play inside or fish in the shallow creek running behind what was left of the barn. I caught crawfish and perch and dreamed of all sorts of things, pretending I was a cowboy, or a soldier, or anything I wanted to be. I came here to cry where no one would see my tears. I cried once when my father invited Howard to go on a trip with him, leaving me here—I don't recall where they were going—it didn't matter. All that mattered was that Howard would be somewhere with Dad for three days, and I wouldn't. I'd cried hard that day, and got a scolding from Helen for coming home late. I hadn't wanted to come home at all.

"What's so special about this ol' place, Dad?" David asked.

"I did a lot of growing up here, figuring out who I was and that sort of thing. I played cowboys and Indians, and fished in that creek sometimes."

He gave me a sideways glance. "You had a swimmin'

pool an' all kinds of neat stuff at home. You said you had a
motorcycle an' a pony an' three electric trains, a pool
table, even.''

I could see the creek had gone dry during the drought.
"I had just about everything I wanted . . . except
friends."

"You had friends at school, didn't you?"

"One or two. They didn't come out to see me very
often and I wasn't allowed to go to town to see them.
Helen said they were oil-field trash and I shouldn't asso-
ciate with them."

I felt Cathy's hand on my arm.

"Grandma can be real mean sometimes," David said.
"That's why I call her the Ice Queen, 'cause she's like a
piece of ice. Even when she smiles it doesn't look real, like
she's fakin' it. I guess I'd have come here too if I had to be
around her all the time."

"That's enough, David," Cathy said. "Helen is dying
and I know your father feels bad today. We can do without
your comments regarding Helen."

"It's okay," I told her. David was only saying what I'd
been thinking for thirty years, give or take. I was lucky. I
found a woman like Cathy and discovered I could give her
and my son the affection I was denied. My brothers and
sisters had not been so fortunate. Howard's marriage was a
convenience, a loveless partnership formed to raise children and for the sake of appearances. Martha's marriage
collapsed because she had insulated herself long ago from
even the remote chance of giving a part of herself to anyone else. Tommy Lee was too busy humping his secretaries
and any other woman who would give up her charms without much of a fuss to look for a lasting relationship—as if
he were on some sort of quest to see how many women he
could buy with expensive gifts and trips to Las Vegas or
Europe. Suzan settled for a man she could control, a brain-

less college football hero who saw dollar signs when he met Suzan King. I truly felt I was the only one who found what we were all looking for, someone who cared about us and not our balance sheets.

I looked across the hills, remembering how Tom taught me to appreciate the ranch. To most people this is dry, rugged, almost barren country with few trees, very little water, brutally hot summers and bone-chilling winters when arctic winds blast from the north across the Caprock region of the Texas Panhandle. Low mountains and table-top plateaus decorate the skyline and it seems almost everything that grows here has thorns——hardy mesquites with spikes like razors that will cut a horseman's legs to shreds should he pass too close. Cactus beds awaiting those unsuspecting creatures who know nothing of desert flora with bristling needles, nature's way of protecting a hapless plant that must exist on scant rainfall, yet are still rich with life-giving protein for cattle and horses if the spikes are burned off with a blowtorch. Men like Tom Walters knew these secrets and during the worst of times kept starving animals alive with burnt prickly pear. Seep springs lay hidden all over the ranch in what appeared to be bone-dry creekbeds, but when a spade was used to dig down only a few inches water slowly filled the holes, and kept cattle and deer from dying of thirst. Broomweed grew in abundance in dry washes, considered a useless plant by most men. Yet old-timers like Tom knew broomweed served to prevent soil erosion when rare heavy rains threatened to wash away the precious topsoil that nourished grasses the cattle herds needed to stay alive. So many secrets hidden by land that made us rich with its oil, things even my father never knew, and Tom shared them with me. Despite the other periods when I felt so lonely and confused, I longed for a return to those parts of my life, the times I spent with Tom Walters.

"Let's go," I said in a strangely melancholy mood after revisiting the old house. For some odd reason I'd thought it might cheer me up.

I stopped at Tom's house on our way out. "I'll only be a minute," I said, leaving the motor and air-conditioning running. I knocked on Tom's back door, greeted by the angry barks of his cow dogs.

Tom peered out. "Come in, Matt," he said.

"I can't stay," I told him, inclining my head toward the car with Cathy and David inside. "Just wanted to say good-bye, and thanks for the great barbecue. I'll call you in a few days to tell you what's going on, but I want you to know the ranch won't be sold and you'll always have a job here and a home, for as long as you want it. Howard will be managing Mother's estate after she dies, but I know he'll let you stay on."

He stared at me a moment through his screen door. "Did Miz King say how long it'll be before . . . she passes on?" He sounded like he hadn't wanted to ask.

"Six months. Perhaps less. She'll be hospitalized toward the end."

"Sorry to hear it, son," he said. He pushed open the screen and came out on his back porch, eyeing our car to see if Cathy and David were watching us. His gaze returned to me and I saw something in his eyes then I hadn't seen for years, not since I was a boy—understanding. "I know you're gonna be in for one hell of a rough time with your brothers an' sisters," he continued, looking past me toward the main house, even though it couldn't be seen from here. "Don't mean to keep your wife an' boy waitin' in this heat, but I've got a couple of things to say even if they ain't really none of my business."

"Take all the time you want," I said.

He was quiet as though it required a moment to collect

his thoughts. "I love this ol' place. Been here more'n thirty years," he began, "but it won't be the same with your ma gone. She loves this land too, but for different reasons, I 'spect. She's like your pa was in lots of ways, lovin' the money this ranch gave 'em. She left it up to me to see to the cattle an' ranch chores, so I reckon it was like this place was my own, in a manner of speakin'. But I ain't so sure I'll work for Howard after Miz King passes. Howard don't give a damn 'bout anythin' besides money. Miz King, she understood the money came from this land, an' because of that she respected it. Never once asked me to overgraze pastures or let them oil companies drain their salt water an' sludge into the creeks like they wanted. She always asked me to see to it that the cows was fed proper, an' when the grass got thin in a dry year she sold off the calves an' older cows, like a cowman is supposed to. There never was a hungry animal on this place, but when Miz King dies, all that's gonna change. I won't work for Howard, or nobody else who don't care what happens to the ranch. I'd just as soon move to town as watch this land go to ruin on account of wantin' to make more money. Won't be nothin' personal between me an' you, understand, but I won't stay on if Howard is of a mind to change things."

"I understand completely," I told him, as something twisted inside my stomach. I couldn't conceive of this ranch without Tom being a part of it. "I'll let you know as soon as I find out what Howard's plans are. That's about all I can promise you. Helen made him administrator of her estate, so I suppose what happens will ultimately be up to him."

Tom merely nodded.

For the time being, there really wasn't anything else for us to say to each other. I shook hands with him, gave him a weak grin, and headed for my waiting family.

DURING MOST OF THE DRIVE HOME CATHY and I said very little to each other, while David spared us the irritation of listening to rock music by wearing the headset on his CD player. Light traffic on Highway 71 from Brady to Llano allowed me to think about today's events without having to concentrate on slower cars or oncoming trucks. It seemed fitting in some dark way that the King family's last Fourth of July reunion was our all-time worst. We provided the usual forms of entertainment, insults, backbiting, and name-calling, and this year we added bloodshed: both rabbit blood and our own. Threats of more violence were an appropriate finishing touch, all in honor of our mother's announcement she was dying.

"What do you think will happen?" Cathy asked later on. "Or would you rather not talk about it?"

"There'll be lawsuits," I said. "Tommy Lee and Martha will join in a suit to have Helen declared incompetent. Carl made the suggestion too that Helen isn't of sound mind. It'll be nasty. They'll name Howard as a conspirator in a scheme to control her fortune. A judge will have to decide if the suit has any merit. Then he may order a psychiatric evaluation, or dismiss it as being without sufficient merit. I haven't seen Helen's will. Dana Fullerton and Harold Haynes handle all Mother's legal work, but I suspect my sisters and brother will try to have her will challenged on grounds of insanity. It'll be complicated and difficult to prove. Both Haynes and Fullerton will attest to

Helen's mental fitness. I don't think a psychiatrist will find anything wrong with her thought processes.''

"Is she crazy? That isn't the right word, is it?''

"She's no different than she ever was, in my opinion, which will be crucial in any attempt to prove she's incompetent. When Fullerton and Haynes give their depositions and Howard proves his procedures having to do with her financial affairs are virtually like they've always been, with the exception being the creation of a permanent trust for her estate, I can't imagine a judge breaking her will or blocking the formation of the trust.''

"You'll be asked for your opinion, won't you?''

"Without a doubt.''

"And if you say she isn't incompetent, Tommy Lee and Martha and Suzan will turn against you.''

"I expect it. I don't suppose it'll matter all that much. We were never close anyway. I wish I could simply stay out of it. I don't really care what happens to the ranch, except for Tom. We have more than enough to live quite comfortably for the rest of our lives and I'd rather avoid the squabbling, in or out of court.''

"Tommy Lee has a terrible temper. If things don't go his way he might confront Howard physically. He was in a rage today. If anyone's crazy, it's him. And the way he uses guns frightens me.''

"He wouldn't shoot Howard, Cathy. Shooting rabbits is quite a different matter. Lots of normal guys hunt deer and elk and so forth. He may threaten Howard with another bloody nose, but that's as far as it'll go. On the other hand, who knows what Carl will do if he doesn't get what he wants. Although surely all of us are sane enough not to indulge in any more violence. It'll be settled in a courtroom, not with fists.''

Cathy stared thoughtfully through the windshield as we drove through what Texans call the Hill Country, a beauti-

ful section of rocky canyons and mountains covered with
some of the state's most varied flora. "You don't have to
answer this question if you don't want to, Matt, but I was
wondering which one of your brothers or sisters you felt
closest to while you were growing up."

"I suppose it would be Martha. She was most like me
in a number of ways. A loner. She wanted friends and
Mother would never approve of anyone she met at school.
We talked about it a few times. As she grew older she
became more distant, removed from what went on in our
family. She spent a lot of time alone in her room. She read
a great deal, about southwestern history and art and ar-
chaeology. We grew farther apart yet I always felt closer to
her than my brothers or Suzan. We were kindred spirits.
We shared the same feelings about many things, and I'm
sure she was acutely aware of how dysfunctional things
were in our family."

Cathy's brow furrowed. "You don't seem close now.
She has a cold personality, an unfriendliness toward everyone. She rarely has a kind word to say about anything."

I remembered Martha when she was younger. "I think
that's her tough outer skin. She was deeply hurt when
Helen cut off all funding to her foundation, although she
refused to show it today. The foundation has been her life
for years, even before she and Ray got a divorce. I don't
know what she'll do with herself when she's forced to
close it. I found out this afternoon why Helen cut off the
donations. Martha refused to change the name of the foundation from Carter to King, after she and Ray were divorced. I think it's tragic Helen allowed something like that
to interfere with all the work Martha put into her collections and the foundation itself. It's like she's punishing
Martha."

Cathy said, "I would have guessed you felt closer to
Howard because of your ages."

"Howard never allowed anyone to get close to him He spent more time alone than any of us. We have ver little in common. I always resented the fact he was close to my father than I was."

"Tommy Lee is the one who frightens me," Cathy said. "If you hadn't stepped between them when you did, wonder how far Tommy Lee would have gone. He was s angry I was afraid he meant to kill Howard with his bar hands. There was something about his eyes when he struc Howard . . ."

"Carl's reaction will be the worst," I told her "When he has time to realize what Helen's trust does t them, that he and Suzan will only receive interest earning and there won't be any more loans, nor can they pledg Suzan's trust funds as collateral for a loan, he'll hit th roof. I am quite sure we haven't heard the last word fror him."

Cathy looked down at her hands. "Every year I tol myself our visits to Eden couldn't get any worse, and ever year I was wrong. I'm sorry your mother is dying, but won't be the least bit sorry never to go there again. Afte Helen dies there won't be any reason for your family to ge together again. Except for the funeral, of course."

"Surely everyone will behave themselves at her fu neral," I said. "By then I'm sure we'll have met more tha a few times in court. And even if a judge allows it to go t trial, which I seriously doubt, it's highly unlikely you'd b asked to testify as to Helen's mental fitness. After th funeral, you won't ever have to be around any of the again."

We drove into Llano. David pulled off his earphone and pointed to a Dairy Queen. "Can I please have a Coke Dad? I'm real, real thirsty."

"I suppose." I turned the car into a shaded parkin area in front of the door. I glanced at Cathy as I turned o the motor to ask if she wanted anything, and when I saw her I was overcome by an unexpected rush of emotion. I reached for her and pulled her close, kissing her lips gently. "I love you so very much," I said. Unaccountably, my voice was on the verge of breaking. "You and David are the best things that ever happened to me. I don't know what I'd do without you. I'm sorry I put you through this today. Always remember that I love you."

"And I love you," Cathy whispered, returning my kiss with her palms pressed to my face.

"This isn't cool," David protested from the rear seat as he slumped down to avoid being seen. "You guys are too old to be kissin' where everybody can see you."

PART

II

13

"**I** HOPE YOU AREN'T BUSY." MARTHA'S VOICE sounded different over the telephone, strained.

I had been preparing a brief for presentation at the Board of Arbitration when she called. We rarely ever went to trial for personal injury cases, but a judge ordered arbitration in this case and I wasn't familiar with it. "I'm not busy," I said, cradling the phone with my shoulder while I closed the file. Martha wouldn't have called without something important to say.

"I had my accountants go over the financial statement with a fine-tooth comb. There may be some big irregularities. Howard may have converted some of Helen's assets for his personal use and certificates of deposit are not in the banks where the report says they are. We may be talking millions here."

This wasn't the approach I'd expected from Martha, not after a San Antonio district judge ruled no grounds were present for a competency hearing last month. It was November now and for weeks after the ruling all remained calm. Until today. Helen was in Southwestern Medical Center in Houston. Howard called me a few weeks ago to tell me, and to say she had asked us not to visit her. "Have you talked to Howard about any of this?" I asked.

"Not yet. Not until I'm sure."

"I don't believe he would do it. I don't think he *could* do it. He can't simply cash in a certificate of deposit and pocket the money. He doesn't own the certificates, he merely controls them for Helen's trust. He can move them to banks paying higher interest, but he can't sell them and keep the money without being guilty of theft. I think you're grasping at straws."

"I think he's a thief and I intend to prove it before Helen dies, if I can."

"Good grief, Martha. This is ludicrous. Howard is required by law to furnish us and the IRS with an audited statement and a tax return every year. He knows money can't simply vanish into thin air and he's not going to hide it under his mattress, for Christ's sake. What does he stand to gain? How does he spend the money?"

"He may have moved it out of the country to a Swiss account, or a bank in Honduras or Belize. They fly to Belize two or three times a year, you know, calling it a vacation. Diane claims it does wonders for her sinuses. Nothing like a few extra million to clear someone's nasal passages."

"I'm sure Howard has a simple explanation for any money you believe is missing. Why don't you call him?"

"I don't want him covering his tracks. A one-million-dollar certificate of deposit listed as being at Victoria Bank and Trust isn't there. My accountant called them. It bore a maturity date in January of 1996. Selling it early means a substantial penalty and Howard wouldn't do that unless he's up to something. Now I'm convinced there are others missing. There's no telling how much he may have embezzled."

If what Martha said was true, it didn't make sense. Selling a CD before its maturity would cost Helen's trust a lot of money. "I'm sure there's a logical explanation somewhere."

"Why the hell are you defending him, Matt? Can't you make yourself believe Howard is capable of stealing? I don't have any trouble imagining it. My CPA says the only possible reason for selling a CD before its maturity would be fear that a bank might be failing. Victoria Bank is supposed to be one of the strongest small banks in the country, according to its statement of condition filed by bank examiners last year.''

In my mind's eye I saw Helen lying on her deathbed with a row of vultures perched on her headboard—five vultures, her five children waiting for her to draw her final breath, all but one overly anxious to feed. ''Let me see what I can find out,'' I said.

''Don't tell Howard what I told you. I'd hoped you would be as concerned as I am.''

''I *am* concerned, if there's anything to be concerned about. I'll call you back as soon as I know anything.''

''Listen, Matt, don't rule out the possibility Howard converted some of Helen's assets. Stole is a better word. He's caught up in this power thing.''

''I'll call you. By the way, have you closed the foundation yet?''

''I'm running on my own money until the first of the year and after that, I'll have no choice.''

''Have you any intentions of going to see Helen before . . . ?''

''No. Do you?''

''She asked us not to, but I thought it might be a good idea to pay her a visit. She can have me thrown out of her room if it bothers her, I suppose.''

''Don't tell Howard we know about the CD at Victoria Bank. I have my accountants checking on some other things. This may be worse than any of us dreamed.''

''I don't dream about it,'' I said. ''Maybe you shouldn't. It isn't likely Howard would commit this type of fraud. He'd know he would be caught eventually.''

A pause.

"You're being naive. Howard controls millions. He thinks he's smarter than the rest of us."

"I'll call you if I find out anything either way." I hung up before she had a chance to say more.

For a moment I stared out my office window at the capitol building, its dome and the statue on top, not really seeing it. Texans brag our capitol is seven feet taller than the nation's capitol in Washington. I tried, but I couldn't imagine Howard being brazen enough to steal money from Helen's estate.

Ten minutes later I dialed his private office number.

"Howard, this is Matt. How's Mother?"

"I talked to one of her doctors. She's in a great deal of pain. Dr. James believes it will only be a matter of weeks."

"Have you seen her?"

"She asked that we not come and I respect her wishes in that regard."

"I guess you've seen to closing up the house and so forth."

"Yes. I asked Tom Walters to attend to it. It's also time to sell off the cattle herd. I was wondering if you'd drive over to sign an authorization at the auction company in San Angelo. I understand they can't sell the cows without a signature from one of the owners. Helen's will provides for retaining a part of the herd; however Mr. Walters informs me it has not rained and there is no grass. He's feeding them almost every bite they get and it is an added expense we don't need."

I was surprised to learn Howard had seen Mother's will. "If she stipulated keeping a few cows on the property, I don't think we ought to sell them all."

"It's not cost-effective. Tom can remain in the house until he dies, at the same salary, but those cattle are losing too much money. They have to be sold immediately. And it's closer for you to make the drive."

"I suppose I can go this weekend. Are you sure this is what we have to do?"

"Absolutely. The cost of feed is far too high. Any profits will be eaten up by feeding expenses. It's the drought."

"But it also violates a tenet of Helen's will. You've taken it upon yourself to make this decision despite what Mother wanted us to do."

"These are special circumstances. I'd hoped you would agree with me. We can't justify losing more money on cows. If you'll refer to the financial report, you'll see we lost thousands of dollars on them last year and we simply can't afford sentiment."

I sensed Howard's feeling of power, control. He was making choices without regard for Helen's wishes, or the provisions of her will. "I'll go to San Angelo this Saturday," I said, wondering if Martha could be right. Had Howard also sold a CD before its maturity date, spiriting the money away to Belize or Honduras? "While I've got you on the phone, let me ask you a rather obvious question. Why would anyone sell a certificate of deposit before it matured? A big one?"

"In these times the answer is simple," he replied. "A bank may not be on solid ground due to problems with its loan portfolio. Bad loans on real estate or in the oil industry. When a bank has unusually high default rates on commercial loans it is wise to pull out early, rather than suffer the consequences if a CD is above FDIC insured amounts. An investor could lose everything above the insured limit. Of course, the other possibility is that the owner of the certificate needed money."

"Makes sense," I said. I had to find out if Victoria Bank was in any trouble with bank examiners. Martha had insisted the bank was sound. "A client asked me something about it and I didn't know," I lied, "beyond the obvious reason that somebody needed money in a hurry."

Howard cleared his throat, a habit when he was bringing up a touchy subject. "Tommy Lee called me the other night. He'd been drinking. He threatened me. He said he was going to get even for what he believes I've done to him. He won't listen to reason and he says he's been talking to Suzan and Carl about it. They intend to try again to have Mother declared incompetent. They've hired another attorney, an Anthony Marcus from Houston who specializes in this sort of thing. Marcus is good, I was told, although his ethics are in question. He uses medical experts with impressive credentials, boarded psychiatrists and neurologists, who'll say just about anything for a fee. Mother's in no condition for any of this and yet they persist. I'm sure Martha will join them in a second petition to have Mother examined."

I didn't say anything.

"That isn't the worst of it," Howard continued. "Tommy Lee threatened to kill me. He actually said it over the phone and I have it on tape. I always record telephone conversations, both at the office and at home, for backup when someone gives me a quotation on a stock or a bond. Tommy Lee said he was going to kill me, unless I agreed to join them having Mother declared incompetent. I've got it on tape."

"He was probably just drunk, Howard. Forget about it."

"I don't think you'd be so cavalier if he had threatened to take your life."

"I wouldn't believe it, and neither should you. He's your brother. He may be irresponsible and have a bad temper, but he wouldn't kill you. Blood is supposed to be thicker than water."

"I wonder at times. We're all so very different."

It was the understatement of the decade. I wondered now if Martha knew about this second attempt to have Helen's sanity questioned, and Tommy Lee's death threat against Howard. "We are very different," I agreed. "Surely we won't resort to killing each other, in spite of our differences."

Howard sighed. "I suppose not. I'd appreciate it if you'd take care of this cattle business as soon as possible. Keep all your receipts for expenses and send them to me so I can reimburse you."

"I'll call Tom and tell him I'm coming on Saturday. I'll bring David along. We'll play cowboy this weekend." I said good-bye and hung up, lost in a tangled mass of thoughts. Since the Fourth I hadn't given our family bickering any more attention than absolutely necessary, when one of my brothers or sisters called to keep me informed on their legal battles. I listened with feigned sympathy and took no position either way. It was disturbing that Tommy Lee would call Howard with a death threat, although I was sure he was too drunk at the time to really know what he was saying.

I picked up the phone and dialed Cathy. "I love you and I lust after you," I said as soon as she answered. "If I wasn't so busy I'd come home right now and throw you down, ripping off all your clothes, ravaging you, biting your neck like a vampire while I buried my throbbing member inside you."

"The garbage disposal is broken," she said, then she laughed and blew a kiss into the phone. "I called the repairman. Since you're too busy to come home to ravage me, I think I'll seduce the guy from Sears. If you see toothmarks on my neck tonight, they'll be his."

"Business before pleasure, my dear. Sorry. Ask David if he wants to go to the ranch with me this Saturday to round up all of the cows. Howard is selling them and I have to sign something at the auction barn. Tell him we'll ride horses and all that cowboy stuff.''

"You won't let him shoot any rabbits, will you?''

"No. As you know, we don't own any guns. But speaking of guns, Howard told me something really strange just now. He said Tommy Lee threatened to kill him. He was drunk, according to Howard, but he said he would kill him unless Howard joined the rest of them in another suit to have Helen declared incompetent.''

"Dear God,'' Cathy gasped.

"Howard even has a recording of it. Apparently, Howard records all his telephone calls.''

"Tommy Lee is the one who's insane,'' she said. "Remember I told you his eyes looked funny just before he punched Howard in the face. He's crazy, Matt. Do you think there's a possibility he might . . . hurt you?''

"He wouldn't try to kill me, if that's what you mean. He might break my nose or something.''

"They'll never stop, will they?''

"They aren't likely to give up until they get what they are after, which is Helen's money. Only I don't see any way they can get it.''

"Let's not talk about it. Your family gives me the creeps. I'll ask David if he wants to go on Saturday. Actually, I sort of hope he won't. He doesn't belong there.''

"All we're doing is rounding up cows. He'll enjoy it. He's bored on weekends anyway.''

"I'll ask him. Bye, honey. I've got to slip into something comfortable and sexy for the repairman.''

"That black lacy thing is my favorite. See if he likes it as much as I do.''

She blew another kiss into the phone. "I may dispense with formalities and wait for him completely naked. Don't come home too early or you might catch us in bed. The garbage disposal can wait.''

14

WE RODE ACROSS MILES OF UNDULATING hills covered with clumps of brittle gamma and curly mesquite grasses yellowed by sun and lack of rain. Cracks in the reddish-brown topsoil were several inches wide in places. David rode a gentle, smooth-mouth gelding belonging to Tom Walters. I rode an old bay mare with saddle marks on its withers. Crossing so much wide-open land is almost a spiritual experience, and humbling in a way when you know all of it belongs to one owner. There are few cross fences and for hours we saw nothing but empty grasslands like the cowmen of old saw, before barbed wire came into existence. Three Mexican vaqueros from town had been hired to push our herds toward corrals and hay barns north of Tom's house. Our role was more supervisory than actually being a part of the roundup. Tom rode between us, slumped over his saddle like a man accustomed to the uneven gait of a horse moving at a trot. By way of contrast, David bounced all over his saddle, clinging resolutely to the saddle horn. I did my best to ride as well as Tom—it was a poor imitation and I knew it. But I was enjoying our ride, the fresh air and a feeling of isolation, although there was something changed about the ranch as I remembered it from my childhood. Swirls of dust rose from our horses' hooves as we crested one hill, then another.

"Kinda sad," Tom remarked in his typically understated way, "to see this ranch without no cows. The hell of it is, we ain't had any rain for so long there ain't hardly nothin' fer 'em to eat. If Miz King was here today she'd be cryin' her eyes out, seein' all them cattle trucks backed up to the loadin' chutes.''

My mother could cry over selling cattle, I thought, but she wasn't able to shed tears for any of her children. "One of these days it'll rain," I said. "Then my brother might consider giving you a grass lease for cattle of your own."

Tom shook his head like he didn't agree. "If you'll pardon me fer sayin' so, Howard ain't likely to show me no favors. It's just money to him. I feel like I hardly knew the boy when he was growin' up an' things ain't changed any. I'd hate like hell to owe him money I couldn't pay. He never cared a damn bit about this ranch. Fact is, none of your brothers or sisters did. Never could figure why. This land's some of the best grazin' in middle Texas, when it ain't so dry. I've rode this ol' place thirty years an' there's spots where all a man can see is King property in every direction without a cross fence. It's like it was before the white man got here, when it was still Injun country, if you don't count all the oil wells. Blue sky an' a bunch of hills, like what you see right yonder, every direction you turn. It can be peaceful as hell too. If a man's got any troubles he can forget 'em out here. Biggest country on this earth is Concho County. Empty as a bucket with a hole in it. Hardly any houses for miles. Place like this is where a man comes to understand he don't amount to much. Never was a real religious feller myself, but when I ride this ranch I get a notion of what the Almighty is all about. Somethin' this big an' beautiful don't get here by no accident.''

David wasn't impressed. "I'm sure glad I don't live here, but if I did I'd have a gun an' I'd be shootin' rabbits all the time because there wouldn't be anything else to do. I'd be so lonely I couldn't stand it. There's nothin' but grass an' oil wells to look at. I'd go crazy here all by myself.''

Tom chuckled. "That's because you're from another generation. Back when I was a boy kids didn't mind bein' alone. We'd go rope a cow or ride a green bronc. That was plenty of excitement fer us. We'd swim our horses across the river or go fishin' for catfish."

"What's a bronc, an' how come it's green?"

"It's a horse, son, a horse that ain't been rode much," Tom explained. "It takes some doin' to make a horse gentle enough so you can rope a cow off its back."

"It sounds boring," David said.

I gazed across empty hills. I'd been very lonely here too, yet I always had a sense this land was something special—because Tom taught me to appreciate it. The size of it was a part of the feeling, although back then I had no scale by which to judge ranches or houses. Until I was old enough to attend school in Eden, and I must have assumed everyone had a ranch like ours. I remember Helen wanted us to go to Dallas to a private boarding school to get a better education, until my father said he wanted us here, so he could teach us the oil and ranching business. "It isn't boring," I said as we trotted our horses over the crest of a hill with a view of a shallow valley dotted with live oak trees. "It's different, like Tom said. It all depends upon what you're accustomed to." One thing Tom was wrong about—being alone on the ranch didn't allow everyone to forget about their troubles. I'd had plenty of problems growing up here and being by myself only seemed to worsen them. Tom's willingness to spend time with me and listen to things that were bothering me probably kept me from turning out to be just like my brothers and sisters. I'm sure that is why I felt so close to him now, even though we only saw each other once a year.

A large group of black Angus cattle was being pushed toward the corrals by three cowboys. Dust rose in lazy spirals from so many cloven hooves. I wondered what my father would think if he were alive to see what Howard was doing, selling off the last of our cows.

"Those cattle sure are gettin' thin," Tom observed. "I've been feedin' 'em every day, but when it's dry like this a cow can't gain no weight. Here it is November already an' we ain't seen a cloud in the sky."

It was chilly enough this morning for light jackets. "It'll rain sometime," I said, taking note of rib bones showing on some of the older Angus cows. Several hundred head of cattle plodded ahead of the cowboys, too many to count easily. "I remember when this place had grass so high it touched a cow's belly . . ."

"Pow! Pow! Pow!" David cried, aiming an imaginary pistol at a jackrabbit bounding away from a prickly pear bed. "That'd be one dead rabbit if I had Uncle Tommy's automatic."

"It was more like a howitzer," I said. "I don't see any sport hunting rabbits with a gun like that. It's like killing butterflies with a sledgehammer."

"I *really* want a rifle, Dad, a twenty-two like the one he let me shoot."

"It would be over your mother's dead body."

"I'll get one when I grow up. You can't stop me from ownin' a rifle when I get old enough to buy one."

"I guess not, but your mother probably wouldn't ever speak to you again."

David watched the jackrabbit disappear over a hilltop. "Mom wouldn't have to know. I wouldn't tell her. It's dumb, the way she acts about rabbit huntin' and havin' guns."

"We don't believe in guns," I said, and that brought a slow grin to Tom's face as he looked over at me.

"Your little sister is the one who can shoot," he said. "I never told Miz King about it. After your daddy died, when Suzan got to twelve or thirteen, she used to beg me to teach her how to use a gun, sayin' it'd have to be a secret on account of Miz King would throw a fit if she knew. Suzan wanted to learn to shoot real bad, so I took her off to a corner of the ranch where nobody would hear us shootin' an' I showed her how to fire my ol' Smith an' Wesson thirty-eight. She got to where she could close one eye an' put a hole through a beer can every time. Then she got interested in boys a year or two later an' that was the end of it. More'n any of the rest of you, she sure did change.''

"I had no idea," I said, genuinely surprised. "She never told me." As far back as I could remember Suzan had only been interested in boys or the way she looked. She had never played with dolls or done little girl things.

"It was supposed to be a secret," Tom said again, returning his attention to the horizon.

"That's what I'll do," David warned. "I'll get somebody else to buy me a gun and I'll keep it someplace where you an' mom won't ever find it."

I gave up arguing with him about the gun when we rode past a rusted pumpjack and a dried-up saltwater run-off pool. A pipe lay on top of the ground running downhill to a crude oil collection tank. For a number of years oil prices had been too low to justify operation of a pump. The cost of running the pump was about equal to what a well could produce. And then I knew what was different about the ranch today—the quiet. In the past there had always been the rhythmic thumping sound of pumpjacks sucking oil out of the ground, and now there was absolute silence all around us.

I considered what Tom said earlier, about being able to see King land in every direction without a cross fence the way it was back in Indian times. Like me, he'd become so accustomed to the presence of oil wells that he didn't actually see them anymore. I wondered if he noticed the absence of noise.

We stopped in front of the house. Tom drove us over in the pickup to show me what he'd done to close it down—I hadn't really wanted to see it yet Tom insisted, so I could tell Howard his instructions had been followed to the letter. Shutters now covered every window, even the smaller ones on the third floor where Martha's and Suzan's rooms had been.

"I drained the swimmin' pool an' put the cover over it," Tom said, leading me around to the back. "I had to put plywood over them glass patio doors, just in case we had a big hailstorm like the one back in '86. The water's cut off at the pump an' the electricity is off at the meter. The refrigerators an' both freezers are emptied out an' cleaned. Maria cried the whole time she was cleanin' up."

I gave the house only a passing glance through the gate into the patio. "Everything looks fine to me, Tom. I'll tell Howard you got it all taken care of."

"I'd be obliged. He can be real fussy 'bout some things."

It was an understatement of grand proportions. "I'll tell him," I said, suddenly in a hurry to leave now that I found myself in the shadow of our house again. I hadn't wanted to come back this time, not for the chore Howard had in mind, which went against Helen's wishes to sell off the last cow on King land. But I'd done it anyway, and it was good to see Tom again, to ride open range with him, and even something as simple as the sound of his voice, the quiet confidence in it, was reassuring.

Tom hooked his thumbs in the pockets of his faded denims. "Will y'all be back next Fourth of July? I can have the place ready if somebody calls ahead of time."

"I'm quite sure we won't be back. Maybe some of the

others will, although I doubt it. Cathy and I won't be coming."

Tom seemed somewhat reluctant to say what was on his mind. He looked up at the roof a moment. "I reckon I can say this to you, Matt, 'cause you was always the most levelheaded. I never saw a family act like yours, everybody fightin' over this or that all the time. Your pa, he was basically a good man, a good cowman an' one hell of a good oilman. He was mighty good to me. Miz King treated me nice too, I 'spose. A time or two we got cross-ways over little things, but she was real generous an' treated me fair. She could be a mite on the cold side. Howard, he's a lot like her. You always reminded me a little bit of your pa, when he first started out in the ranchin' business. Tommy Lee don't remind me of nobody. Suzan . . . I used to call her Missy 'til she got bigger, she's a dandy, only she's got a mean streak. Martha hardly ever talked to me so I never really got to know her. All I was thinkin' was, after Miz King passes on it ain't likely any of you will come back here. I 'spose it ain't none of my business. I was just wonderin' about it."

I was surprised and a bit flattered that Tom thought I was like my father. "We won't be back as a group," I said, watching David toss rocks at a tree limb in the front yard. "You're right about my family, Tom. Normal people do not behave the way we do toward each other. Something went wrong from the very beginning, although I've never known exactly what it was. I've always blamed my mother. She had a difficult time showing her feelings, I think, and perhaps the rest of us grew up without knowing how to show our own. I was fortunate. I found a woman like Cathy who was patient with me until I learned how to express the way I felt toward her. My brothers and sisters weren't so lucky. I guess it's wrong to blame our mother

for everything. I just wish she'd shown us that she loved us.
I don't believe she knew how.''

Tom nodded, scuffing a tuft of dry grass with the toe
of his boot. ''She loved all of you. She couldn't hardly wait
from year to year to have you back on the Fourth of July.
She'd talk about it for months ahead of time, an' after
everybody left she'd cry for days.''

Something twisted inside me. ''She cried after we
left?''

''Her eyes stayed red an' she'd be snifflin' tears for
nearly a week. She tried to hide it, but I seen it just the
same.''

I looked up at a shuttered window of the study. ''I
wish I'd known,'' I said quietly. Why couldn't she have
shown us, or told how she truly felt?

Tom offered his simple explanation. ''Some folks ain't
got it in 'em to show what they're made of. Miz King
could be hard as nails. No sense talkin' 'bout her now, I
don't reckon. How much longer do you figure she's got,
now that she's down in that hospital?''

''Not long,'' I replied, following Tom when he turned
to head for the truck. ''A few weeks would be my guess.''

''I 'spose she'll be buried next to Lee at the Eden
cemetery plot,'' he said, taking longer, bowlegged strides
away from the house. ''Me an' the wife'll come to pay our
respects if you give us a call.''

''Of course. One of us will let you know.''

We got in Tom's pickup. David sat in the backseat
looking out a window. ''Grandma's house looks like it's
got its eyes shut with all the windows covered up,'' he
said.

Neither Tom nor I looked back when he looped around
the drive to take us back to our car. The last possum-belly
cattle trailer would be loaded by now, headed for the auc-

tion barn in San Angelo with what was left of Helen's prize Angus cows.

I shook hands with Tom before we left. I'd learned several things from him today, secrets that I might have been better off not knowing. I wondered if I was truly anything like my father, as Tom thought I was. Or was he only being kind to me?

"I'll be in touch, Tom," I said.

He thumbed the brim of his sweat-stained gray Stetson back and looked me in the eye. "Like I told you before, I'll probably be movin' to town later on. I ain't gonna stay here an' watch Howard turn this ranch into an oil dump. It's costin' money to haul off them truckloads of salt water an' sludge from the wells, an' if Howard gets his way he'll cut costs by dumpin' it here in surface pools. Won't matter what them Environmental boys say if they don't know about it. Afore you know it these creeks will run black as tar an' even our water wells won't be fit to drink. I ain't gonna stay on an' watch that happen, Matt. I'd rather draw a little Social Security an' live in town than see this ol' place ruined for cattle. Maybe I sound like a sentimental old fool, but I couldn't stand it."

"I'm sure Howard won't break any laws," I said.

Tom's eyelids drooped a little. "You got more faith in him than I've got," he said, turning for his back porch.

Tom's shoulders seemed a little more rounded than I remembered as he walked away.

15

CATHY AND I SAT IN THE DEN DRINKING LONG-stemmed glasses of red wine after David went to bed. She sensed something was on my mind. The back wall of our den in West Lake Hills is all glass, overlooking Lake Travis and expensive lakefront homes built when Austin was in an economic boom. It's a beautiful view night or day, but tonight my thoughts were not on scenery.

"I learned several things from Tom Walters today," I began, staring idly through the glass at a starlit sky. "Tom told me Mother cried every time we left on the Fourth. According to him she planned our get-together for weeks in advance and when it was over, she wept for days. Why she never revealed her emotions, that she felt something, still puzzles me. I suppose it's senseless now to try to figure it out or understand her. I told you she had tears in her eyes the day we left, but I wrote that off because she knew she was dying. Now Tom tells me she cried *every time* we left on the Fourth of July. Even after all our bickering and the annual insult-trading contest, she wept when our visit was over. I wish he hadn't told me . . ."

"You shouldn't feel guilty, if that's what's bothering you. It was *her* choice to hide her emotions. I've told you before she is the coldest woman I ever knew, at least on the outside. Your brothers and sisters are exactly like her. When I first met you, you couldn't show your feelings very well, remember?"

I reached across the sofa and took her hand. "You

taught me how, you and Tom. I didn't know how to let go of my feelings in front of you or anyone else. As a boy, I went off by myself to cry or found Tom and told him how I was feeling. I don't suppose I really knew what love was until I fell in love with you. You helped me reach a part of myself I didn't know existed, even though Tom kept reassuring me I wasn't like the rest of them. And now Tom tells me there was a side to my mother I didn't know about, only it's too late . . .''

"You feel very close to Tom, don't you?"

"Closer than I ever felt to any of my family, I suppose. If I needed to talk to someone he was the only one who'd listen, and when I felt lonely, he took the time to talk to me about what was bothering me. He took me with him to work out on the ranch even though I wasn't much of a cowboy. Most of the time I was just in his way, I guess. But what mattered then was he'd listen, and explain things to me when my father didn't have time, or wasn't around. He told me it was okay to cry, when I'd been trying to hide it from everyone else. It didn't make me any less of a man to shed tears. He told me about the time he cried when his favorite old cow pony died. Tom buried him under a big live oak tree behind his house, and he says he still feels sad when he passes that particular tree. Then today, he tells me Helen used to cry when all of us left on the Fourth of July, when all my life she never showed any emotion or allowed us to show any—except anger when one of us did something she didn't approve of. I wish I'd known how much she really cared. It might have made a difference to all of us."

"Maybe you should go to see her before she dies. The two of you could talk."

"She said she didn't want us there."

Cathy toyed with her glass. "Consider the possibility that she didn't mean it, that she was only sparing you from having to see her in the final stages of cancer. Maybe it was her pride that wouldn't allow her to let you see her suffering.''

I thought about it. "I'm afraid she'd only ask me to leave before I had a chance to say a word."

"You could try."

"I suppose I could. I could fly down tomorrow. It's Sunday and getting a flight should be easy." I was torn between fear of what Helen would say when she saw me and a need I felt, to make her explain why she held back her feelings. "Tom told me I reminded him of my father in some ways. He said I was more like him than either of my brothers, which makes it even harder to understand why my dad chose Howard as his favorite. Helen always said it was because he was their firstborn son. I felt like an outsider most of the time. When Dad went away on trips he took Howard with him. That really hurt me. I couldn't understand why I was never allowed to go."

"Let's not talk about it anymore."

I nodded. "It's in the past and I'd just as soon forget it. I'll fly down tomorrow and see if Helen will talk to me. I can tell her what Tom did to close up the house, if nothing else."

"David came back talking about guns again," Cathy said. "He told me what Tom said about teaching Suzan how to shoot a pistol, as an argument for getting us to buy him a rifle. He said Suzan was only thirteen when Tom gave her shooting lessons. I told him we would never allow him to have a gun as long as he lived under this roof. He threatened to run away from home."

"He's only bluffing. We talked about it on the drive back and I told him he couldn't have a gun under any circumstances."

"Suzan doesn't seem the type to like guns. Come to think of it, she doesn't seem to like much of anything."

"Except money. Let's go to bed. It's been a long day for a cowboy like me, a forty-two-year-old cowboy. I've been ridin' the range, and I'm tired."

"Too tired to ride a filly like me tonight?"

"I thought you'd given all your charms to the repairman. I forgot to ask if the dishwasher was fixed."

"It wasn't the dishwasher, it was the garbage disposal. You never listen when I'm talking to you. Yes it's fixed and the guy from Sears was really great in bed. It took him fifteen minutes to fix the disposal and over an hour to satisfy me. Maybe it was two hours . . . I was lost in ecstasy and didn't really keep track of the time." She leaned over and kissed me. We put down our wineglasses before I pushed her gently on her back across the sofa cushions.

"Ride 'em, cowboy," I whispered, unfastening the buttons on her blouse.

Southwestern Medical Center is one of those sterile hospitals where everything smells like rubbing alcohol. I was shown to Helen's private top-floor suite by a nurse. I'd stiffened my resolve to go through with this by means of several drinks on the plane to Houston, but as I approached Helen's doorway my hands were damp. The nurse had been instructed there were to be no visitors in her room, until I convinced the woman I was Helen's son and an exception should be made. After all we were spending a lot of money for special accommodations on the top floor where only VIPs and wealthy patients could afford to stay.

When I walked in I found the room dark. Drapes were pulled across the windows. And when I saw her lying on the bed with an intravenous tube in her arm I almost didn't recognize her. She couldn't weigh a hundred pounds. Her cheeks were sunken and her arms were like matchsticks. As I approached the bed her eyelids fluttered open.

"Hello, Mother," I whispered.

Her deep blue eyes looked cloudy when she fixed me with a stare.

"Why are you here?" she asked in a phlegmy voice.

I took a deep breath. "To tell you about the house, how Tom got it fixed up just the way you wanted with the shutters closed and things like that. I also came to tell you that I love you."

"I asked everyone not to come. No one wants to be seen in this deplorable condition. I'm asking you to leave. I'm gratified by what you've told me regarding the house. Please thank Tom for me when you talk to him. Now go away, Matthew. Respect my wishes in this matter. I'd like to be left alone."

"Did you hear what else I said? I said I love you. It was very important to me to say it, and I also wanted to thank you for everything you've done for me."

"You've said it. There is nothing wrong with my hearing. I love you too, Matthew, as I do all my children. It shouldn't have to be repeated, especially at a time like this."

"I thought this might be a good time to say it. I'd hoped it might ease your suffering to hear me say that I love you and I'm grateful for everything."

Her eyelids were slitted. "I've never asked for expressions of gratitude, nor do I want a demonstration of sentiment now. We said our good-byes at the ranch."

"You cried, Mother, and Tom told me you cried every Fourth of July after we left. You never let us see your tears and I've been wondering why. What's wrong with showing how much you care for us by shedding a few tears?"

"Are you here for the sole purpose of irritating me? I've asked you twice to leave."

My nerves were coming unraveled yet I didn't want it

to show too plainly. "I'm sorry, Mother. I guess I was looking for some answers. You always seemed to have such a hard time showing emotion of any kind. It made me wonder if . . . you loved me. I don't remember you saying it."

"How can you accuse me of not demonstrating my love for you? Lee and I gave you the best of everything and when he died, I did nothing less."

My mouth felt like it was full of sand. "It wasn't what you gave us, Mother. It's more a matter of what you didn't, or could not give us, that I wondered about. I'm just curious why it was so difficult for you to tell us that you loved us, why you never cried or laughed or put your arms around us. What was wrong with telling us how you felt?"

Her eyes bored holes through me and the cloudiness I thought I saw in them earlier was gone.

"I expected more from you, Matthew," she said evenly, with no suggestion of understanding.

"I don't think it's too much to ask to want to know why you kept so much distance from us emotionally. I found it very hard to show affection toward Cathy because I didn't have any experience with demonstrations of affection. She taught me how, but I should have already *known* how."

"Get out!" Helen snapped, turning her face away from me. "If you don't get out of my room immediately I'll have you taken out of my will entirely. You can't make it on your own, Matthew Lee. You'll starve to death without income from the trust. Howard is the only child I have with enough business sense to survive without my help. Please refrain from doing anything else to further convince me I have raised four children who are utter fools and financial failures."

I'd heard enough. "Good-bye, Helen," I said, backing away from her bed with tears brimming in my eyes.

I walked quickly down a carpeted hallway to the elevator gritting my teeth. I'd been wrong to hope I could reach Mother with anything I said. Even facing death, she could not change. I had the sudden urge to strangle Howard with my bare hands. I calmed myself with a recollection of something Howard told me over the phone—Tommy Lee had threatened to kill him when he called the other night. Maybe we all resented the amount of trust Helen placed in Howard. Right at the moment I didn't care if Tommy Lee carried out his threat.

In the elevator I dried my eyes. This was madness, I told myself, the same madness ingrained in all of Helen King's children. I wasn't going to have any part of it. I had a wife and son who loved me and I loved them dearly. Why did I ever talk myself into believing I could change the way Helen expressed her feelings? And why was I jealous of Howard simply because Helen believed he had better business judgment? I was allowing emotions to get in the way of more important things, like David and Cathy, and the happiness the three of us shared.

I signaled a taxi and directed the driver to Hobby Airport before I lit a cigarette. My flight to Houston had been a waste of time. Somewhere deep inside I'd known I would fail, trying to get my mother to say things she'd never been able to say. I suspected her marriage to my father was as loveless as Howard's union with Diane. I couldn't ever remember seeing my father and mother kiss or embrace.

I lit another cigarette with the butt I was smoking. The taxi driver was watching me in the rearview mirror.

"You nervous about flyin', mister?" he asked. "If you've got time, have a couple of drinks at the airport bar. It works for me. I have to get plastered to ride on one of those fuckin' things, 'specially after all those crashes they've been havin'.''

"I intend to have several doubles," I told him, filling my lungs with smoke. I didn't bother to explain it wasn't because of a fear of flying.

16

$\mathbb{S}$UZAN WAS WAITING FOR ME AT THE OFFICE when I got there at ten Monday morning. She was filing her fingernails, snapping chewing gum, dressed in loose-fitting slacks and a sweater. I was surprised she hadn't called to tell me she'd be here and yet I knew, instinctively, she was on a mission to sway me to support the next piece of legal wrangling she and Tommy Lee and Martha were planning.

She smiled when she saw me, a plastic smile. "I didn't ask for an appointment, Matt," she said, standing up. "If we could talk for just a few minutes? I flew in early."

"Of course," I said, nodding to my secretary as I showed Suzan into my office and closed the door. Suzan took a chair opposite my desk, still toying with her fingernail file, chewing gum furiously.

"You know we've hired another lawyer," she began, crossing a heavy leg over her knee.

"Anthony Marcus," I replied.

Suzan stared at me. "We need to have you with us on this."

"You've wasted a trip. I won't have any part of an action to have Helen declared incompetent."

"Why are you suddenly so loyal to her, and to Howard? You know she never gave a damn about the rest of us, and you know Howard has been influencing her all along to gain control of the whole estate. Why can't you see what he's done to us?"

"I don't really think it was his doing, Suzan. I think it was Helen's idea all along. As to the part about Mother not giving a damn about us, I think you're wrong. She just didn't know how to show it. Tom told me this past weekend that she cried every time we left after the Fourth of July gathering. In fact, he said she cried for days afterward. She cared for us, but in a way none of us will ever understand."

"The estate belongs to all of us. It isn't right that she can fix it so we can't use it. Howard gets control of everything like it all belongs to him. It's bullshit that she can tie up all the money in some fucking estate trust fund so we can't spend any of it. We have our own lives to live, you know, and it was Daddy who really made all that money in the first place, so how come she gets to decide what happens to it after she's dead?"

"It's perfectly legal, what she's doing. I'm not saying it's fair, but it is legal."

"It's all that bastard Howard's doing," Suzan snapped. "Tommy Lee is right. Howard's trying to screw us out of our inheritance."

"It isn't our inheritance unless Helen leaves it to us in a will, which she isn't. She's putting it in trust; however, we get equal shares of the trust's earnings, which is a hell of a lot of money, I might add."

"Anthony Marcus says Mother's estate is worth two hundred million, conservatively. She put a lousy five million bucks in trust funds for each of us, so all we get is the interest."

"Five million dollars is lousy?" I asked, quickly tiring of Suzan's attitude. "We each make over a million a year in total earnings from her investments. What the hell is so lousy about that?"

"The rest belongs to us too, only Howard got his hand in the cookie jar first so he doles it out, like we were still children. Carl and I can't buy that ranch in Alpine because of some credit trouble, and Howard won't make us a loan. I'm so mad at Howard I could kill him.''

"Get in line," I said. "Tommy Lee has already threatened to kill him and Howard has a tape recording of it." I added a touch of sarcasm out of sheer frustration. "You'll have to hurry if you want to kill him before Tommy Lee does. Tom said he taught you how to shoot a pistol when you were a kid, and that you were a good shot. We saw how many rabbits Tommy Lee could kill this summer, so if both of you show up at the same time I don't see how Howard stands a chance of surviving the deadly cross fire. He'll have more holes in him than a screen door.''

"You aren't funny, Matt. I'm asking you as a sister to join us in a petition to have Mother's will challenged. We all think she's crazy, and that Howard has been manipulating her.''

"You can save your breath, dear sister," I said, disgusted by her attempt to make our sibling relationship a part of my decision. "I won't sign it, and if it goes before a judge I intend to say I believe Helen is of sound mind and always has been, in her own peculiar way. There is no point in discussing it further." It was apparent Martha had not said anything to Suzan or Carl about her suspicions that Howard was embezzling from the estate. I would leave that allegation up to Martha to make, and leave it to the rest of them to prove it.

"You can be such a bastard at times, Matt," Suzan said as she got up.

"So I've been told a number of times," I replied, turning to my desk for a file I needed for today's first appointment. Suzan stalked out of my office without saying another word.

•   •   •

Anthony Marcus called the following week while I was out of the office meeting with representatives and a claims adjuster for Allied Insurance Group, a Houston-based underwriter of Workers Compensation. I'd settled a two-million-dollar claim against the company for three hundred thousand plus attorney's fees the week before, which they felt sure they couldn't win in court. In front of a jury, Consuelo Gomez might easily have gotten everything she wanted, had her attorney not gone too far trying to put on a performance for the benefit of Arbitration with neck and back braces and a doctor whose report stated that Mrs. Gomez's X rays revealed serious damage to a disk between her fifth and sixth lumbar vertebrae that would limit her mobility for the rest of her life, without surgery. One of my investigators took several minutes of video of Consuelo weeding her garden in Waco without either of her braces, bending down and using a garden hoe without the slightest difficulty.

I knew, of course, what Anthony Marcus wanted. When I did finally return his call, he sounded peeved.

"Don't you have a cellular phone, Mr. King?" he asked.

"I never use it while I'm in an important meeting with a client. I turn it off."

"I've been warned you will not be sympathetic to the view that your mother isn't competent."

"She's fully competent and my testimony will be to that effect. In my opinion, some members of the family simply want larger shares of her estate."

"The preponderance of depositions will say otherwise. I have four given by your sisters, a brother, and your brother-in-law, all stating their belief that your mother's intellectual faculties have been impaired for a number of years. They cite any number of examples. Loss of memory. Extensive periods of deep depression during which she isolated herself at her ranch house and did not make contact with anyone or return telephone calls from concerned relatives. They also state your older brother, Howard King, has manipulated her to his advantage, enabling him to control her fortune."

"It isn't true. Howard has always controlled all financial dealings for her. It was our father's wish. Nothing of any real consequence has changed except that Helen is dying."

"I understand you are next in line. Should anything happen to Howard, you become administrator. He has had health problems in the past, seriously elevated liver enzymes and very high blood pressure. Could your brother's health be a part of the reason you won't join the rest of your family in an action to have your mother's sanity examined by qualified experts?"

"I suppose I should resent that; however I hope you won't be disappointed if I don't. My brother is in good health for a man his age and I have no interest whatsoever in controlling Helen's trusts. I assure you she is of sound mind. Her law firm there in Houston will be your biggest obstacle in any attempt to have her sanity questioned. Dana Fullerton and Harold Haynes have handled Mother's legal affairs for years and she knows them personally. They will depose and testify, if necessary, that nothing is wrong with Helen's mind. I'm certain you know them, if not personally, then by reputation. I'd call them heavyweights in front of a judge. You've got your work cut out for you."

"You've counted me out too soon, Mr. King. I may have a few surprises. Some have called it airing dirty laundry."

"I hadn't counted you out, Mr. Marcus. I'm well aware of your reputation. I said you had your work cut out for you. As to the part about airing dirty laundry, your clients will have a great deal more to worry about in that regard than Howard or my mother. Before you start peeking under too many skirts I suggest you brace yourself for a few moments of embarrassment in your own camp. Mudslinging is a King family specialty. Howard knows all their soft spots."

"Are you charging me for this legal advice?" Marcus asked.

"Not a cent," I replied. "I'm quite sure you're being well paid on the other end. But I've got an additional word of warning, at no charge, of course. Howard has retained a very influential law firm to challenge any attempt to have Helen examined by your experts and I'm sure you know a good lawyer will be able to postpone and delay your petitions for months. By then Helen will be dead, and all your efforts will have been for naught. You'll be left with nothing but testimony from my sisters and Tommy Lee, which Howard and I will contradict, as will Fullerton and Haynes, in the unlikely event a judge allows this to go to a sanity hearing."

"I have documents, examples of recent and dramatic changes in your mother's signature. Several expert handwriting analysts are prepared to offer testimony there are signs of brain damage, possibly Chronic Brain Syndrome and hardening of the arteries."

"Your experts will be challenged by other experts. The lawyer Howard has retained is Joel Murchison. Be prepared for a lengthy battle."

Silence on the other end of the phone.

"Are you still there, Mr. Marcus?" I asked, enjoying the first signs of Marcus's discomfort. Joel Murchison had never lost a civil case in eighteen years of practice, according to a recent article in the *Dallas Morning News*.

"Your family hoped you would be reasonable," he said.

"I am being reasonable. Helen is of sound mind. As to

the five of us being a family in any sense of the word, there might be room for debate.''

"Good afternoon, Mr. King. We'll be seeing each other in a judge's chambers very soon.''

"I doubt it," I said, hanging up the phone. I had to hand it to Howard. Retaining Joel Murchison was not only a stroke of genius, it virtually assured no action could be taken before the funeral at Eden. Murchison was a master in the art of delaying tactics, I'd been told, and he had influence in judicial circles few Texas attorneys could match.

Forty-five minutes later, as I was preparing to leave the office before evening traffic clogged Austin's downtown maze of streets leading to West Lake Hills, my secretary's voice came through the intercom. "Your brother, Tommy Lee, is on line five and he says it's important.''

I put my briefcase down and settled into my chair. Marcus hadn't wasted any time spreading the news of my refusal to depose in behalf of his clients. "Hello, Tommy,'' I said, fully expecting my brother to be drunk, so late in the day.

"What the fuck are you tryin' to do, Matt?''

"What do you mean?''

"You know goddamn well what I mean. Anthony Marcus called just now an' he said you were bein' a complete asshole about our lawsuit against Howard.''

I'd been right about both the call from Marcus and my brother's drinking—some of his words were mushy. "The suit is not against Howard. Marcus is filing a brief to have was Helen's sanity questioned.''

"Howard's gonna control every fuckin' dime if we don't do somethin' to stop him. Besides, you know Mother's always been nutty as a fruitcake.''

"Therein lies part of the problem. She hasn't changed any, as far as I'm concerned, and a judge will wonder why you waited until now to challenge her mental fitness. If you believed she was crazy, the three of you should have done this a long time ago.''

''Howard talked her into this shit. He kisses her ass every fuckin' time he gets the chance an' now she's leavin' everything to him.''

''But she isn't leaving everything to him. He is administrator of her estate. He has always managed her money, the investment end and so forth. Nothing substantial has changed.''

''Like hell! He talked her into puttin' the ranch into some kind of fuckin' trust so we can't ever sell it, besides keepin' his chickenshit fist around all her CDs. He's screwin' the rest of us blind! How come you can't see that?''

''I don't think that's what he has in mind, Tommy. Calm down and think about it. It was Helen's idea to keep the ranch in a trust . . .''

''He *told* her to do it! He had his nose buried in her ass when he told her what to do. The crazy bitch listened to him.''

Tommy Lee's anger was almost out of control. I wondered if he might have been in this same frame of mind when he called to threaten Howard. ''Take it easy,'' I said. ''I can't believe Helen could be talked into anything she didn't want to do. She loves that ranch and I think she merely wants to preserve it intact for her own peace of mind, not because of anything Howard did.''

''Marcus told me you wouldn't listen. He said you were next in line an' that you hoped Howard would croak so you'd be the big cheese. You're the administrator if anything happens to Howard.''

''That's true, but I'm not hoping he'll croak, as you put it. I don't want the responsibility. I'm staying out of this.''

I heard Tommy Lee swallow and I was sure he was drinking beer.

"So you've turned chickenshit on us too. Suzan said all along you'd be a prick about it. You were a prick for steppin' between me and Howard in the den. I was gonna bust his fuckin' skull if you hadn't stopped me. If Howard wasn't such a wimp he'd have gotten up off the floor so I could hit him again. He's a yellow son of a bitch who'll stab you in the back, but he won't fight face-to-face like a man."

I took a chance. "He said you called and threatened to kill him."

More swallowing sounds. "He's a goddamn liar. I've sure as hell *thought* about it. He hates me. He was always tryin' to fix it so Helen wouldn't loan me any money. He hates my guts and I hate *his* guts. He's a rotten chickenshit prick."

There was no point in telling him Howard had made a recording of the threat. "I'd better head for home on account of the traffic. After you calm down I think you'll see things differently."

"Bullshit! The only thing I see differently is that you've turned on the rest of us. I didn't think you'd do it, Matt. I thought you'd come around, but I guess you're becomin' the same kind of prick Howard is. Stay out of our way, Matthew. Don't try to stop us. I'm warnin' you . . ."

I recalled something Cathy said, and I asked him, "Are you planning to beat me up if I don't play along? We're adults, not a bunch of schoolkids."

"Just remember what I said, Matt. Don't fuck around with us on this lawsuit thing or you're liable to regret it." He hung up before I could say anything else.

·   ·   ·

Cathy handed me a Scotch as I was taking off my necktie in the bedroom.

"Something's wrong, isn't it?" she asked. "I could see it in your eyes the minute you got home."

I took my drink and gulped half of it. I'd already decided not to tell her everything, so she wouldn't worry. "The attorney representing my brother and sisters called today. He wanted me to give a deposition saying Helen is losing her mind. He hasn't got any grounds, but he implies he has some kind of dirt. By the time he can get it before a judge, after Howard's attorney delays things, she will be dead and hopefully that will be the end of it."

"They'll still try to prove she wasn't sane when she turned everything over to Howard, won't they?"

I slipped out of my shirt and tossed it on the bed, remembering Tommy Lee's unbridled anger. "They'll try, but it's very unlikely to succeed. Without expert psychiatric evaluation of Helen's thought processes, I don't think a judge will rule. It isn't insanity when someone is merely eccentric. Perhaps Helen was a step beyond eccentricity, but she wasn't insane. Her law firm in Houston will say she functioned in virtually the same way she always had, right up to the end."

Cathy sat on the edge of the mattress watching me undress and change into my bathrobe and slippers. A fire was burning in the fireplace when I came in and it looked so inviting I wanted to be downstairs in front of it with Cathy beside me. Something garlicky and wonderful in the kitchen had also reminded me I was hungry. It was one of those nice, chilly fall evenings in Austin.

"If you ask me they're all crazy," she said. "Everyone but you, my darling. How you came from that family with all your marbles in the same bag is nothing short of a miracle."

I'd had enough of the whole mess for one day. "Where's David?" I asked.

"Basketball practice. The Thompsons picked him up. I've got you all to myself for a few hours. They're stopping off someplace for a pizza." She looked into my eyes. "There's something else, isn't there?"

I drained my glass and took her hand to lead her downstairs. "Tommy Lee phoned. He was furious because I won't join them in their petition to have Helen declared incompetent. He called me a few names, stuff like that. It came at the end of a very long day at the office with representatives from Allied. I'm just tired and I'd rather be with you than discuss it, if you don't mind. It didn't amount to anything except some name-calling, which as part of the King family, I'm quite accustomed to."

Cathy halted me at the top of the stairs. "Did he threaten you like he did Howard?" she whispered.

"No," I lied. "He called me a chickenshit and a few more choice things. Sticks and stones. C'mon. Let's sit by the fire and have a drink. Something smells good down there."

We sat in front of the fireplace watching flames lick the sides of artificial logs as the skies darkened. Before I could get a swallow of my second Scotch, the telephone rang.

Cathy picked it up and said "hello," then she put her hand over the mouthpiece and said quietly, "It's Suzan. Shall I tell her you haven't come home yet?"

I sighed. "It wouldn't do anything but delay it. Let me talk to her. Please bring me the bottle of Scotch and the ice bucket. I have a feeling this may take a while."

With her hand still covering the phone, Cathy whispered, "Don't let them drag you into this, Matt."

"I'm already into it," I replied. "I was born into it."

17

"**H**EY, MATT." SUZAN'S VOICE SOUNDED DIStant, as though we had a bad connection—or someone else was listening on an extension. "We need to talk."

"I was about to eat supper. Can I call you back?"

"This won't take long. I talked to Tommy Lee and our lawyer this afternoon. Nobody can understand why you're doing this to us."

"I'm not doing anything. I'm staying out of it."

"That's what I mean. Nobody's mother would do something cruel like this to her children if she was sane. Mother has always been off in the head. Don't act like you don't remember. She was so loony we couldn't bring friends out to the house back in high school. We were all embarrassed by her. I was miserable being around her and so were you. That's why I can't understand why you're standing up for her now. You *know* she's nuts. Howard took advantage of her, and look what's happening to the rest of us."

I rolled my eyes when Cathy brought me a bottle of Scotch and the ice bucket. "Nothing has actually happened to us, Suzan. We haven't lost anything we had. Helen put the ranch in a trust and we can't sell it, but we couldn't sell it before so what's the difference?"

"It was supposed to be ours when she died, but because she wants to be a bitch about it, she's tryin' to take it with her to her grave. She wouldn't have done this if Howard hadn't stuck his nose in it."

I was certain Suzan was being coached. "Howard doesn't gain anything, really. He has seen to Mother's financial affairs since he went to work at the bank. He can't spend any of her money. It's all in trusts and he manages them, making the right investments and so forth. He's been doing the same thing for twenty years."

"Our lawyer says he can prove Helen has been losing her mind for quite some time. Her handwriting changed, and some of what she did with all those trusts proves she got paranoid at the end to keep us from getting what's rightfully ours, because Howard manipulated her. Mr. Marcus says it happens all the time to old people. They get real childlike in some cases and she may even have been coming down with Alzheimer's disease."

"Helen doesn't have Alzheimer's. She's almost seventy and people her age tend to forget things, but that doesn't mean she's incompetent to manage her own affairs."

"I can't believe you, Matt. It's like we aren't talking about the same person. She's nuts and you know it. She never *took* us anywhere or allowed us to go anywhere until we were old enough so she couldn't stop us from leaving. As soon as I got my T-bird I drove the wheels off it going to town. She tried to keep us in prison. You think that's normal?"

I drained my drink and poured another. I heard Cathy in the kitchen. "I'm not a psychiatrist. I told Marcus I was staying out of it, and that I'm convinced Helen was not unfit to manage her estate. I'll agree she was never what I'd call a normal mother. We're not a normal family. We never talked or did things together, except on the Fourth of July. Tom Walters told me she cried every time we left. She planned our get-togethers months in advance. Mother never knew how to show us she cared about us, but that doesn't make her crazy. She left us five million dollars apiece and we all have good income from earnings off her investments. As far as I'm concerned, that's enough."

There was a change in Suzan's voice. "Carl says you're in on this with Howard."

"I frankly don't give a damn what Carl says. I won't give Marcus what he wants. I don't want any part of this fight between the rest of you and Howard. Call him if you want to talk about this."

"I don't ever intend to speak to him again in my whole life. I *hate* Howard for what he's doing, and I can't believe you'd turn against the rest of us. How can you say that Martha and Tommy Lee and I are wrong about Mother's craziness? Did you forget how we couldn't have any friends because Helen said they were all trash? Howard was always Mother's pet and he could do whatever *he* wanted, but the rest of us were treated like shit. Like *we* were the ones who were trash. Do you ever remember Helen giving us a hug or a kiss? Or telling us that she loved us?"

"We're talking about whether or not Helen is competent to manage her own affairs. Which she is. Nothing about our childhood was normal, but that doesn't mean we have a right to put her through a series of psychiatric exams simply because we don't like the way she has decided to leave her estate. If she wants it put in a managed trust there's nothing we can do to stop her."

"But she's dying," Suzan protested. "What sense does it make to have all that money and a big old ranch if nobody benefits from it? Carl and I want a ranch of our own, and if Mother would only loan us what we need, we could have it. Instead, she wants to hand everything over to Howard, like he's so much smarter than the rest of us, so he can play god managing all those millions and write us checks on the first of the month. What has Howard done to *deserve* being in charge of everything?"

"He was Helen and Lee's firstborn son, and in some

families it's traditional for the oldest son to manage the family business matters. Besides, it was Helen's decision to make and she's made it. It is my suggestion that you take it gracefully and go on with your lives."

"*Gracefully?*" Suzan screamed. "When the rest of us are being *screwed* out of what's rightfully ours by our own brother?"

"I honestly don't think Howard had anything to do with it," I said, wishing this conversation were over.

A moment of silence passed. I took a swallow of Scotch.

"I'm begging you, Matt," Suzan said quietly. She'd regained her composure. "Please don't let Howard or Helen do this to us. Please call Mr. Marcus back and say you'll join us to have her will changed. Tommy Lee will have to file bankruptcy in another month or two unless he gets some help. Carl and I will lose our escrow money on the Alpine property if we don't get that loan. Martha is having to close down her foundation, the only thing that matters to her in the whole world, if she doesn't get contributions from Mother's estate. I can't believe you'd sit there and watch all those things happen to your own brother and sisters."

"I just don't agree with your methods, Suzan. A bank in Midland will surely loan you the money for your ranch."

"Not now," Suzan replied quietly. "Carl has some bad credit from an investment deal in a shopping center. We tried to get a loan from Helen to cover the losses, but she turned us down flat. Howard said it was throwing good money after bad."

It was obvious Martha still hadn't told the others about her suspicions concerning Howard's embezzling—perhaps it wasn't true after all. "I'm sorry," I said, "but I had nothing to do with it whatsoever. Neither Helen nor Howard consult me on those kinds of things.''

''Please call Mr. Marcus and tell him you'll sign the thing. If you love us . . . if you love me or Martha or Tommy Lee, you'll do it.''

''I simply can't, Suzan. Helen isn't incompetent and I won't sign anything saying I believe she is. It would be a lie.''

A longer silence. ''Then I guess the rest of us will have to take matters into our own hands. Good-bye, Matthew. We hoped you'd listen to reason. You've become just like Howard with your selfishness. You have no feelings left. I'm never speaking to you again *either!*''

She slammed the phone down in my ear. I closed my eyes for a moment. Perhaps we were all insane, some genetic fluke making us incapable of feeling. To tell the truth, I had no real feelings for my mother or my brothers and sisters. If I never saw or heard from any of them again it would have suited me, with the possible exception being Martha. While she could be as acerbic as any of us, she had the most unselfish motives for wanting a change in the will, yet in her own way she was as cold and insular as anyone I ever met—preserving southwestern art and history had become her life, an obsession, and beyond her passion for these things she was very much like Helen. But I did have the capacity to feel—Cathy and David were proof of that. I knew what love was, but why was I incapable of feeling love for my sisters or brothers? Or Helen? I'd told Helen I loved her when I visited her at the hospital yet I knew they were only words. I said them out of a sense of duty, an obligation.

Cathy came into the den, finding me staring out our glass wall at the lights of west Austin.

''Was it bad?'' she asked in a gentle voice, sitting beside me with an apron tied around her waist.

"Same old thing. I'm a chickenshit because I won't join in the petition. She told me I'm being selfish."

Cathy touched my forearm. "Until I met your family I would never have believed any family was like yours. They despise each other yet they'll make a pact among themselves, like making a deal with the devil if they have to, to get what they want. I'm so very glad you're not a part of what they're trying to do to Helen, but I worry they'll take it out on you."

"Suzan promised she'd never speak to me again."

"Fat chance of that. None of them will stop until this is over, one way or another."

"I'm sure you're right, only the trouble is, a thing like this can drag on for years. The lawyers will be the biggest winners until every legal avenue has been tested. I don't see any way they can win, but I know they'll keep trying."

"Maybe the worst of it will stop after Helen dies. You said it would make things harder to prove."

I wasn't so sure. "Let's talk about something else. What's that delicious smell?"

"A surprise. Follow me to the dining room, Mr. King, and I'll let you experience it by candlelight."

"I love you," I said, pulling her over for a kiss.

Martha sat across from my desk smoking a cigarette, one leg propped over her knee, foot twitching, a tiny tremor in her hands when she touched the drink I gave her or her cigarette. She had dark circles under her eyes and today looked much older than her forty years. She'd driven up from San Antonio without giving me a call, taking a chance I'd be in the office.

"I suppose I'm an emissary of sorts from the enemy camp. I can wave a white flag if you wish . . . I brought a handkerchief."

I knew why she was here. She hadn't visited my offices but once in the past ten years.

"No need for white flags," I said, loosening my tie before I tasted my Scotch on the rocks. Two weeks had passed since Tommy Lee and Suzan called and I guess I should have known things were too quiet too long.

"Without your testimony agreeing with ours, Judge Huffman is going to dismiss our petition for a sanity hearing. He told our attorney there wasn't enough to justify it and Howard's hotshot lawyer has promised Mr. Marcus he'll file a motion for a continuance. Marcus says this could go on forever."

"It shouldn't be going on at all. Helen wasn't incompetent when she had her will drawn and she probably never was. She is odd, eccentric, taciturn, downright cold, a lousy mother . . . all of those things, however those aren't sufficient grounds to have her declared insane."

"You left out being a bitch. She is the biggest bitch I ever knew. If things weren't done *her* way, she'd turn to stone and make everybody so miserable they wanted to die. I wanted to die a thousand times when I lived at home. I cried so often I made Niagara Falls look like a trickle. She knew it and didn't give a damn. Nobody in this whole family gave a damn about anything or anyone else. You may have been the exception."

"We gave a damn about money," I said.

"It was Helen's carrot. She got us to do what she wanted by dangling a green carrot in front of us. She never *asked* us to do anything . . . she *told* us, and if we didn't, she withheld our money. I used to wonder what it was like when Dad screwed her. I bet she charged him for it."

"You have a gift for creating ugly visual images, Martha."

"Our lives were ugly. All I have to do is remember

what it was like to live with Helen and bingo, something ugly comes to mind.''

"We were all unhappy children, but that doesn't make Helen insane. She may have been the worst mother on this planet, but she wasn't crazy. She could be generous at times and she always listened to our troubles . . .''

"She enjoyed hearing about them. She *wanted* us to fall on our faces so we'd have to come crawling to her for money. She hated it when I married Ray because he made a fortune. She was afraid I wouldn't need her money any longer. Can I have another drink?''

I got up and brought a bottle and ice over, placing them in front of Martha. "Don't have so many you can't drive home.''

"Why, Matthew, you sound like you're genuinely concerned. It isn't like a member of the King family to show concern for anyone else.''

I sat down without offering any objection to her sarcasm. She wasn't in the mood for it. "I won't join you in the petition or in any attempt to break the will,'' I said. "That's final. I don't think she is or ever was incompetent and I don't care what happens to the ranch.''

"Maybe you'll change your mind when you see this,'' Martha replied, taking an envelope from her purse. "I caught our dear brother Howard with his dirty little hands in the cookie jar.''

"You're kidding.'' I took the envelope, but did not open it.

"Read it, when you find time. Howard has a numbered bank account in Tegucigalpa, Honduras, and a numbered Swiss account. The bank in Honduras has a branch in Belize City. You'll also find a list of certificates of deposit that are no longer where Howard said they were in the financial report. He's skimming, and he has the balls to do it before Helen's body turns cold. I paid a private snoop a lot of money to follow Howard's tracks, and even more to find out how he's doing it.''

"How does . . . he do it?" I couldn't believe Howard was guilty of stealing from the estate, yet Martha sounded so sure.

Martha smiled, lighting another cigarette. "He's clever, I have to admit. He started by playing on Helen's sympathies, if you can believe she has any. Dad was always interested in racehorses, remember? Really good racehorses. Thoroughbreds. When Lee died she sold off his interests in several breeding studs in Kentucky and that was the end of it. A couple of years ago, our clever brother convinced Helen to reinvest in some Thoroughbred breeding program in Australia, of all places. In the financial report it's called Kenbarra Limited, a foreign stock not listed on any exchange. I never checked on it and neither can the IRS because it's a privately held Australian corporation. Howard put millions into it and none of us thought to find out what Kenbarra Limited was because we *trusted* him. But my private dick found out everything. It's a front. They don't actually own a horse, not even a saddle. An agent for Kenbarra buys some high-priced Thoroughbreds at private treaty, they call it, with a check which is cashed and then the money is given back, in cash, to the investor, for a percentage. Now it's untraceable money in American dollars, and the so-called investor hides it in a numbered account in another country. Who the hell's going to fly all the way to Kenbarra, Australia, to check on some phony horse-breeding program? Or a stock called Kenbarra Limited?"

"I hadn't taken time to read the financial report," I said, though I had a vague recollection of the name Kenbarra Limited on a list of Helen's extensive stock holdings. "How do you know Helen approved of the invest-

ment in racehorses? Maybe she had no idea what Howard
was doing."

"She knew. I talked to Dana Fullerton personally.
Helen told him about the investment in Australia. She said
Howard was interested because he knew how much his
father loved good racing Thoroughbreds and he thought
Helen would enjoy knowing some of Lee's money was
invested in champion racehorses. Fullerton told her it
sounded okay to him, that he was sure Howard understood
the risks of a foreign investment and wouldn't make a
costly mistake. You see, Helen trusted Howard and he used
that to siphon off several million, making it look like an
investment."

I opened the envelope now, glancing at a report from a
man named Wesley Wise, calling himself a "Private Investigator" in bold print at the top of the first page.

"The trouble will be proving it," Martha continued,
adding more Scotch and ice to her glass. "Kenbarra Limited isn't required by Australian law to report earnings or
losses or its assets to an outsider. They pay Australian taxes
on what they say they earn and we can't get a copy of their
report. It isn't public record there, even if they're audited
by their version of Internal Revenue. It's all in Wesley's
report."

"Wesley?"

"He's kinda cute, but I'm not interested."

"You haven't been interested in another man since you
and Ray divorced, have you?"

"Ray taught me to hate men. Dealing with you and
Howard and Tommy Lee hasn't given me any reason to
change my mind. Men are arrogant, condescending bas-
tards for the most part. I'm whatever you call the opposite
of a misogynist."

"But you don't mind joining a petition with Tommy

Lee to get at Helen's money. Getting in bed with the devil?"

"She cut off all donations to the foundation. And now I can prove dear sweet Howard is stealing her and the rest of us blind. What the hell did you expect me to do? Send Howard my congratulations for devising such a clever scheme? And send a 'Thank You' note to Helen for being so considerate? After all the years of hard work and sacrifice I've put into the Carter Foundation?"

I wouldn't tell her the problem lay in what she named it. I couldn't.

"Do the others know about this?" I asked.

Again, she smiled. "Not yet, but I'm about to put a skunk under everybody's bed. In case you ever wondered what it's like to see sparks fly, you're about to see some. I wanted you to be the first to know."

My mind began racing, wondering what Howard would do when his scheme was exposed. Martha seemed very sure of her investigator's information. I needed to do a little checking myself. "I want to ask you a favor and you don't owe me one. Let me have a friend of mine look into this. Give me a couple of weeks. You said it may be hard to prove what Howard is doing and I might be able to get that proof, if it exists. I'm still having trouble believing Howard would do this; however your boy Wesley obviously covered a lot of ground."

"You'll call Howard and tell him I'm onto him."

"No I won't. You've got my word."

"I'll take a chance and trust you," she said, after a brief hesitation. "I'll give you two weeks, Matthew. Then I'm giving copies of Wesley's report to everybody else and we'll go to the district attorney. This is a criminal offense, as I'm sure you know."

I knew, even though criminal law isn't my specialty.

18

A COLD GRAY RAIN FELL ON EDEN CEMETERY. It was the fourth day of December, precisely six months after Helen told us she was dying. Hundreds of mourners, bankers and corporate chairmen and stockbrokers and literally everyone who stood to benefit from doing continued business with the King estate, were there, standing under umbrellas. Nothing else would have brought out so many company dignitaries, shivering in drizzling rain with mud clinging to the soles of expensive shoes, umbrellas shedding water, overcoats darkened by raindrops, gathered around a coffin suspended above a six-foot hole where a giant marble marker bore the name Helen Rathbone King. The very fact that it was raining was bitter irony, after selling off the last of Helen's cows. It was as if the forces of nature waited until Helen died to unleash nourishing waters for King ranch grasses.

I was more concerned with who was not there than with those who were present. I found it hard to believe Tommy Lee, Suzan, and Carl refused to attend. Howard stood beside a preacher from Eden's First Baptist Church with Diane clinging to his elbow, a dazed, glassy look in her eyes. The elderly minister read from his Bible in a sonorous voice while his wife held an umbrella to keep wind-driven rain from dampening the pages. There was a tent roof erected over the gravesite, too small to offer much protection from the weather for more than a few mourners. Eden's lone funeral home could only provide bare essentials, a few folding chairs and small carpets of artificial turf around the casket. Huge sprays and arrangements of soggy flowers sent from half a dozen states where Helen kept money in CDs offered evidence of how much worried bankers cared about keeping her money in their electronic vaults.

Cathy stood beside me, shivering when a gust of wind blew rain under our umbrella. David had stayed in Austin for a ninth-grade basketball game. Martha was on my left, her features drawn into an expression so severe it was impossible to read, clinging to the handle of her umbrella. We'd talked just once since our meeting in my office that afternoon. I called to tell her about my investigator's findings thus far. A man I knew in Miami dealt in highly specialized security arrangements for insurance companies and banks across the country. He was an expert at tracking funds spirited out of the United States by clever embezzlers, and if anyone could prove Howard was robbing Helen's trust, it was Robert Kincaid. He was in Sydney, Australia, now checking on the history and officers of Kenbarra Limited. Kincaid was expensive and well worth it. He'd already bribed someone at the Banco Central del Tegucigalpa to find out Howard King had six million and some change on deposit there, transferred from a bank in Sydney in small increments over the past three years. But with Kincaid's revelation came a warning—it would be hard to prove the original source of Howard's funds. Proof would have to come from documents at Kinbarra Limited, or bank records in Australia that were much harder to obtain, if not impossible. Martha hadn't greeted my news with much enthusiasm at first, but she found some satisfaction in my admission that it appeared she was right about Howard's fraudulent activities. I hadn't mentioned any of this to Cathy, although I'm sure she sensed I was preoccupied. Now, as I looked across Helen's casket at Howard

while the graveside service began, I was almost certain I
was looking at a thief—my own brother who was stealing
from our mother's estate and apparently had been for a
number of years. We shook hands at the funeral parlor
before Helen's memorial service and spoke briefly to each
other's wives. Howard said nothing about Tommy Lee's or
Suzan's absence. Martha had shown up late at the cemetery, avoiding Howard in the throng of mourners plodding
across mud and sodden grass to Helen's grave. She merely
nodded to me and to Cathy when she arrived, wearing a
black dress and black overcoat. Her face was flushed and I
suspected it was Scotch, not the cold, coloring her cheeks.
We endured a typical Southern Baptist funeral eulogy, un-
necessarily long and animated when conducted by a generously paid preacher. Howard had made all the funeral
arrangements—when he called to tell me Helen had died
in her sleep on Monday he told me it would be a simple
service.

"Amen," the preacher said, closing his Bible.

A few murmured "Amen"s came from mourners as
people began to head for their cars, trudging over slippery
sod under gray-black rainy skies.

"Let's go," Cathy whispered when I stood looking at
Helen's casket too long. "I'm freezing."

Martha spoke to me as we were leaving the tent. She
kept her voice low. "I need to see you, Matthew. Can you
come down tomorrow? I have something I'd like to show
you."

It was a strange request, coming from Martha. "I suppose I can cancel some afternoon appointments. Where
should I come? To the foundation?"

"Yes. Come to the back door and knock. We're closed
to the public now. Friday was our last day. I ran out of
money."

"I'll try to be there by two o'clock. If I'm running late I can give you a call."

She nodded and turned her umbrella into the wind, walking away as quickly as muddy conditions allowed, her shoulders rounded. I took Cathy by the arm and led her toward our car. I didn't say good-bye to Howard or Diane. They were surrounded by too many sympathizers.

"I wonder what that's all about?" Cathy asked.

I sighed, tilting our umbrella to keep raindrops off Cathy as much as I could. "I'm sure it's more of the same. Another request to join them trying to break Helen's will. Let's not discuss it now."

"I understand," she replied, struggling to keep her balance in high-heeled shoes while holding on to my elbow. "I couldn't help but notice one thing, darling. Nobody shed a tear the whole time, not Howard, not you or Martha. I've never been to a single funeral before where nobody cried."

I thought about it. "I think we shed all our tears years ago," I told her honestly. I hadn't felt the least bit like crying today—I felt numbness, and a vague feeling of dread. Martha wouldn't have asked me to drive down to San Antonio unless she wanted something from me.

As I was closing Cathy's car door, Tom Walters and his wife, Bonnie, walked up to me. I said "Hello" to Mrs. Walters and she returned my somber greeting, continuing toward their pickup truck while Tom stayed a moment, dressed in his best blue jeans and a tan canvas duster, rainwater falling off the brim of his hat in tiny rivulets.

"Real sorry 'bout your mother passin' on," Tom said, as if he'd rehearsed what he was supposed to say for a funeral. "After things get settled down a bit I'd like to talk to you. Me an' my wife have found us a little house we can rent in Eden. Hell, I feel like I'm stealin' the money Howard sends me every month on account of there ain't really nothin' to do. Got to thinkin' on it some an' decided we'd move off the place. Without no cows it don't seem like a ranch no more.''

"I wish you'd stay on awhile longer," I said. Hearing his gentle voice now reminded me of how much I truly owed him. "If it's all the same to you. Don't worry about the salary. Maybe now that it's raining Howard will agree to put some cattle back on the place.''

"I'd just as soon not work for your brother, Matt. It won't be the same. But if you want me to stay fer a spell I'll do it, but only because it was you who asked.''

"I'd appreciate it, Tom. Right now things are getting a bit nasty between the five of us. I'd feel better knowing you were here looking after things.''

"Nothin' to look after now," he said, and I sensed, rather than heard, the sorrow in his voice. "No cows. You can hire a man to open the gates for them oil-field trucks.''

"I wish you'd stay until things get worked out.''

"I'll do it, son," he told me, offering his hand. "I reckon you've got enough on your mind right now. We can talk about the place some other time.'' He looked up at the sky briefly. "This rain sure as hell will give the ranch a bunch of grass, come the spring. Tell David I said hello.''

I watched Tom walk off with mud caked to the soles of his boots, feeling strangely lonely.

The Carter Foundation Museum and Exhibit Hall of Southwestern Culture is on Broadway near Brackenridge Park adjacent to the Witte Museum, not far from Trinity University. I'd only been inside once, almost twenty years ago when Martha and Ray decided to open it. I remembered walls displaying dozens of oil paintings of southwestern scenes, glass cases full of Indian and early Spanish relics, antique guns and old saddles and wagon wheels and the like. Collectors sometimes loaned rare items for showings lasting a few months to a year, Martha told me. But today, as I drove into its empty parking lot, the Carter Foundation building looked forgotten, forlorn with its glass doors darkened, and I had a better understanding of my sister's grief. I drove around to the back and parked beside Martha's dark blue Mercedes, dreading our meeting more than ever. I knew it wasn't going to be a pleasant visit.

My knock produced a clicking noise in the door's lock a few moments later. Martha stood back to admit me wearing faded jeans and a sweatshirt. Her hair was uncombed, tangled, hanging in a careless manner around her face. I smelled liquor on her breath when she said, "Hello, Matt."

"Sorry I'm late." I apologized even though I'd called her on my car phone to explain the delay.

She led me toward a lighted office. The rest of the building was dark, musty-smelling. The whine of a central heating fan came from a duct above her office door. The temperature outside was close to forty degrees, unusually cold for early December.

In a room crowded with boxes of files and papers, open file cabinets and clutter I didn't recognize, Martha's desktop held a mound of unopened mail and magazines. Two chairs were placed side by side across the desk from her swivel chair. I took one as Martha removed a glass from a desk drawer and poured me a Scotch from a half-empty bottle near her telephone. Under the harsh glare of fluorescent light from the ceiling, Martha's face looked pale, waxy, and deeply wrinkled, as though she'd lost a lot of weight.

"This place doesn't look the same without cars around it," I said, before realizing it was the wrong thing to say.

She tossed back half a glass of Scotch without ice, giving me a blank stare.

"No shit," she said, handing me my drink. "How the

hell do you think I feel? Eighteen years down the drain. Poof! Just like that!"

I noticed an old pistol in a wooden display box resting on a corner of her desk. "Are you planning to shoot someone?" I asked by way of changing the subject.

She glanced at the rusted revolver. "It's on loan and I'm sending it back to El Paso. It's the gun John Selman used to kill John Wesley Hardin. Shot him in the back with it. He was a lawyer, you know, after he got out of prison for shooting twenty-three men. Apparently killers make good lawyers, and vice versa. Hardin passed the bar right after he was released from jail."

"I'm glad you weren't planning to shoot me."

She smiled weakly. "It probably wouldn't fire anyway. It's too old to be useful—like me."

"Feeling sorry for yourself? Life doesn't end because some worthwhile enterprise closes down. You did your best to keep it open. Stop blaming yourself."

Martha's expression turned cold. "I'm *not* blaming myself. I blame Howard and Helen and their sick relationship. This whole family is sick, Matt. Really sick. Mentally ill. Have you heard the latest? Tommy Lee threatened to kill Howard. Suzan told me about it. Tommy Lee actually bragged about it and he doesn't even *know* about Howard's embezzling yet. Carl told Suzan he wished Tommy Lee would go ahead and do it, that we'd all be better off if you were administrator of the estate. At least you'll *listen* when somebody talks to you."

"Howard told me about what Tommy Lee said," I admitted, drinking warm Scotch from the smudged glass. "He has a tape recording of it. He records every telephone conversation, at home and at the office. He says it's because he forgets things. I think he's paranoid and won't admit to it."

"I'm going to give him ample reason to be paranoid in

a few more days. You said you only needed two weeks to find out what Howard's been doing."

"Kincaid is in Australia now. If anyone can get proof it'll be him. I told you he found over six million in Honduras before he left. He told me the key to everything is with Kenbarra Limited and their records."

Martha poured herself more Scotch. "I'm going to enjoy it when Howard is sent to prison. Do I sound too bitchy for your taste?"

"We have no proof yet, nothing that will stand up in court. It isn't a crime to have money in foreign banks, so long as you report it to the IRS. Since we can't get a copy of his tax return we have no way of knowing if it's his money, or money he may have embezzled from Helen."

"I'm glad she's dead," Martha said quietly, staring into my eyes. "I know it's a rotten thing to say about your own mother, but I'm actually glad. She used us like puppets, pulling our strings, putting words in our mouths like 'I love you' when none of us loved her at all. She wouldn't *allow* us to love her like a mother. She kept us at a distance from her all our lives. The only exception was Howard, because he was Lee's favorite and the first to be born. What a lousy fucking system for determining who gets any attention. She really was crazy, you know . . ."

I needed more liquor as our conversation changed directions. I held out my glass. "Maybe now you can get on with your life. She won't be around to make you miserable."

Suddenly Martha began to cry. "She ruined everything I've worked so hard to build here. I was happy. I found something I could do that made me feel good about myself instead of feeling miserable all the time the way I did when we were growing up. All the bitch had to do was make tax-deductible contributions to my work here, but she stopped when Howard told her it wasn't a 'significant tax advantage' over some fucking tax-free municipal bonds. She would rather own bonds issued by the city of Cleveland than help her own daughter with a project to preserve historic parts of southwestern culture. How can she say she ever loved me when a fucking bond from *Cleveland* was more important to her? A goddamn *municipal* bond, of all things, whatever the hell they are . . .''

"That was probably Howard's idea," I lied, omitting what I knew about Helen's problem with the name of the foundation. "He saw it as sound financial advice, I suppose."

"While he was *stealing* millions!" she cried, anger replacing sorrow and frustration.

"What did you want to show me?" I asked when Martha began to cry again. "I ought to be heading back to the office. I had a late appointment at six o'clock I couldn't cancel."

She sniffled and dried her eyes on her sleeve. "My museum. You'll be the last person to see it before everything is shipped off to other collections. I wanted you to see it, Matt. You're the only member of the family I ever cared to show it to."

I resisted a temptation to glance at my watch. "Sure. I'd like to see it. Fix me another drink and give me a guided tour."

"You know why, don't you?" Martha asked, filling my glass again. "I think you're the only member of this sick family who can understand what I've done here, how much of my heart and my soul is in it. It's all I have that I care about, and now I'm closing it down forever."

ROBERT KINCAID CALLED ME FROM MIAMI THE following Tuesday morning, five days after I visited Martha.

"It's a scam," he said, "but you'll never be able to prove it. Those guys play hardball Down Under and the minute I started nosing around, I was followed. I can't get any bank records or any cooperation from the government, so the scam may run pretty high up in political circles. They're laundering money, probably dirty money from all over the globe. The registered agent for Kenbarra Limited is Douglass A. Washburn, but he doesn't exist. He listed his home address as a rural route miles from Kenbarra, but the postman never heard of him. But I did talk to a horse trainer who winked when I asked about buying a racehorse from Kenbarra Limited. He said I had to have an 'introduction' to the right people, from the right people, or I was wasting my time. Another trainer told me that Kenbarra occasionally buys a high-priced Thoroughbred stud, to look legitimate, then they insure it for big bucks through a Lloyds of London agent and kill the horse a few months later to collect the insurance. The guy I talked to was a retired needle man—that's what they call the bastard who kills the horse. He agreed to talk to me anonymously for five thousand dollars, so he tells me how he goes into the stud's stall at night and pulls out a tail hair, then he sticks a needle full of a neurological poison like curare into the hole where the hair shaft was so nobody will find a mark made by a needle, and the horse drops dead. In a few hours the poison dissipates so it won't show up in a typical veterinary autopsy. Sorry, old chap, as they say down there, but I can't get you a thing other than heresay. I did find out that it's relatively easy to send a bank wire transfer from Sydney to Honduras through a British offshore bank down in Belize. That may explain why your brother goes to Belize City from time to time. Several Honduran banks have affiliations with Belizian banks for wire transfers. It's called correspondent banking. The deposits in Tegucigalpa arrived in amounts of a few hundred thousand or so, over a period of several weeks. That's about all the girl could tell me. I had to get her drunk that night to tell me anything at all. She works in their International Department. A real cute little bitch. I hope it doesn't bother you that I had to fuck her all night. I'm not charging you for the extra time.''

"Send me a bill," I said, frustrated. "There is no way to prove what Howard is doing, right?"

"Follow the money is my rule of thumb. I did that. It's a dead end in Australia. If you can get a DA somewhere to accept an embezzlement charge, he may be able to get your brother's tax returns, if a grand jury will indict him. But you're barking up an empty tree if you think selling off a few big CDs early will be enough to convict him. If he's as smart as he seems to be, he has those tracks covered by now. Moving money around is the way the big boys do it. Changing the amounts, moving deposits back and forth. Money loses its identity, if you know what you're doing in this game. You'll never be able to prove he doesn't own a bunch of racehorses in Australia, and even if you do he'll claim he was cheated by Kenbarra Limited and you can't prosecute them. Howard gets off free as a bird by saying he was an innocent victim of their scam. You can't touch his bank records in Honduras or with the Swiss banking system to prove he got money back for the investment checks he wrote.''

"Shit," I whispered into the phone.

"Cussing is about all you can do, Matt. By the way, I was sorry to hear you lost your mother while I was gone."

"Yeah. Thanks. Send me a bill. And thanks for looking at this so quickly. I know you're busy." When I hung up I spent a moment staring at the wall of my office, pondering what to do with what I'd just learned. Martha had to be told.

"You bastard," I whispered, discovering my fists clenched on my desktop. Martha had been right all along about Howard.

Although I'm not the confrontational type, I wanted to hear Howard's denial. It was four o'clock and with luck I'd catch him at the bank. As I dialed his private number I wondered why he kept office hours in the first place, with several million hidden away as a cushion. He didn't need to work. I suppose because the trust owned a significant share of Texas Bank stock Howard felt he should be there, a watchdog, perhaps, though in his case I was reminded of the fox guarding the henhouse.

"Howard King," he said with authority, like he knew his name meant something.

"It's Matt. Are you alone?"

"I was leaving. Is it important?"

"You tell me. How important is stock in Kenbarra Limited?"

A pause. I remembered we were being recorded.

"Why do you ask?" Howard's voice had changed, softened to a degree, possibly wary.

"Because I know it's a scam, and so does Martha. I think we know a great deal more than you wanted us to know. She was the first to suspect something. She hired an investigator to look into it. He found your money in Honduras and traced Kenbarra Limited. They don't own any racehorses, as you know. They are in the money-washing business, and they kill expensive racehorses for the insurance.''

A much longer silence. Howard was collecting his wits. He would not have entered into an embezzlement scheme like this without planning what he'd say if he were about to be caught.

"I'm shocked. They had an excellent rating for a private corporation in Australia. I was referred by a friend. I am puzzled by your remark, about finding my money in Tegucigalpa. There is nothing wrong with depositing my own funds in a foreign bank. What's the connection to Kenbarra?''

"I'm sure you know the connection. That was money from the estate. You laundered it through Kenbarra Limited and sent it in smaller amounts to Honduras by bank wire. I had a guy who knows the banking business trace it. You've been embezzling Helen's estate, Howard. You knew there weren't any racehorses, or even if there were, they'd wind up dead.''

More silence.

"You've become smitten with the same delusions of grandeur as our sisters and brother, Matthew. You've joined them in their legal action against me, it would appear. Otherwise I'm sure you wouldn't make such groundless accusations. I'm disappointed. If you believe you can prove I've done anything illegal, then by all means attempt it. I invested in racing Thoroughbreds in Australia, with Mother's written consent. I have her letter authorizing the purchases. As to your wild accusation that I embezzled funds from the estate, you'll have to prove it in court. I acted within my authority as administrator. Now, if you have nothing more to discuss, let's end this fruitless effort to discredit me over the phone. My attorney is Joel Murchison, and if you have anything further to say to me, put it in writing and send it to him.''

"Martha wants to take it to the district attorney. The others don't know about it yet."

"Poor Martha," Howard said. "Because she has to close down her artist's colony, or whatever the hell it is, she is depressed to the point of making false charges against me. She has been unstable since her divorce. She's always been a schizophrenic personality."

"I didn't know psychiatry was your field, Howard."

"Good-bye, Matthew. I was about to wish you a Merry Christmas, although now it seems like wasted breath. Don't call me again. I don't care to hear from you."

The phone went dead in my ear. I hung up, lost in thought. Howard hadn't been the slightest bit ruffled by my charges. He'd been prepared for the day when someone questioned the Kenbarra investment.

I dialed Martha's cellular number.

"Hello?"

"It's me. I've got bad news. Shall I call you back at the foundation? I wasn't sure where you'd be."

"Give me the bad news. Somehow I knew the news would be bad all along."

"Kincaid says we can't prove a thing. He was followed when he started asking about Kenbarra down in Australia. It's a scam, like your private investigator said. They launder money from all over the world, but it's big and powerful, well connected at least in the Australian government and there is no way to get any records. There aren't any racehorses and even the people running the company don't exist."

"We'll take it to the DA anyway."

"I called Howard to confront him, to see what he'd say about Kenbarra. He says he has a letter from Helen authorizing everything and he claims he didn't know there were no horses. He has his ass covered on the money in Honduras too, I think. He didn't deny having money there, only he says it's his. According to Bob Kincaid we can't subpoena foreign bank records and if the money isn't on Howard's tax return, even a subpoena for his personal bank records and copies of the IRS filing for the estate won't be proof of anything illegal. I don't think Howard will do it again because he knows we're watching him. I can call for an independent audit of the estate's tax return and financial statement every year as a beneficiary of the trust, and so can you. But it appears there is nothing else we can do. He's done this sort of thing for years and he'd know—''

"We can't let Howard get away with this," Martha snapped. "There must be something we can do."

"Nothing I know of, but I'm not a criminal lawyer. Without some sort of documentation, all we've got is a bad investment in a foreign stock and suspicions of foul play."

"I'll bet the asshole's laughing at all of us right now."

"He wasn't laughing, Martha. If he's guilty, which I'm sure he is, he'll cover his tracks and lay low."

"But he's already stolen *millions*. Doesn't that piss you off?"

"Of course. The problem is, I don't know what we can do about it."

I heard Martha lighting a cigarette.

"I'll call Tommy Lee and Suzan to tell them about it. We can take what we have to the DA," she said.

"Tommy Lee will be furious. Howard may get another broken nose."

"The bastard has one coming. Carl said a good ass-whipping was what Howard needed."

"Even our in-laws have a tendency toward violence."

"Now will you join us in the petition to have Helen's will broken? Haven't you seen enough?"

I took a deep breath. "I'll think about it, but I'm afraid it's all in vain. Helen wasn't incompetent. Dana Fullerton and Haynes will testify to that. I don't see any way we can win."

"I need a drink," Martha said. "I'll call everybody else. Think about joining us, Matt. We can't let Howard get away with this."

"I'll give it some thought, but don't count on me. If I had my way, we'd leave the whole thing alone. Howard won't try this again . . . I'm sure he won't, now that we're on to him."

"I'm not so sure. He has Helen's ice water in his veins. He may think he's smart enough to pull it off again and again if we ignore it this time."

I wondered if Martha could be right. I tried to change the subject. "How's the packing going?"

"Sadly. I cry all day when I take down one of my favorite exhibits. The girl who's helping me says I'm a manic depressive without a manic phase. And I've lost my appetite. I keep thinking this is all because of Howard, because his greedy fat ass wanted everything under his thumb. If I were a man I'd choke the shit out of him until he turned blue."

"Now you're showing me *your* violent side."

"I wish I had one. Every side I've got is too depressed to function properly."

"It's Christmas. I read somewhere people get depressed on certain holidays. Maybe that's it."

"Howard is the reason I'm depressed, not Santa Claus. I don't give a shit about Christmas."

"I'm wishing you a Merry Christmas anyway."

"Humbug. Maybe Howard is giving us all an invisible

racehorse for Christmas. Good-bye, Matt. I'm heading for the closest liquor store. Think about signing our petition. With all of us saying Helen was nuts, we stand a better chance.''

"I'll think about it. Good-bye, Martha.''

20

I WAS AT HOME, MAKING A FAILED ATTEMPT AT
helping David with his algebra homework, when the phone
rang. I never understood a need for algebra. Solving for
"X" has to be the biggest waste of time in the universe.
David knew more about the equations than I did, however
maintaining a knowledgeable fatherly image kept me from
admitting to my deficiency until Cathy summoned me to
the den for a call.

"It's Martha," she said.

"Christ. More family affairs." I'd told Cathy about
Howard and Kenbarra before David got home from basketball practice and she didn't act the least bit surprised.

I took the phone and sat down while Cathy fixed me a
Scotch and rocks—she knew to dispense with the water
when I was facing a phone call from anyone in my family.

"Hello," I said, really noticing for the first time our
Christmas tree Cathy put up near the fireplace, decorated
with the same balls and lights and tinsel every family ac-
cumulates as years pass.

"Cath said you were doing algebra. I figured you
needed a break anyway. Algebra is stupid, busywork for
morons. The guy who invented it must not have had a dick
or anything else to play with."

"You have a way with words."

"Listen to these. Tommy Lee is headed for Dallas with
a gun and a case of beer. He swears he's going to kill
Howard. I told Suzan. Carl wasn't home, but she's leaving

him a message on his voice mail. She's flying to Dallas to try to stop Tommy Lee from doing something stupid. She's renting a car at the airport. Tommy Lee usually stays at the Marriott when he's in Dallas, according to her. She's hoping he'll get a room first, before he . . . I tried calling his car phone. He won't answer."

"A loving family, gathering for a Christmas celebration," I remarked, envisioning Tommy Lee speeding along an interstate with a beer in one hand, a pistol in the other. Our family was truly showing off its emotional cracks tonight.

"Only some of us are bringing loaded weapons," Martha said. "Maybe Santa will get his ass shot off coming down the chimney, struck by bullets fired at each other by the King brothers. It may make the OK Corral look like a church social if it makes the ten o'clock news."

"Surely he won't go through with it. Besides, Howard does not believe in guns. Tommy Lee wouldn't shoot an unarmed man."

"Don't bet against it. Tommy was shouting over the phone. He was drunk. I should have known better than to tell him about what Howard did when he was in that shape. I suppose I should drive up there too, to keep Tommy from doing something dumb. It was my fault he flipped his lid. I can be there in four hours. He may go straight to Howard's house. If I step on it I can get there at about the same time. According to the resident slut this week at Tommy Lee's house, he left about an hour ago. She's the one who told me he had a gun."

"Call the police in Dallas," I suggested.

"Tommy Lee would never forgive me if the cops picked him up with a loaded gun in front of Howard's house. I'll try to stop him myself. He won't shoot me."

"He's a grown man, Martha. Call the police and let

them handle it. I don't think he'd actually go through with it."

"He's changed. His Buick dealership is in serious financial trouble. He owes hundreds of thousands he can't pay. He drinks all day, he told me. It's like Nero fiddling while Rome burns."

"I'd stay out of it, if I were you."

"I feel responsible. I'll call you from Dallas if anything happens. Don't call Howard. He'd love having Tommy Lee arrested for attempted murder. It would make his day."

She hung up before I could object further. I wondered if I should ignore Martha's warning not to call Howard. It was six-thirty. I was three and a half hours from Dallas myself. If I hurried I could park in front of Howard's house to head off Tommy Lee before he got there and Howard would never have to know about the death threat. I might be able to keep Tommy Lee from going to jail.

Cathy brought me my drink. "I have to go to Dallas. Tommy Lee is headed for Howard's house with a gun," I said in a voice too low for David to hear in his bedroom.

"Why don't you call the police?"

"I suppose it's because he's my brother," I replied, getting up slowly, wondering if I might be doing the wrong thing. "It's not that we actually are like brothers, but I guess I owe it to him to stop him from doing something really foolish. If he truly intends to see it through . . . I think it's just drunk talk. He's more likely to kill himself on the highway driving drunk than to cause Howard any harm."

I drained my glass and started for the garage.

"Please don't go, Matt," Cathy said.

"It'll be okay," I assured her, taking my overcoat. "I'll call you when I get there. Don't worry."

PART

III

21

DALLAS HOMICIDE DETECTIVE TONY GARCIA entered my office at ten in the morning wearing a cheap suit and clip-on necktie. He was about what I expected, judging by his voice. We had had several phone conversations during the previous week and I almost felt like I knew him personally. He was fortyish, graying, slightly overweight with most of his extra pounds centered around his middle. I noticed he had fleshy jowls with deep wrinkles below his chin. He didn't look Hispanic and there was no trace of an accent in his speech.

"Good morning, Mr. King," he said, offering his hand.

We shook and I pointed to a chair. Since Howard had been found murdered in his study I was in something of a daze, getting almost no work done. I hadn't been able to sleep or eat much of anything. Scotch was the only thing that helped. I sat down, eyeing Garcia, wondering what he'd found out. He did not strike me as being particularly bright.

"Sorry to trouble you," he began, taking a notebook from his inside coat pocket. "I keep finding things, things I don't understand. I need to go over some of them with you, if you have the time."

"I'll take the time," I said.

Garcia looked at his notes. "As you know, your younger brother Tommy threatened to kill your older brother. Howard King's wife gave us a tape recording of

what he said, although this was more than three weeks
before Howard was murdered. I've been wondering why
he waited so long, if he did it. At first we were sure it was
a simple robbery. The White Rock Lake area is prime
pickings for thieves and sometimes a burglar makes a mistake when he thinks nobody's home. But when Diane King
told us about Tommy threatening to kill Howard, we questioned him and his answers didn't add up. He was in Dallas
that night. He had a gun and he'd been drinking heavily all
day. The hotel where he was staying says he checked in at a
few minutes before midnight. The coroner's report indi-
cates your brother was killed about ten-thirty or eleven.
Tommy says he was driving around and he admits he drove
by Howard's house, but according to him, he didn't stop.
He was driving a dark blue Buick Roadmaster, a demon-
strator owned by his dealership, he said. At about eleven
the next morning he checks out of his hotel and drives to
San Antonio. That's when he says he found out Howard
had been murdered. We haven't arrested him, as you must
know by now. We sent his pistol to the lab. It had been
fired recently, but we have no bullet, so a ballistics test is
out. Whoever killed your brother took the time to dig the
slug out of the back of his chair, so we know he's smart.
On the other hand our forensics expert says it was probably
a forty-five, so it could have been from Tommy's gun. A
forty-five makes a very big hole. Now I come to another
troubling part. Howard King's secretary at the bank gave
us another tape recording of a conversation between you
and your older brother, in which you accuse him of embezzling from your late mother's estate. Howard was the administrator, but documents were filed making you
administrator if anything happened to him. Do you remember this particular telephone call?''

   ''I remember it quite well. My sister, Martha Carter,
paid an investigator to check on some apparent discrepan-

cies. I also hired a private investigator and he came to the same conclusions the other fellow did. Howard had been misappropriating money for his own use. I called Howard to confront him with what we found. If you have the recording, you already know what I said.''

Garcia's brow furrowed. "Three brothers, and all of you are mad at each other. Unusual, don't you agree, when a brother threatens to kill another brother?''

"Yes, it's unusual. We never got along all that well. We had a rather unusual upbringing. None of us were close. But as you know, I did not threaten to kill Howard or anything of the kind. I called to tell him what my investigator found out and to hear what he had to say about it.''

Garcia shook his head and referred to his notes again. "I also know you drove to Dallas that night. You returned, according to your wife, at about five-thirty in the morning. You told her you never saw Tommy and that you did not go inside Howard's house. You waited outside, hoping to stop Tommy from carrying out his threat.''

"That's the truth. Tommy Lee never showed up, and after I saw Diane and the kids come home around midnight I drove back to Austin.'' I hadn't known the police talked to Cathy and I could not imagine why she hadn't told me about it. It wasn't like her to keep secrets from me.

"You can understand, surely, why someone might find it a bit strange when one brother does not go inside to warn the other of a possible murder attempt,'' Garcia observed.

I nodded. "Howard said he never wanted to speak to me again and I took him at his word. It's all on the tape. I was there to keep Tommy Lee from doing something he would regret. He was drunk and wasn't thinking straight, my sister said. She talked to him about the embezzlement and that's when Tommy Lee got mad.''

"But you were at the scene of the murder from around

ten that evening until midnight, according to what you told me over the phone, and the coroner says Howard was killed between ten-thirty and eleven o'clock."

"I drove around the neighborhood some. I didn't just sit in front of the house all that time. I drove to a convenience store to buy cigarettes. I have no idea what time that was."

"And you never saw a thing? Nobody going in or out?"

"Nobody."

"Maybe you're covering for Tommy. You could have seen him going in and you won't tell me about it. I would expect it, coming from a brother. Now, here's another strange coincidence. Your younger sister, Suzan Westerman, was also in Dallas that same night. She flew in on Conquest Airlines flight ninety-six, arriving at Love Field at eight-forty. She rented a Cadillac and drove to the Marriott Hotel, inquiring if Tommy King had checked into a room. She rented a room herself and left a message for Tommy to call her, then she went out, leaving a phone number at the desk. It's a Midland cellular exchange. As you must have guessed, I'll have to question her at length. Maybe you can tell me . . . does she own a gun?"

"Not that I'm aware of. We don't see each other very often, so I wouldn't know."

"Tommy says Mrs. Westerman is part of a legal action to have your late mother's will changed. Are you also a party to it? As a lawyer, maybe you were handling it . . ."

"I'm not involved. An attorney in Houston by the name of Anthony Marcus is their legal counsel. I do not agree with them or what they are trying to do, so I stayed out of it."

"However, you accused Howard of embezzling funds from the estate."

"I did. The proof is in documents outside the country and no one can subpoena it."

"You mentioned Honduras and Australia, I think," Garcia said as he turned a notebook page.

"That's correct. I paid a security specialist to fly down to Australia, to see if he could trace some money missing from a trust fund of Helen's. His name is Robert Kincaid and his offices are in Miami. I'll give you his number if you need to talk to him."

"At this point it doesn't seem necessary," Garcia went on. "I need to talk to everyone who was in Dallas on the night of the murder to compare their stories."

"I'm a suspect," I said. I'd known I would be.

Garcia smiled. "Right now, all of you are suspects. You and your brother and possibly your sister were near the murder scene, at or very close to the estimated time of your brother's death. And you were at odds with each other over money."

"What makes you so sure Howard wasn't killed by a burglar? You said it was a bad neighborhood for robberies . . . prime pickings you called it. Someone could have come from the alley, and when Howard saw him, the burglar didn't want to be identified, so he shot Howard and robbed him before he took off. You said Howard's billfold was empty . . ."

"At first, we believed that's all it was. Forced entry at a side door near the garage. The alarm system was off because Mrs. King and the children were shopping. It was Mrs. King who made us start looking at other motives. She told us about years of difficulties between the five of you, and then she gave us the tape recording of Tommy King threatening to kill Howard, and told us about another incident in which Tommy broke Howard's nose with his fist. She told us what she knew about the legal matter with regard to your mother's will. When we searched Howard's office, I found the recording of your phone call. In any homicide, the first place you look is at those who knew the deceased. It's almost always someone they were acquainted with, sometimes someone they knew quite well. Random killings are rare and often accidental. There's usually a personal motive when a murder takes place. And here's another thing . . . I'm sure Howard knew his assailant. The gun was fired at close range, close enough to put powder burns on his face, yet there was no sign of a struggle or any indication he tried to escape. He was seated in his chair like he didn't suspect anything until it was too late."

"But you said there was forced entry."

"The killer didn't have a key. He used a screwdriver, which is even more evidence he wasn't a professional burglar. They use more sophisticated tools, in most cases."

I found myself wishing for a drink even though it was early. "Tommy Lee didn't do it. He'd have driven up in the driveway and I would have seen his car. I drove around a little bit, and when I saw Diane come home I left for Austin. Nobody parked near the house while I was there. Tommy Lee didn't know Howard was dead until three or four the next afternoon, when Suzan called him to ask him what he knew about it, or if he'd done it. She'd been trying to reach him all morning. He didn't have his cellular phone with him in Dallas. I found out about it when I got home at around five-thirty that morning. Diane was hysterical when she called Cathy, my wife, screaming something about Tommy Lee blowing off Howard's head. Cathy told me Diane was the one who found him."

"And you say you didn't see anyone enter the house. Which brings me to another question, Mr. King. Do you own a gun?"

"No. Never have. Surely, if I'm a suspect, you've checked gun registration records."

"It's easy to buy a gun by other means. As an attorney you already know this."

"I've never owned a gun. You have permission to search my house any time you wish."

Garcia seemed bemused. "The Austin Police Department is at your house now, conducting a search. They got a search warrant at nine this morning for your residence, based on a reasonable assumption that you wouldn't keep a murder weapon in your car, or here in your office. Your wife was instructed not to call you until the search is completed. Sorry, but you must understand I felt I had no choice. Even if they find a gun it will only be circumstantial evidence, since whoever shot your brother took the slug with him. No ballistics test. A good lawyer would know these things, if he wanted to get away with murder."

"It sounds like I'm your prime suspect."

"You have several motives. You become the administrator of your mother's estate and trusts when Howard dies. You called to accuse him of embezzlement. You admit you were there at the time of the murder, so this gives you both motive and opportunity. On the other hand, we have no fingerprints or witnesses, no murder weapon, and no ballistics report. A circumstantial case at best. So we'll keep looking. Howard's wife is of the opinion Tommy did it. She does not believe you would be capable of such a thing. She describes you as mild-mannered and retiring, not the type to commit murder. Way out in left field I have your sister, Suzan Westerman, who was also in Dallas and could have been motivated by the disagreement over money and the way Howard was disposed to use it, or not use it. Howard's wife told me Mrs. Westerman was angry over the denial of some sort of loan for real estate. As we speak, Mrs. Westerman's home is being searched by the Midland Police Department for guns, although of course it's highly unlikely the killer would keep the murder weapon. He, or she, probably ditched it. We've conducted a thorough search around Howard's house. You also have another sister, Martha Carter. Her house will be searched. I have not had an opportunity to question her yet. She hasn't returned any of my phone calls."

"She's probably at the Carter Foundation on Broadway in San Antonio," I said, "but I can tell you now she doesn't own a gun or know how to use one. She ran a museum, until it closed a few weeks ago. She's packing things up."

Garcia scribbled something in his notes. "As far as I know she's the only one of you who wasn't in Dallas at the time the murder was committed, so I won't consider her a primary suspect until I've questioned her as to her whereabouts."

I decided to let Martha answer for herself. I had to call her as soon as Garcia left, to warn her about Garcia's questions. I wasn't going to tell him Martha and I had talked at Howard's house that night, because he didn't *ask*. Nor did I intend to tell him I'd seen Suzan there. "I am unable to make myself believe my brother or either of my sisters would kill Howard, and I know I didn't do it," I said. "None of us really got along all that well, although neither can I believe any of us would be capable of murder."

Garcia tilted his head. "You evidently believed Tommy was capable of it or you wouldn't have driven all the way from Austin to Dallas and back in the middle of the night."

"He was drinking. I wanted to prevent an ugly scene. I'm quite sure Tommy Lee wouldn't have actually shot anyone, despite what you heard on the tape recording. I was hoping to stop him from making any more threats while he was drunk. Howard would have sent him to jail if he tried to start a fight."

"Like the one at your mother's house on the Fourth of July, when Tommy broke Howard's nose?"

"That's right. Tommy Lee was drunk that day."

Garcia put his notebook away. "I can't think of anything else right now, Mr. King. Sorry about the search warrant, but I have to make sure. Your wife was upset and I'm sorry for that too. It's my job." He got up and half turned toward my door before he stopped. "By the way, how did you know Tommy was going to Dallas that night with a gun?"

"My sister Martha called me. She'd just told him about the embezzling scheme and he blew up. She was wondering what to do."

"Why didn't you call the Dallas police?"

I looked down at my hands. "In retrospect, I suppose it was the proper thing to do. I only wish I had . . ."

I DIALED MARTHA'S UNLISTED CELLULAR NUM-
ber, not sure where she would be this time of day. I got an
answer on the third ring.

"Where are you?" I asked.

"At my office."

"I'll call you back. We shouldn't use a cell phone. But
I have to call Cathy first. The police are searching my house
for a gun. That detective from Dallas is probably on his way
to see you today. He left my office just now and San Antonio is an hour and fifteen minutes from here."

"What did he ask you?"

"Everything. I'll call you back at your office number in
a few minutes. I have to talk to Cathy." I hung up quickly
and called home.

"Hello?"

"I know the police are there. Can you talk?"

"Oh, Matt. Three of them are tearing this place apart.
What is going on? They think you're hiding a gun here, and
that must mean they think you did it. They told me not to
call you at the office until they were finished. They have a
search warrant."

"Did you talk to a Dallas detective by the name of
Garcia?"

"He called this morning, asking questions about when
you got home and what you said and what time you left. I
started crying. That's when these three guys knocked on
the door. If they know I'm talking to you they'll probably

make me hang up. What the hell is happening? Everybody acts like they think *you* did it.''

''They're just doing their job, Cathy. They have to ask all these questions. I was just curious about when Garcia talked to you.''

''Why does the time matter? It was about an hour ago, before these cops showed up. One of them has this great big dog sniffing around in all our closets . . .'' I heard her sob quietly. She lowered her voice. ''I don't understand, Matthew. What the *hell* is going on?''

''They're doing the same thing to everybody. Suzan's house is being searched this morning. Tommy Lee's already been through it. Martha will be next.'' I hadn't told Cathy about Martha or Suzan being in Dallas, or of any meeting at Howard's. Not that I had things I wanted to hide from my wife. I simply saw no point in dragging my sisters into it. After all, Garcia found out about Suzan on his own. ''Calm down. We don't have a gun, so stop worrying.''

''They're tearing everything to pieces. The guy with the dog ordered me around like I was a Nazi war criminal. I don't understand why they're doing this to *us*. Tommy Lee is the one who did it. I think you *know* he did it and you won't say anything. You shouldn't be protecting him . . .'' She started crying softly again.

''I don't know that he did anything. I wouldn't keep something like that from you. Please don't cry. I love you and I'm sorry you're having to go through this. It'll be over soon. I can come home if you need me there.''

''No. It's okay. Don't come. I'll manage.''

''Have a drink,'' I suggested, glancing at the clock. ''It's five o'clock somewhere. Pretend you're in China.''

She sniffled. ''Here comes the guy with the dog. I'd better hang up. Bye, honey.''

I dialed Martha's number as soon as Cathy hung up. Martha caught my call on the first ring.

"I didn't tell Garcia you were there that night," I began, "but if he presses the issue, maybe you'd better tell him, or figure some way to explain why you weren't at home. If anybody called and you didn't answer, or if a neighbor noticed you driving off when you say you were at home, it'll make Garcia suspicious. You have to convince him you've got nothing to hide. They intend to make a search of your house, and probably the foundation as well. I think Garcia still believes he's going to find a murder weapon in somebody's closet or under the bed."

"You said they were searching your house now."

"Cathy's upset. She's never been through anything like this before. She told me again she thinks I know Tommy Lee did it and I'm covering for him."

"About all I can do is wait for this Garcia guy, I guess. I have messages from him on my answering machine but I didn't want to trouble you with a call. I can handle him. I'll tell him I called you when I heard Tommy Lee threaten to kill Howard, and you said you'd drive up there and stop him from going inside."

"He'll want to know where you were and if anybody saw you, someone who can vouch for you. He may not buy the 'I was home alone' story. You may still be a suspect."

"Hell, everybody in this screwy family is a suspect. Suzan was there. And so were you. Carl may have been there, only I think he was probably sleeping with his secretary. Suzan told me she believes he's having an affair."

"Tom Walters told me he taught Suzan how to shoot a pistol. He said she was a good shot. I'm convinced Detective Garcia believes Tommy Lee did it, but without a murder weapon or a bullet, he can't prove it. If Suzan admits to being able to shoot, she may become a prime suspect along with me. At this point Tommy Lee's the one Garcia thinks is guilty."

"He called last night. He's scared to death," Martha said.

"As well he should be. He shouldn't have threatened Howard over the phone. And it might have looked better if he'd attended the funeral."

"Tommy said he was glad Howard was dead, but he didn't kill him. You're the lawyer. Can they convict him without the bullet or a witness, even if he insists he didn't do it?"

"Probably not, although I'm not a criminal attorney. Garcia admitted he had a circumstantial case."

"I'll talk to Garcia. I'll say I went out to buy some Scotch and came home to get drunk. I'm known for my drinking."

"I told him where to find you. Hope it was okay."

"Why not? He'd have found out sooner or later anyway." I could hear Martha lighting a cigarette.

"Let me know what he says. All this shit has me drinking my head off and I still can't sleep."

"Try a Valium and Scotch cocktail. It works for me if I put enough Valium in it to make it cloudy."

"That could kill you."

"So who cares? I think I'm dead anyway. I have no life, no reason to live, with the foundation closing. I'm so depressed I can't even masturbate. I'm hoping that will change when a court makes you administrator of the estate."

"My hands will still be tied as to how I can spend money, unless the trust is flawed. What you need is a good man in your life."

"That's an oxymoron. There are no good men. You come close but you're my brother."

"You've stopped looking."

"It's like looking for the Loch Ness monster. If something only surfaces every twenty or thirty years, most people give up and do something else. Like drinking.''

I tried to change topics. "Are you almost finished packing up? I think getting away from that building and its memories for a while would be good for you.''

"I sent out the last important shipments a week ago. All I have left is a few odds and ends and tons of paperwork. At times I feel like setting fire to the whole thing. The only faint hope I have is reopening after you get the estate's checkbook.''

"Call after you talk to Garcia. I had the feeling he was on his way to San Antonio. He'll ask Tommy Lee more questions and come looking for you. And he said he needed to question Suzan.''

"This is like having Howard's ghost hanging over all of us. He's probably enjoying watching the rest of us sweat. Tommy Lee is suffering the most. He was so drunk last night I could barely understand him.''

"He's feeling the pressure," I said.

"Aren't we all?" Martha hung up, as though she didn't need an answer.

I leaned back in my chair wondering if Martha could be right about Howard's ghost. He knew the truth of what happened and if anyone could come back from the grave to make our lives miserable it would be Howard.

I pondered the wisdom, or lack of it, in suggesting to Martha that she lie to the police. I told myself it was smart to keep her out of it as much as possible. She had enough problems of her own. Like Tommy Lee, it would have looked better if she had attended Howard's funeral and the same could be said about Suzan and Carl. As it was, Cathy and I were the only family members there . . .

23

IT WAS ON THE TWENTY-THIRD OF DECEMBER.
Cathy and I were attending our second funeral this month,
our second family funeral in less than twenty days. Howard's body lay in a closed casket at Wilkerson Funeral
Home in Dallas for a private ceremony, including family
members and a few close friends. But Cathy and I were the
only family members in attendance, other than Diane,
Timothy, and Rebecca. Fewer than a dozen others stood
quietly in pews while somewhere out of sight behind a silky
white curtain an organist played soft music. Diane wept.
I'd been informed by the funeral director of Diane's request to keep the coffin closed—she did not want to be
reminded of the damage done to Howard's head no matter
how skillfully a mortician might repair it cosmetically. According to what Diane told Cathy over the phone that night
in the midst of her hysterics, Howard's head had been
blown off . . . blown off by Tommy Lee.

When the music stopped a Baptist minister from High-
land Park read a few words in his most somber voice.
Cathy stood beside me at the back of the funeral chapel.
We'd arrived late because of heavy holiday traffic. David
asked to spend the night with the Thompsons and we both
readily agreed, fearing an ugly scene could develop if
Tommy Lee showed up for the funeral. I didn't think
Tommy Lee would come, although I was somewhat surprised when Carl and Suzan didn't make it, and neither did

Martha. Apparently the bitter enmity over Howard's control of the estate did not end when he was killed.

After the service, the few handpicked mourners filed by to offer condolences to Diane and the children, and Cathy and I waited until the others were gone. I walked up to Diane and gave Timothy and Rebecca an understanding smile, before an elderly woman ushered them out of the chapel.

"I'm very sorry, Diane," I said as she wiped tears from her eyes with a handkerchief.

"So am I," Cathy said gently, clinging to my arm.

Diane sniffled and then suddenly her expression changed from sorrow to anger. "I'm sure you noticed, Matthew. Not one of his sisters had the decency to come. I thought Martha and Suzan were capable of putting differences aside long enough to attend their own brother's funeral, but I was wrong. I'm glad that *murderer* Tommy Lee didn't show up . . ."

"It hasn't been proven Tommy Lee did anything," I said. "I know he threatened Howard. A threat doesn't mean he would do it. He was drinking and he probably said things he regretted later. I think Martha and Suzan stayed away to spare your feelings, because of all the unpleasantness over the trust funds and the ranch. I'm sure Tommy Lee wasn't here for the very same reason."

Diane looked me in the eye. "I told the police he did it. I gave them the recording Howard made. They've already questioned him about it and taken away his gun. I *know* he did it. You saw what he did to Howard's nose. The police said his gun might even *prove* he did it. Howard told me a hundred times Tommy Lee was crazy. He *had* to be crazy to strike his own brother like that."

"I think that was only a spur-of-the-moment thing. Tommy Lee wouldn't commit murder. They'd hired lawyers so they could settle their differences in court."

Diane began sobbing. "You should have seen what Tommy Lee did to Howard. There was blood all over everything! The kids saw it too. It was the most awful sight anyone can imagine, to find your husband and the father of your children with this huge hole all the way through his head! It's the most cowardly thing Tommy Lee could have done, shooting Howard like that. He's crazy and he should go to prison forever. Rebecca wakes up screaming during the night when she dreams about it. Timmy stays in his room and won't come out. That *murderer* ruined our Christmas, our whole lives . . ."

"I know you're upset, Diane."

"You're damn right I'm upset! Wouldn't you be?"

"Of course. I just think you'll be better off if you calm down and let the detectives do their job."

"You know perfectly well *he* did it. It's right there on the tape recording. He's a stark raving lunatic who ought to be put in prison or an insane asylum for the rest of his life. Can't you see he's the only one who *would* do something like this?"

I wanted to end what was clearly a pointless discussion as quickly and gracefully as I could. "Is there anything Cathy or I can do for you or the children?"

Diane wiped her eyes again. "No. Thank you for coming. I'm taking the children to my mother's. I'm selling the house. Too many things there remind me of dear Howard."

"Call, if we can help," I said, turning for the chapel door.

Skies were clear and the wind was cold when we got outside. Cathy waited until we were in the car before she said anything.

"You know Tommy Lee did it, don't you?" she asked. "You're protecting him."

I started the engine and pulled away from the curb.

"That simply isn't true. I didn't see anyone go in or out until Diane got home. I never saw Tommy Lee. Why don't you believe me?"

"Because I don't think you're like the rest of your family. I think you'd keep quiet rather than send your brother to prison, even if the two of you aren't like real brothers."

I let it drop. Like a number of other things having to do with my family's affairs, I was tired of talking about them.

I was spared further recollections of Howard's funeral when my telephone rang.

24

A MESSAGE WAS WAITING FOR ME WHEN I GOT back from lunch to call Tommy Lee. Following Detective Garcia's questions that morning my lunch consisted of three double Scotches on the rocks with a handful of black olives at my favorite bar over on Congress Avenue, The Cloak Room. Learning Garcia considered me a prime suspect in Howard's murder unsettled my already badly shaken nerves. I'd received a call from Cathy as soon as the policemen left our house with their dog and as before she was crying. It had been her call that came while I was thinking about Howard's funeral, a straw that broke my camel's back. I rarely ever drank before the middle of the afternoon, with today being an understandable exception—in my opinion.

Betty, my secretary of eleven years, handed me the message. "You look so tired, Mr. King. I understand you're having a difficult time. Perhaps you should go home for the rest of the day . . . I can cancel your afternoon appointments, or have Gene take them."

"I'm okay," I said. "I don't get much sleep. Hold all my calls while I'm talking to my brother unless it's from Martha or Cathy." Gene Williams was my senior partner and while I trusted him, I had a conference scheduled with representatives from SEMA and I couldn't blow it off— SEMA was our second largest client in personal injury cases.

I closed my office door. I'd soundproofed the room

when I had it decorated, spending almost forty thousand dollars on good furniture and oil paintings and drapes, an investment I believed at the time was worth it to impress clients. I scarcely noticed any of the furnishings now. I dropped into my chair like my ass was girded with lead weights and dialed the number Tommy Lee left for me. I hadn't talked to him but once since Howard's murder—he never bothered to explain why he hadn't come to the funeral when he called for the name of a good criminal attorney. I'd suggested Marvin Miller in San Antonio. I met Miller once at a party and found out from friends he was a courtroom showman with an excellent defense record. Tommy Lee had been drunk the day he called, right after Detective Garcia questioned him and took his automatic to a forensics lab to see if it had been fired recently.

A soft voice answered.

"Tommy Lee? This is Matt."

"Thanks for callin'. That fuckin' cop just left here again, after he asked a bunch more questions. I called Miller. Miller said I didn't have to answer a damn one of 'em unless they were gonna charge me. But I think they *are* gonna charge me, Matt. I didn't kill Howard. I swear I didn't. I know I said I was gonna do it, only I didn't. I was real pissed off after Martha told me about the racehorse deal, the millions of bucks he stole, when I can't keep my dealership doors open without some help. Howard could have loaned it to me, only he wouldn't because he was too goddamn busy stealin' money for himself."

"The problem you've got, as I see it, is that you don't have a good alibi. You can't explain where you were that night, other than to say you were driving around with a gun. And you admitted you were drinking. Listen to Marvin Miller. Do exactly what he tells you to do and nothing else. They don't have a witness or a bullet or any fingerprints. The tape recording of the threat you made to kill

Howard is about the only evidence they have. Saying you intend to kill somebody doesn't make you a killer. We've all said things in moments of anger. Let your attorney tell you what to do and don't talk to the police without having him present.''

''That makes me look like I've got somethin' to hide.''

''Not necessarily. It's good legal advice. Detective Garcia also believes I could have done it. I went to Dallas right after Martha called, to see if I could stop you. If Garcia persists in his suspicions that I could have killed Howard, I'll hire my own criminal attorney. Right now, I'm a suspect and so is Suzan.''

''I didn't do it, Matt. Please believe me. I know I said I was gonna kill him, but those were just words. I was really mad an' when Howard refused to make me that loan, I could see everything goin' out the window. Then I find out he's been stealin' millions from Helen's estate an' I just blew my lid. I lost my temper an' said things, but I'd been drinkin' all day when Martha told me what he did. When I get drunk I sorta lose my temper, but I never would have killed anybody.''

''I'm not saying you did. Just be sure you follow Miller's advice. Don't answer any questions unless Miller is there.''

''Garcia asked me about Martha, about what she said when she called and how she knew I was takin' a gun to Dallas. The cunt I had stayin' here that weekend told her, when Martha called back. If she didn't give such great head I'd throw the bitch out on her ass for sayin' that. She had no business tellin' anybody I took a gun.''

''It's too late to worry about it now. Just tell the truth when you talk to Marvin Miller and let him tell you what questions you can answer.''

''They're gonna charge me. I can tell by the way Garcia acts he thinks I did it. Hell, if I did it I sure as hell

wouldn't be keepin' the same gun around my house. I'd
have thrown it in the river or somethin'."

"Where *did* you go that night? If somebody saw you
someplace else at the time of the murder, you'd have an
alibi."

"I was so goddamn drunk I don't really remember. I
drove around. Stopped to buy more beer somewhere, I
think. Ain't you ever been real drunk before? You can't
hardly remember shit . . ."

"That isn't going to sound too good to a jury," I said.

"They can't find the bullet. Whoever shot Howard
took it with him. Miller says that may save my ass, only I
didn't kill Howard in the first place."

"They have to prove you did it beyond a reasonable
doubt. With no bullet, they don't have much of a case."

"Who do you think really did it, Matt? Do you honestly believe I'd shoot Howard?"

"No. I don't think you killed him; however my opinion won't matter to a jury."

"Suzan was in Dallas. Martha told her what I said
about how I *wanted* to kill him, so she flew up there to try
to stop me just like you did. I'm grateful for what both of
you did, only there wasn't any need. I never *really* meant to
kill him. I was just so damn pissed off about him stealin' all
that money when I'm too broke to keep my dealership
open."

I wondered if Garcia was talking to Martha now. "Just
take Miller's advice whenever they question you. He's
good, maybe the best in Texas right now. You don't have to
say a word without an attorney being present."

"I was just thinkin', Matt. Do you suppose Suzan
coulda got mad enough over that ranch deal to do it? She
don't know a damn thing about usin' a gun. What the hell
does *any* woman know about shootin'? I was wonderin' if

you thought Suzan could pull a trigger aimin' a gun at Howard. She don't seem like the type . . .''

I wasn't about to offer conjecture, or tell Tommy Lee that Suzan did know a few things about guns. ''I have no idea. I still say it's possible a burglar broke into the house thinking no one was at home. Howard saw or heard him and the burglar shot him to keep from being identified to the police.''

''That detective don't believe that. He thinks I did it.''

''He has to prove it,'' I said again.

''By the way, Matt, when will you become the administrator of our estate?''

''It could take months. I haven't looked into it yet.''

''Jesus. I can't wait that long. I need some money, just a loan real quick, or General Motors is gonna shut me down. I need a couple hundred thousand. I used everything in my bank account. Then I sold some new cars an' didn't pay the loans off. Hell, I couldn't.''

''I probably can't loan you money from the estate anyway,'' I told him. ''It's fairly cut and dried.''

''But I *have* to have that money.''

''I can't promise you anything, Tommy Lee, but I'll see what I can do.''

''The bank won't loan me any more. The assholes say I'm up to my neck in debt already, borrowin' against next year's interest check from the trust. I gotta have that loan, Matt.''

''Sounds like you went to Vegas too many times.''

''That ain't it. It was our chickenshit brother stealin' all Helen's money that fucked me. He fucked you too, and all of us. I wouldn't say this in front of that cop, but I'm glad Howard's dead. He was a thief an' a chickenshit. I'm not a goddamn bit sorry he's dead. I didn't kill him, but whoever did was doin' us a favor.''

''You're talking about our deceased brother.''

"He didn't act like a brother. He acted like a chicken-shit."

I closed my eyes a moment, remembering when Martha told me she wasn't sorry our mother was dead. Now Tommy Lee was saying he was glad Howard was dead. I wondered if anyone on earth would believe these remarks came from members of the same family. "You shouldn't say anything like that in front of Detective Garcia. He's having enough trouble imagining how we function as brothers and sisters, suing each other, breaking noses, making death threats over the phone . . ."

"I gotta run, Matt. My secretary said Suzan's on the other line."

I wondered idly if it was the same secretary who gave great blow jobs. "The Midland police are searching her house for a gun and I'm sure Garcia intends to question her about where she was the night Howard was killed. We're all suspects. She'd better have a good alibi."

"I'll call you back tomorrow. See what you can do about gettin' me that loan. A couple hundred thousand will get them off my back. I'd sure appreciate anything you can do an' I swear I'll pay it back. Business is gonna get better this spring. I know the rest of you don't approve of the way I live, the women an' all, but when I put my mind to it I really do know the car business. I can pay the loan back in practically no time. I'd like to come up an' see you anyway, Matt. We live so close, only an hour's drive. We oughta get together more often."

I heard the phone go dead in my ear. I knew I could loan Tommy Lee the money myself, but I also knew he'd never repay it. It would be like tossing money out a window.

I hung up and reached for a fresh bottle of Scotch. Martha would be calling after Detective Garcia left. I wondered when, or if, this madness would ever end.

25

I CAME BACK FROM MY MEETING WITH THE SEMA adjustors and attorneys at four-thirty. A message from Martha was waiting for me, as I'd known it would be. I autodialed her number at home with a drink in my hand.

"It's me," I said when I heard her voice.

"Garcia reminds me of Columbo. He's playing dumb, but he's smart. I think he only *pretended* to believe me when I said I was at home. He asked me a hundred questions about *you,* how you and Howard got along and what would happen now that you'll be administrator of Helen's estate. If things would change so you would benefit from it. He hardly asked me anything about Tommy Lee or Suzan. A couple of San Antonio detectives searched the foundation from top to bottom and then they told me I had to drive them out to my house. They looked everywhere. All that time Garcia was asking questions—where I bought liquor that night, what time it was when I called you, what time I got back from the liquor store, what time I went to bed, if I watched television and what I watched on TV, did anybody call. A fucking inquisition. He wrote down shit the whole time, like it mattered, like he was going to check on every damn thing I told him."

"He's very thorough."

"Suzan just called. She's mad as hell because they searched her house, but she's even madder because Carl can't come up with a story about where he was while she was in Dallas. She knows he's having an affair. She said she told the Midland police you probably did it. She told them you were an asshole and she never wanted to speak to you again as long as she lived, that you were just like Howard when it came to money. She told them she hated your guts.''

"How touching," I said, tossing back a mouthful of Scotch.

"You mean, how typical, don't you? Suzan hates everyone. You shouldn't take it personally simply because she happened to mention your name this time.''

"Your sense of humor is warped. There's nothing funny about what's going on. Tommy Lee called. Garcia questioned him, and I'm sure Garcia intends to question Suzan and Carl.''

"Garcia says we all have a motive," Martha said and I could hear the click as she lit a cigarette.

"I suppose he's right, in a way. By now I'm sure he knows he's dealing with an utterly insane family. He shouldn't have much trouble convincing himself we all could have done it.''

"I was puzzled why he asked so many questions about you.''

"It's because my financial motive appears the strongest. I become administrator of Helen's estate now. He sees that as my reason for wanting Howard out of the way. He apparently doesn't know that much about trust management. Hardly anything of real significance will change.''

"You could decide to make charitable donations to the Carter Foundation with some of the income, couldn't you? Couldn't you dump some of those fucking bonds from Cleveland, or wherever the hell they're from?''

"I suppose I could. I haven't looked into it. Managing a trust can be complicated, depending on how it's set up and the nature of the income earned by it. Dana Fullerton would know if I'll have that kind of leeway. Tommy Lee says he'll be forced out of business by General Motors unless he gets a loan, as he calls it, of two or three hundred thousand. I'm quite certain the trust structure won't allow it. After things cool down a bit I promise I'll look into your question about donating to the foundation."

Martha paused. "I have this feeling Detective Garcia isn't going to go away."

"Probably not. Just stick with your story about being at home and let the rest of us paddle our own canoes. The important thing to remember is that he has no murder weapon, no bullet, no fingerprints, and no witness. I cut a few classes in criminal law but you don't need to be Perry Mason to know he can't make a case against anyone without evidence."

"How does it feel . . . to know?"

I sat up straight in my chair. "To know what?"

"That one of us is a murderer." She said it quietly.

"I told Garcia I still believe a burglar did it."

"Garcia doesn't believe that," she said. A second later she hung up.

David met me at the door when I got home. I could tell from his expression that he was worried.

"Mom's asleep upstairs," he said, following me to the coat closet where I hung my overcoat. "She's been cryin' all day. I think she's had more than she can take. Those cops tore the whole house up when they came this mornin'. Mom said they acted like they think you shot Uncle Howard. They were lookin' for a gun. I stayed home after I got home from school when I saw how upset Mom was. She's been asleep for about an hour."

I headed for the den to make myself a badly needed drink. "Thanks for staying with her. I didn't shoot anyone, son. The police are simply doing their job, looking for evidence, asking everybody questions. It doesn't mean they think I killed him." I poured a generous Scotch on ice, reminded of the example I was setting in front of my son, drinking when I felt the slightest bit of stress. I put my arm around David's shoulder and led him to the couch in front of the fireplace where he sat beside me, watching me with a look I'd never seen on his face before.

"You didn't do it, did you, Dad?" he asked in a voice so small I scarcely heard him.

"Of course not, David. I'm a little bit surprised that you would ask. I've never owned a gun in my life and I could never shoot another human being, much less my own brother. I couldn't shoot rabbits or doves when I was a kid because I didn't believe in killing anything. Tom Walters taught me how foolish it was to kill something without a good reason. I still feel that way. I shouldn't have allowed you to go rabbit hunting with Tommy Lee last summer. It was a mistake."

David was still trying to read my expression. "Mom says you know it was Uncle Tommy Lee who did it an' you won't say anything to the cops because he's your brother. If I had a brother I wouldn't squeal on him to the cops, no matter what he did."

"I never saw Tommy Lee the night I went to Dallas. When I got there I parked in front of Howard's house for a while, then I bought a pack of cigarettes and came home. I didn't shoot Howard. I've never lied to you, son, and I certainly wouldn't lie about a thing like this."

"I told Mom she was wrong, that you didn't like Uncle Tommy all that much an' if he'd killed anybody, you'd tell the cops if you knew about it."

I gazed out at an evening sunset above the lake. "I know she thinks I'm protecting Tommy Lee. She's asked me about it several times. I don't think she believes me when I tell her I didn't see him that night."

"This whole thing's so weird," David said, cupping

his chin in a hand and resting his elbow on his knee. "Nobody in this whole family liked Uncle Howard, 'specially not Uncle Tommy. He busted his nose that time. You've got a real weird family, Dad. All of 'em are weird. Grandma was weird too. Aunt Martha always acts bitchy an' so does Aunt Suzan. I liked Uncle Tommy best of all."

"He's very irresponsible. He spends more money than he can make selling cars."

"But he's cool, an' he can shoot rabbits with a pistol from the back of a pickup. He showed me how to aim an' everything."

"It isn't something you need to know. Your mother and I are against guns."

"That's what I told Mom she shoulda told the cops, about how you threw this big fit when all I did was shoot one lousy rabbit. That'd prove you couldn't shoot a real person like they think you did, because you couldn't even stand to *look* at a dead rabbit."

"They don't necessarily think I did it. They have to check everyone's story about where they were and what they did at the time Howard was killed." David's fourteen-year-old wisdom seemed more insightful than my own at times.

David was watching me again. "Who do you *really* think it was? *Could* it have been Uncle Tommy?"

"I don't believe he'd be capable of it. A burglar could have broken into Howard's house while Diane and the kids were at the mall. The burglar might have been armed and when Howard got a good look at him, this guy decided to get rid of a witness to keep from going to jail later if he were identified."

"Mom said the cops don't believe it happened that way. She says they think it was one of you . . . maybe even Aunt Suzan because she was in Dallas that night. Mom can't stand Aunt Suzan. Mom told me one time that you came from the weirdest family she'd ever seen, but that you weren't like the rest of 'em at all. You really ain't weird like they are, Dad.''

"Please stop saying 'ain't.' You know your mother doesn't like it. I'd better go upstairs and check on her." I tousled David's hair affectionately. "Don't worry about any of this. I appreciate you staying home this afternoon with your mother. She is having a very difficult time right now and she needs all the support and understanding we can give her.''

David grinned, although it lacked real substance. "She used to only get depressed on the Fourth of July when we had to go to see Grandma, an' that's nearly the only time I ever saw her drink whiskey. I told Bobby I couldn't come over to shoot baskets at his house because Mom was cryin' over the cops bein' here. Bobby said maybe Mom was an alcoholic. His dad used to get drunk every night, until he started goin' to some kind of meetings. He only gets drunk on the weekends now.''

"Your mother isn't an alcoholic," I said, standing up with a drink in my hand, and feeling guilty holding it. "She's been under a lot of stress because of what's happened in my family. With any luck at all it'll be over soon.''

"Can I call an' have 'em deliver a pizza? Mom told me she didn't feel like cookin' supper . . .''

"Order anything you want," I replied, aiming for the stairs. "I'll leave twenty bucks here on the bar.''

"You've been drinkin' an awful lot too, Dad. Maybe you oughta try goin' to one of those meetings with Bobby's dad once in a while.''

I refilled my glass and put a twenty-dollar bill on the bar. "I've had a rough day. Let's talk about it some other time.''

I climbed the stairs feeling terrible about David's concerns over our drinking, and what the police investigation was doing to him, to us. He'd actually asked me if I'd killed my brother and I wondered what he saw in me that would allow him to consider the possibility.

I found Cathy asleep in her bathrobe. I sat beside her on the mattress and kissed her cheek lightly. She opened her eyes, red-rimmed, puffy eyes, and immediately began to cry.

"I'm so glad you're home," she sniffled. "This has been the worst day of my life."

"I'm sorry," I said gently, trying for a smile.

"It's never going to end, is it? It's like a curse, the King family curse that keeps following us wherever we go, whatever we do. It's like the Midas touch in reverse. Ever since the Fourth of July, everything we touch turns to shit. That detective made it sound like he *knows* you killed Howard. He kept asking me the same questions over and over again."

"I don't think he believes I did it, but he suspects me of protecting Tommy Lee. He thinks I saw something and I won't talk about it. I keep telling him he's wrong."

"Is he wrong, Matt?"

"Why don't you believe me? I've told you several times I did not see Tommy Lee anywhere near Howard's house. No one was there." But I was lying. "When Diane and the kids came home I drove off. That's the entire story. Tommy Lee never arrived while I was sitting in front of Howard's. I shouldn't have gone in the first place and I know that now. It was a spur-of-the-moment reaction to Martha's phone call when she told me about Tommy Lee taking a gun to Dallas."

Slowly, shakily, Cathy pushed herself up on her elbows to look into my eyes.

"I believe you, honey. I'm sorry for what I said. I've had a little too much to drink, I suppose, after watching them let that damn dog sniff every inch of our house. They threw our clothes all over the floor and opened every drawer. One of them spilled a box of Cheerios in the sink and all he did was laugh. The dog raised its leg and urinated on my potted ivy, the one in the front hall. I threw it away. The carpet still stinks like dog pee.''

"Have a cleaning service come out tomorrow. Buy new carpet for the whole house if you . . .'' I was interrupted by the ring of our telephone. "Maybe it's one of David's buddies,'' I said as I raised my glass for a drink. Maybe I did need to attend an AA meeting.

"It's for you, Dad!'' David shouted from downstairs.

I picked up the bedside phone. Martha's voice sounded like she'd had too much to drink.

"Suzan called,'' Martha began. "The Midland police found a forty-five caliber pistol in a dresser drawer. They say it was fired recently. Suzan told them she flew to Dallas and any idiot knows you can't carry a gun on an airplane, but Detective Garcia said she could have checked it through in her luggage. He had her detained for questioning until he could fly out to Midland tomorrow morning. The Midland police told her she's now a suspect in Howard's murder.''

I took a deep breath. "They'll also find out she's a good shot. Tom Walters told me she could hit a beer can every time.''

"Now Suzan is yelling her head off that Tommy Lee had to be the one who killed Howard. She only flew to Dallas to keep him from doing it and now she's pointing her finger right at him, trying to save her *own* ass. That's true sisterly love. First she wants to save him and now she's ready to hang him.''

"I don't think any of us knows the meaning of brotherly or sisterly love,'' I said.

"I'm getting drunk tonight,'' Martha said.

"What's new about that?" I asked, suddenly angry over her intrusion at a time when Cathy needed me. Then it occurred to me that Cathy had also seen the need to drink today. "I may do the same thing. We should invest in good distillery stocks this year. Tommy Lee gets drunk every day before noon. You and I drink enough Scotch to float a battleship and Carl enjoys a cold beer as much as any man I ever knew. My wife prefers Wild Turkey and wine. When I take over as administrator of Helen's estate I plan to invest heavily in the booze market simply because our personal consumption will send stock prices skyrocketing."

"Helen said we were all drunks. Remember?"

"Peculiar, unstable drunks. Good night, Martha. I've heard just about all I care to hear for one day, one really lousy day."

"Good night, Matthew, however I must leave you with a parting thought. As of now I'm the only member of this sick family who isn't one of Detective Garcia's suspects. It's only a matter of time before he gets around to me, and should he find out I lied to him about being at home I'll probably move to the front of the pack. So I'm getting drunk tonight and probably will every night until my lie is discovered. Don't tell me about your lousy day as though you're the only one having them. I'm sure I'll have a few of my own."

She slammed the phone down in my ear and I winced.

"What was that all about?" Cathy asked.

"The police found a gun, a forty-five, at Suzan's. They say it has been fired recently. Martha called to tell me the list of suspects has just grown longer . . ."

26

I HADN'T REALLY WANTED TO DRIVE OUT TO the ranch at Eden in the midst of so much turmoil, with Detective Garcia's investigation a prime source of my growing anxieties. But when Tom Walters said it was important, I did not question him. I left on Friday at seven in the morning. Tom's call had come at eleven on Thursday night, to tell me Tommy Lee arrived an hour earlier and that he appeared to be drunk, demanding to have the house unlocked. The news that Tommy Lee was drunk was the only bit of information Tom gave me that came as no surprise. Tom said he was worried about what Tommy Lee meant to do.

Driving down the Brady highway under gloomy gray skies with a light mist dampening my windshield, I glanced at our pastures when I was a few miles west of Melvin, a tiny community with but a single grocery and gas station where King ranch property began. Grass lay thick, a winter-brown carpet speckled with green cold-season grasses over the hills south of the highway, strengthened by weeks of rain and the absence of grazing Angus cattle. It was the first time in my life I'd seen our pastures empty and yet I supposed it was fitting, now that the house was also vacant.

Passing miles of fence posts enclosing King property, I saw things I hadn't noticed before and was amazed again by how little I knew about the ranch. Little grottoes hollowed out of limestone were shaded by dozens of live oak trees concealing wet-weather springs I'd never visited. I hadn't really seen but a small portion of the ranch and it should have embarrassed me to be an owner of so much land and never have visited all of it over the years I'd lived here. Distant hilltops bristled with groves of trees, home for any number of whitetail deer, or so I imagined. After my father died no deer hunters were allowed on the property—a big part of Tom's job during deer season was keeping hunters from crossing our fences illegally. But without high deer fences our deer population drifted to neighbors' pastures and natural thinning of deer herds occurred during dry years, or when overgrazing took its toll on grasses. Tommy Lee had hunted deer from time to time until the lure of city life took him away to bars where he hunted a more desirable prey, women, in San Angelo and Abilene.

Driving past our fences now, I knew we'd all taken the ranch for granted. Or had it been something else? A desperate wish to escape the madness we experienced here, hiding in our rooms instead of finding out what this land had to offer us besides its Black Gold, exploring its far corners and secret places, the beauty of it we inexplicably ignored. I was lucky. Tom had taken me to some of his favorite spots and tried to teach me to appreciate natural beauty the way he did. I knew now, years too late, that I'd missed out on so much of what Tom could have shown me while I was feeling sorry for myself, wishing I was old enough to leave the ranch. There were times when I felt like a butterfly in a cocoon, waiting for the time when I could escape Helen's fierce control over my life, our lives. I hadn't understood until many years later, after I married Cathy, that the control I resented so much was Helen's only way of showing love.

In spots I saw oil well pumpjacks working, while most were stilled, going to rust above pools of oil deemed worthless in relation to the cost of pumping it from the ground. It is an oddity beyond all rational explanation how some sections of this vast ranch country bestow its owners with uncommon riches while others yield only what the soil can produce. My father had known the difference. If only he had known as much about raising a son or a daughter.

I turned in at the gate and parked in front of Tom's house, a modest three-bedroom brick with a yard encircled by a chain-link fence. Tom's pair of blue Australian shepherds barked behind the fence, announcing my arrival. Tom came outside dressed in his usual faded denims and a denim jacket, wearing his sweat-stained gray cowboy hat pulled low in front. I got out, pulling on my raincoat even though the mist was slight.

"Morning, Tom," I said, shaking his familiar, work-hardened hand.

"Mornin', Matt. Sorry I had to call you, but I didn't see no other way. Your brother's bad drunk at the house. I turned on the electricity an' water for him. He fell down goin' up the steps. Said he was gonna get a few things an' leave this mornin' sometime, only I figure he was too drunk to git up early. He wasn't in no shape to be drivin' last night. I reckon he was lucky he didn't kill hisself gettin' here."

"What did he mean by getting a few things?"

"He didn't say."

Some of Helen's oil paintings were worth a small fortune and I wondered if Tommy Lee meant to sell them to raise the money he needed. I hadn't asked Howard what became of Helen's marquise diamond necklace and earrings or the rest of her jewelry after she died. There was a safe behind a painting in the wall of her bedroom where she usually kept them. I didn't know the combination. Was Tommy Lee desperate enough to sell some of Helen's valuables? We hadn't talked for several days, since he called to ask me about arranging a loan from the estate the day Detective Garcia came.

"I'll drive down and see him, Tom. Thanks for calling. If you'll give me a key I'll drop it off on my way out."

Tom dug into a pants pocket. "It ain't really none of my affair," he said, handing me a ring of keys, "but this feller in Dallas who said he was a policeman called the other day, askin' questions about Tommy Lee an' the rest of you. He said there's some possibility Tommy Lee was the one who shot Howard, an' he wanted to know if I thought it was very likely. Hell, I didn't know what to say to him. Tommy Lee's always been a little bit on the crazy-actin' side, but I don't figure he's no killer, 'specially not his own brother. That's what I told that Mexican feller anyways."

"What else did he want to know?" I asked.

Tom couldn't look me in the eye. "He asked the same thing 'bout you, an' then he wanted to know 'bout Martha an' Suzan. I told the truth, only maybe I shouldn't oughta done it. I told him Suzan was a right smart good shot with a pistol, 'cause it was me showed her how to shoot an' I knowed how good she was when she was a kid. Only I told him she wouldn't never shoot nobody, leastways for sure not her brother. Said the same thing 'bout you an' Martha. Hellfire, that feller's gotta be crazy himself to believe somethin' like that. I knowed the five of you never got along all that good, but none of you woulda killed Howard."

I pondered how much damage might have been done to Suzan's guilt or innocence in Garcia's mind after he heard what Tom had to say. Lost in thought, I turned for my car. "I'll drop this by on my way out," I said.

I drove down the road a little faster than I should have. I kept thinking about the possibility Tommy Lee had made up his mind to take what he needed from the house to raise

money, and what I'd do about it if he did. The last thing I
wanted was a physical confrontation with him, especially if
he'd been drinking heavily.

I saw a blue Buick parked in the driveway. I drove up
and parked behind it. Glancing at my Rolex, I saw that it
was almost ten-thirty and I'd made the trip in less time
than ever before.

When I got out of the car I promised myself I wouldn't
let my brother goad me into a fight, not over oil paintings
or even a half million dollars' worth of jewelry. I climbed
the steps and knocked several times. When I got no answer
I used the key Tom gave me and let myself in.

"Tommy Lee?" I said in a loud voice, flipping on a
hallway light.

The house was quiet, dark where shuttered windows
blocked out light from every room. I made my way to the
den and turned on another light switch.

The room was empty. And I immediately noticed several oil paintings were missing from the den's walls. I assumed the paintings were already in the trunk of his car.

I climbed the stairs after a brief inspection of every
room downstairs, including the kitchen. The quiet hum of
the refrigerator intruded upon an otherwise total silence.
Helen's room, and the safe, were at the end of a dark
hallway. Helen's bedroom door was closed. I saw light
trickling from a crack at the bottom.

I approached the door carefully. "Tommy Lee? It's
Matt. I let myself in when you didn't answer my knock."

A stirring somewhere in Helen's bedroom, shuffling
feet on carpet.

"What the fuck are you doin' here? Did that ol' bastard Tom Walters call you?"

His voice was filled with antagonism, and some of his
words were slightly slurred. I hesitated before I put my

hand on the doorknob. "Tom called me last night. He was worried you were too drunk to drive."

"Fuck him! It's none of his goddamn business an' it's none of your goddamn business what I'm doin' here. Go away!"

"We need to talk a minute," I said, opening the door slowly.

Tommy Lee sat on a bench Helen used at her dressing mirror with a gun in his hands, watching me through slitted eyelids. I saw tears on his cheeks. An automatic pistol dangled at his side. His hair was mussed, tangled. He hadn't shaved for several days. The front of his shirt hung open as if buttons were missing. Empty beer cans littered the bedroom floor and the scent of stale beer hung heavy in the air.

Then I noticed Helen's safe in the middle of a wall to the left of her bed, a wall filled with dark round holes. The oil painting that normally covered the safe was gone.

"Have you been shooting at Mother's safe?" I asked, pausing in the threshold when I saw his gun.

"Goddamn right I am. That fuckin' necklace is in there an' I can't open the motherfucker, so I been shootin' at it. Don't give me any of your bullshit, Matt. I need that fuckin' necklace real bad. She can't wear it anymore. The ol' bitch is feedin' maggots right now. She owes me that fuckin' necklace . . ."

"I noticed you took some of the oil paintings downstairs," I said quietly, hoping to avoid provoking him further. "I don't think the necklace and earrings are in there in the first place. Howard probably did something with them."

"You mean he stole 'em. The rotten cocksucker stole millions an' he also got the fuckin' jewelry. I shoulda killed him that night, only I lost my nerve. He deserved what he got. If I knew who did it I'd thank him for it. He deserves a damn medal, or somethin', for gettin' rid of the sorriest chickenshit brother anybody ever had.''

"Let me take you somewhere so you can get some coffee,'' I suggested. "Drinking and shooting up the house won't solve a thing.''

"Fuck you, Matt. You're just as bad as he is, playin' like you're some kinda fuckin' god over the rest of us because you get control of everything now. You can kiss my ass. I don't want any fuckin' coffee an' I don't want to look at your fuckin' face any longer. Get the hell outa here.''

"I'm only trying to help.''

"I don't *want* your fuckin' help. Leave me alone.''

I drew in a breath. "It isn't fair to the others for you to take the oil paintings. I know how badly you need money but this isn't the right way to get it.''

"Fuck the others. An' fuck *you*. I'm takin' those god-damn pictures because they're *mine*. I got fucked out of everything else by that prick brother of ours. He stole millions of dollars from us.''

Summoning my nerve, I said, "I can't let you steal the oil paintings. I'll see what I can do to get you a bank loan.''

"You ain't gonna stop me, Matt,'' he said, rising un-steadily to his feet, glaring at me through bloodshot eyes. "I'll whip your ass if you try an' stop me. Are you blind? Can't you see I've got a gun?''

"I see it. I'd hoped you wouldn't threaten to use it on me if for no better reason than because we're brothers.''

"That don't mean shit in this family!'' He staggered toward me and lifted his pistol.

I can't explain where the urge came from, perhaps nothing more than self-defense. When Tommy Lee was within reach I swung my fist at his chin.

I felt the shock of the blow all the way to my shoulder and my knuckles exploded with pain. Tommy Lee's eyes rolled upward, then he sank slowly to his knees and dropped the gun on the floor beside him.

I stepped back and cried, "I'm sorry!" rubbing my knuckles.

Tommy Lee fell forward, landing on his face and emitting a soft groan.

It took an hour to get the paintings from the trunk of his car and return them to their proper places on the walls. I took Tommy Lee's gun and put in in the trunk of my Mercedes, wrapping it in a badly stained hand towel I'd forgotten to throw away that I found hidden behind the spare tire. I made a mental note to get rid of the gun and towel at the first opportunity.

Tommy Lee was still passed out when I finished, surely from booze more than my blow. I revived him with cold water from the sink in Helen's bathroom and helped him downstairs. He didn't seem to remember what happened.

I locked the front door and put Tommy's arm around my neck to put him in the passenger seat—he staggered most of the way. When I got in, I noticed he was crying.

"Look, Tommy Lee, I'm sorry I hit you," I said. "It's the last thing I wanted to do."

He buried his face in his hands. "I'm scared, Matt," he said, his voice muffled by his palms, sobbing. "Scared I'm gonna lose everything, scared I'm gonna go to jail for killin' Howard when I didn't do it. I'm flat busted. Spent every fuckin' dime on women an' havin' parties an' goin' places. I sold cars an' didn't pay off the loans, an' if I don't do somethin' real quick they're gonna close me down. All I ever wanted was to have a good time, to try an' be somebody. I never was as smart as you or Howard an' I couldn't get through college. I wanted people to notice me, to like me. I wanted a bunch of friends. Everybody came to my

parties, an' women liked the things I bought 'em, or goin'
to Vegas. I just wanted to have some fun . . ."

"Maybe you went about it the wrong way, Tommy
Lee. You can't buy real friends."

He took his hands from his face, staring through the
windshield at the house. "We've got all this money, only
Howard got control of it an' he treated us like a bunch of
diaper babies, sayin' he had to do this or that with the
money on account of our mother wanted it that way, fixin'
it so he controlled every cent, makin' us beg for it." He
glanced over at me with tears brimming in his eyes. "I
hated him, Matt, for the way he treated us. But I didn't kill
him. Only, that fuckin' Mexican detective believes I did it
an' he's gonna send me to jail."

"Maybe not," I said quickly, uncomfortably, my hands
gripping the steering wheel. "He has to prove you did it.
Marvin Miller is the best criminal attorney I know. Detective Garcia has a long way to go to convict you of murder.
Listen to Miller and be patient. Let him do his job."

"General Motors is gonna close me down," Tommy
Lee said. "I know sellin' those cars without payin' 'em off
was wrong, but at the time I figured sales would pick up
an' then I'd pay it all back. On top of everything else I'm
gonna go broke, because I believed things would get better.
When I heard Howard had been stealin' millions from us I
just lost my head, goin' to Dallas with a gun, knowin' I was
busted an' him with all those millions in Honduras. I know
I've got a hell of a temper, but I never woulda actually shot
him. I hope you believe me, Matt. I've done a lot of bad
things in my life, but I never killed nobody an' I sure as hell
didn't kill Howard."

"I believe you," I said.

He looked down at his hands. "I'm sorry 'bout what
happened upstairs. I wouldn't have shot you either. I've
been wonderin' if I'm goin' crazy the past few weeks,

worryin' all the time I'm gonna get closed down by Buick an' that I'll go to prison. I've been drinkin' a lot more'n usual. Sometimes, these crazy ideas just pop into my head, like comin' down here to take that necklace an' those paintings. I told myself they wasn't doin' anybody any good in this big ol' empty house, an' how they might bring enough money so I can keep my dealership open. If nobody ever came back here, nobody'd know . . .''

"It wouldn't have been fair to everyone else. I'll see what I can do about loaning you the money. I'll talk to my bank about selling off a few CDs early, or borrowing against them. Haynes hasn't filed the estate paperwork yet, so I'll make you the loan myself."

Tommy Lee looked at me again. "You'd do that for me?"

I shrugged. I wanted this discussion to be over. "You're my brother, Tommy." I started the car and swung around the gravel drive. "I'm taking you to Tom's house until you've sobered up, so you won't kill yourself or anyone else on the highway driving back. I'll call you in a couple of days, after I've talked to my bank."

"I don't hardly know what to say," he said, his voice on the verge of breaking again. "I never figured you'd be the one to help me."

I stopped the car at Tom's house. He met us out on the back porch. "If you'll ask Bonnie to make Tommy Lee some coffee," I began, helping my brother up the steps, "don't let him leave until he's sober enough to drive."

Tommy Lee walked in the back door meekly. Tom stayed with me out on the porch a moment, as if he was awaiting some explanation.

"He was trying to take some of the oil paintings and open Helen's safe," I said softly, when the door was closed. "I talked him out of it. Here's the key, and from now on, don't let him or any of the others in. I'll be the

administrator of Helen's estate in a few weeks or so, and at
that point we'll talk about what to do with the ranch." I
gave the pastures a passing glance. "I'd like to see some
more cows back on the place, and I'd like it most of all if
you'll stay on to run things. You'll be in complete charge,
if you stay."

"I'll think on it," Tom replied casually. "We ain't
gotta decide nothin' just yet, not 'til you get all this *mess*
out of the way."

I looked into Tom's eyes. "The police think I may have
done it, Tom. They say I had the strongest motive because
now I'm in control of everything, and they know I was in
Dallas on the night Howard was killed. I haven't got much
of an alibi."

Curiously, despite the seriousness of the subject, Tom
gave me one of his grins. "Shows how little they know
'bout you, son. You've never harmed a housefly. You never
would even put a spur to a horse when you was supposed
to, back when you was a kid, an' I don't figure you've
changed any. Don't fret over it. Soon as they take the time
to find out who you are an' what you're made of, they'll
start lookin' someplace else for who done it."

"Thanks, Tom," I said, shaking his hand, grateful that
someone other than Cathy and David believed in me.

Driving back to Austin with swollen right knuckles, I
made up my mind to wash my hands of any further affairs
having to do with Helen's estate. As administrator, I could
decide to appoint someone else to my position. I would
appoint Martha, as she was next in line in chronological
age. She could then make all the contributions she wanted
to her foundation, within limits set by the trust. They
could fight among themselves for all I cared, but I refused
to act as some sort of powerless referee. I wasn't going to
spend the rest of my life listening to Suzan's requests for

real estate loans or any more of Tommy Lee's troubles. I'd give him enough money to get General Motors off his back this time and then have Martha appointed administrator. I'd seen and heard enough bickering to last a lifetime.

I remembered the gun in my trunk suddenly. I started looking for a spot along the highway where I could throw it and the dirty dish towel away. Tommy Lee could always buy another gun, but I found it unsettling, knowing the bundle was back there.

But it began to rain heavily and kept on raining all the way back to Austin. I wasn't going to get soaking wet finding a place to hide it. It could wait until the rain stopped. And more than anything else right now, I needed a drink.

27

I CALLED THE OFFICE ON MY WAY INTO TOWN, hoping there would be no reason for me to drive downtown in a pouring rain so late on a Friday. Betty gave me unwanted news. An Austin policeman by the name of Si Menem was waiting for me, and he had a search warrant for my offices.

I hung up the car phone and cursed silently, although I had nothing at the office the police would care to see. I supposed they were merely being thorough, at Detective Garcia's request I was certain, looking at my files on the trust and estate matters. I had to hand it to Garcia . . . he was investigating Howard's death with bulldog tenacity.

I drove into the parking garage and got out, desperately in need of a Scotch. After assaulting my brother and a long drive through a steady downpour gripping the steering wheel with badly swollen knuckles I'd had about all I could take for one day.

Riding the elevator up, I suddenly remembered the gun in my trunk. "Shit," I whispered, attracting a quizzical look from a secretary I recognized from somewhere on the third floor. "I'm sorry," I muttered. "It's been an awful day."

The girl smiled, cradling an Express Mail package against her chest. "It's probably the weather," she said, getting off when the elevator doors opened at the floor below mine.

I reached our suites and found a man with distinctive Arab features seated in a chair in the waiting room. He wore a rumpled navy sport coat and gray slacks. His prominent nose and Fu Manchu–style beard gave him a fierce countenance even when he smiled, rising from his chair to show me his identification card and badge. He looked to be in his early fifties.

"Detective Menem," he said. "I'm with Homicide Division. I got a call from Dallas PD to pick up a search warrant for this office." His voice had a feathery quality that was unnerving and when he looked at me I saw something in his eyes that reminded me of a cat. "I gave the warrant to your secretary. Two of my officers are searching the place now."

I didn't offer to shake hands. "What are you looking for?" I asked.

"A murder weapon, Dallas PD said. Any kind of gun. You can make things go a lot quicker if you'll show us any guns you have in the office."

My pulse started to race. "There are no guns in my offices, Mr. Menem. I explained to Mr. Garcia, the Dallas detective investigating my brother's death, that I've never owned a gun. They already conducted a thorough search of my house some time ago. I wouldn't think Detective Garcia actually believes I keep guns where I have my law practice and I therefore must assume he's looking for something else."

"We'll keep lookin', Mr. King," Menem said, giving me the strangest stare, as if he could read something in my face or behind my eyes that troubled him. "If you don't have a gun up here then there's nothin' to worry about."

I wondered if I should tell him about the pistol in my car and try to explain that it belonged to my brother and it was not in my office, so I hadn't really lied to him. Betty came around her desk and asked, "Can I fix you a drink, Mr. King?"

"Thank you. No water. Just ice." I saw Gene Williams walking down the hallway past my partners' offices. He looked at me and spread his palms in a helpless gesture. His shirt collar was open and his necktie loosened . . . I could tell by the look on his face he was flustered.

"I can't get any work done until they've finished, Matt," he said.

"I understand, Gene. Just go on home. There's no telling how long this will take."

"I'll have to search him before he leaves," Menem· said, "and that goes for everybody else. You understand. A member of your staff could smuggle a gun out. We've gotta be sure."

I shrugged and moved past the detective to my office door. I needed to sit down, and I sure as hell needed a drink. "Do what you have to do," I said over my shoulder. "I'll be in my office if you need anything from me."

"We already searched your office, Mr. King, so you can prop your feet up and have that drink. We shouldn't be much longer."

My office was a mess. File cabinets stood open and every book had been removed from my bookshelves, piled across the floor in careless heaps.

"Don't worry," Betty said, handing me my Scotch. "I'll have everything put back before Monday morning."

"Thank you, Betty," I said, dropping heavily into my chair. "It may sound a bit like gallows humor, but I guess this is what everyone goes through who's suspected of murdering his brother."

"They don't *really* think you did it," Betty said.

"Detective Garcia must believe I've done something," I said, after taking a thirsty gulp of Scotch.

"The phones are ringing," Betty said apologetically as she hurried out to her desk.

"Hold all my calls," I mumbled, distracted by a dreamlike vision of Detective Menem, wearing a ridiculous turban like they wear in movies, searching the trunk of my car. I noticed now, as I shook off the daydream, that my hands were trembling. I looked guilty as sin. More Scotch would settle my nerves.

Later, Betty closed my office door. I turned to a window to watch it rain, convinced Martha had been right when she said Howard's ghost was hovering over us, making our lives as miserable as he could.

"No guns," Detective Menem said, after Betty showed him in an hour later. "Sorry for the inconvenience. The investigating officer in Dallas said he felt sure you were hiding something. I guess he's wrong."

"Garcia is a very thorough man. May I go home now?"

Menem nodded. "After I've patted you down. It's a formality. A female officer will search your secretary in the supply room. After that, everybody can go."

I stood up, hoping my shakiness wouldn't show.

Menem patted my pants legs and pockets in a perfunctory way and stood back, giving me that same hard look. "This warrant includes your automobile, Mr. King, based on probable cause, a legal technicality I'm sure you're familiar with. I assume it's in the parkin' garage. I'll ride the elevator down with you. Won't take but a minute."

I felt as though my knees would give way. "Is this really necessary?" I managed to say without stammering.

"I'm afraid it is, Mr. King."

Detective Menem only needed half a minute to open my trunk and find the pistol. When he turned to me his cat's eyes were hooded. He held out the gun exposed on top of the dish towel.

"You lied to me, Mr. King," he said, holding the gun forth as proof.

"I can explain. You asked if there were guns in my offices and I told the truth. You didn't ask about my car. This is not my gun. I took it away from my brother this morning when he came toward me with it. He'd been drinking. I took it away from him and I'm sure a check of gun registrations will show it belongs to Tommy Lee King, my younger brother."

Menem wagged his head. "As an attorney yourself you know I have to take you to headquarters while we check out your story. You can call your own lawyer when we get there, if you want. I'm not arresting you, you understand."

"I understand. Everything I've told you will be borne out by my brother's testimony and gun ownership records. I've never owned a gun in my life." My heart was beating so wildly I thought I heard it hammering in my ears when it dawned on me gun registrations were not the only thing I should be thinking about—I was having a flashback to the night of December twentieth—not something I'd done, but something I'd forgotten to do.

Menem lifted a corner of the dish towel. "These look like old bloodstains, Mr. King," he said. "If they are, I guess you have an explanation for them too."

"It's . . . not my towel. I think I'd like to call my attorney before I answer any more questions."

Menem folded the cloth over the pistol. "You know what your rights are." He gave me another steady stare. "Kinda curious, what you just told me, about your younger brother comin' at you with this. Detective Garcia told me you were a suspect in the murder of your older brother. Now you tell me you thought your younger brother was gonna try to kill you. A strange bunch you come from. I'm of Lebanese descent. Third generation. We're taught from the day we're born to put family members first, that we have to stick together. I call myself an American, but there's still that Lebanese part of me who can't believe brothers could turn on each other with a gun. If that's the American way, I'm damn glad my ancestors didn't get here on the *Mayflower*. My car's on the lower level, Mr. King. I'm afraid you're gonna have to ride with me to headquarters. You can call your lawyer from there.''

I sat at a metal table with my hands folded in front of me, looking down to avoid the harsh glare of the fluorescent lights. My call to John Albritton reached his answering service, hardly an unexpected result when trying to reach a very successful attorney late on a Friday. I hadn't called Cathy yet to tell her I was at the police headquarters on Seventh Street being questioned in my brother's death because the police found a gun in my possession—I didn't have the nerve. Trying to explain things to her over a telephone seemed too difficult, too impossible, and at the moment my nerves were shot.

And far more impossible to explain would be the bloodstained towel. I felt trapped, wondering how much of the truth I could tell my own attorney.

I told myself life has certain boundaries and obstacles we all encounter. If I could keep my composure I'd make it through this.

I gazed blankly at the interrogation-room walls, a sickly pale green, waiting for Detective Menem to return. That damn dish towel, I thought. Why hadn't I thrown it away where no one would ever find it? Everything I loved, everyone I cherished, could be taken from me because of it. My own stupidity would be my undoing. Carelessness was about to send me to prison for the rest of my life, or even to a death sentence when a crime lab analyzed the bloodstains.

It was Howard's blood on the towel . . .

28

"**I** DIDN'T DO IT, JOHN," I SAID.

Albritton grinned. "I could never be made to believe you did, Matt. They're sending the cloth to DPS labs for a blood analysis. Since I don't need to tell you about attorney-client privilege, tell me whose blood it is . . . if you know."

"It *is* my brother Howard's. It seems like a complicated story but it is really quite simple. I got to Howard's house the night he was killed and when nobody answered the doorbell, I went around to the garage and discovered a side door pried open. My sister in San Antonio had called me to say our younger brother, Tommy Lee, was on his way to Dallas with a gun after threatening Howard's life. Everything had gone crazy as soon as our mother died, fighting over her money, some of my family trying to have her will contested because they thought Helen lost her mind. So I went in, thinking Tommy Lee could have parked in the alley. I found Howard in his study and he was already dead, shot through the head. I believed Tommy Lee killed him while in a drunken state of mind. So I did the most unthinkable thing I could have done . . . I took a letter opener from Howard's desk and removed the bullet from the back of Howard's chair. Howard's wife and kids were Christmas shopping, so I went to the kitchen and got a dish towel, wiping off anything I thought might have Tommy Lee's fingerprints on it, or my own. I took the slug and the bloody towel and left. Nobody saw me."

Albritton frowned. He's a huge man, well over six feet with a wrestler's build, almost completely bald, a graduate of Baylor Law School with a formidable record as a criminal attorney. We met in college and became friends. "What about the gun they say they found in your car?" he asked. "Is it the murder weapon?"

"I have no idea. It's from another incident. Tommy Lee is going broke with his Buick dealership in San Antonio. Our ranch foreman called to tell me he was at the ranch planning to rob it of some valuable oil paintings and jewelry. I drove over there this morning and found Tommy Lee drunk. He came at me with that gun and I hit him with my fist. I took the gun and put it in my trunk, wrapping it in the dish towel I used to wipe things clean at Howard's before Christmas. I'd forgotten it was there. I was planning to throw both of them in a lake someplace, only it was raining too hard and I didn't stop. Detective Menem found them and it makes it look like I lied, like I was trying to conceal my guilt as Howard's killer."

"And you believed your brother Tommy Lee murdered Howard, so you tried to protect him by wiping off fingerprints."

"I worried he might have done it. Howard was dead when I got there. Tommy Lee was in Dallas, although he insists now he doesn't know who killed Howard. He told me he drove by the house a few times and then lost his nerve. He was drinking heavily. He hasn't got much of an alibi, but I'm pretty sure now he didn't do it. He's the family hothead, and he did threaten to kill Howard one time over the phone, when Howard wouldn't loan him any money from the estate for his business. But I don't think he shot Howard. A burglar could have done it, or any number of other possibilities."

"You were also there," Albritton said, rubbing his chin. "I don't need to tell you that makes you a strong suspect. Now they have a bloody rag with your deceased brother's blood on it and a possible murder weapon, found in your possession. What did you do with the bullet you removed from the chair?''

"I honestly don't remember. I was scared to death someone would see me. I recall tossing the dish towel in the trunk after I wiped my hands. The bullet may be in the trunk of my car. I drove off and stopped at a bar near I-35 to have a drink or two, before I drove back to Austin. I was so damn nervous I could hardly hold a glass.''

Albritton glanced at his watch. "It's almost ten-thirty. I think I can convince them to let you go home until the lab report comes back. But when they find out it is your brother's blood, you may be charged with his murder and bond will be set, if the district attorney in Dallas believes he has a case. If the gun they found is the murder weapon, you'll go to trial. The problem the DA faces is, he has no bullet, but it may be in the trunk of your car. If they find it, and if the gun is the murder weapon, we've got a larger problem. As far as you know, they don't have a witness putting you at the murder scene at the time of death?''

"I admitted being there. I didn't think there was a reason to deny it. I told the Dallas cop I sat out front until Howard's wife and kids got home around midnight. That's the part I lied about.''

Albritton took a notepad from a pocket of his gray pinstriped suit. He scribbled something down. "I don't believe they intend to question you any more tonight. I'll ask someone out front if you can go home. This isn't an Austin PD case, so I don't think anybody will give a shit. Dallas hasn't issued a warrant so it's no skin off their noses. The little Arab cop, Sied Menem, can be a real prick when he wants to be. I've dealt with him before. Maybe he went home to beat his wife or something . . .'' Albritton got up and tucked his notepad away. "I'll be back in a minute."

"I didn't do it, John. I swear I didn't do it."

"I believe you, Matt. The way I see it, you've got a real difficult case if that bullet is still in the trunk of your car." He walked out of the interrogation room, leaving me to my dreary thoughts.

I had a real problem, as Albritton put it—a tiny misshapen ball of lead rolling around somewhere in the back of my Mercedes. I closed my eyes, remembering that December night vividly. If I hadn't gone inside, hadn't acted in haste, none of this would be happening.

As a lawyer, I knew I'd committed an unpardonable sin, not telling my own attorney the entire truth. On the one hand I was risking losing my wife and son, the most precious things in the world to me, if I went to prison. But the other option left me with a betrayal I wasn't certain I could live with.

I LIED TO CATHY ABOUT WHY I WAS LATE GET-
ting home, claiming the weather delayed me. My life was
becoming a succession of lies, one to explain another. I saw
no end to it. I told her about Tommy Lee, the paintings,
and the gun incident, making no mention of the hours I'd
spent in an interrogation room at Austin police headquarters. She informed me a call had come from Tommy Lee
and he wanted it returned, no matter what time I got
there.

"Don't call him back, Matt," she said, handing me the
number on a slip of paper. "It'll only upset you."

"I don't really have a choice," I replied. "I can't
dodge him forever and the way today has gone, I'd just as
soon get it over with. It's been one of the shittiest days of
my life."

I went downstairs and walked out by the pool with my
cellular phone, to keep Cathy from overhearing anything I
might say. David was asleep. It was still raining, a lighter
rain, but I stood underneath our patio canopy where Cathy
hung her plants in summertime to dial Tommy Lee's number.

"This is Matt," I said abruptly when a voice answered,
fully expecting my brother to be antagonistic after our
scuffle. "I'm returning your call."

"I'm real sorry about what happened this mornin',"
he said. "I got home okay. I just wanted you to know I feel

awful about it, about what I tried to do by takin' that stuff.''

"In the first place, it isn't fair to Martha or Suzan for you to take them and sell them. It's stealing from them.''

"Howard stole millions. I was gonna pay it back this spring when business picked up.''

"I couldn't let you do it. I couldn't face Martha or Suzan if I did.''

"You're a better brother to me than I ever was to you, Matt. I don't know what happened to the four of us. It's like we all grew up bein' strangers. Howard was born a prick, but you ain't nothin' like him. By the way, where's my Luger?''

"If you're talking about the gun I took away from you, the Austin police have it. They intend to hold it as evidence to see if it can be the murder weapon. They came to my office this afternoon with a search warrant. A detective found it in the trunk of my car. They'll be checking registrations to see who it belongs to. I've been at police headquarters for hours, answering questions. I had to tell them it belongs to you.''

"It ain't a murder weapon. I didn't kill Howard.''

"You'll have your chance to explain.''

"I've gotta have that money, Matt. General Motors is gonna close my doors if I don't get it real soon, like next week. I hope you can make me that loan, an' I'll be glad when you're in charge of the estate.''

"Listen, I'm really tired of everyone calling me a chickenshit or a prick over this estate business. I decided on my way home today to appoint Martha administrator. That way, she can make all the donations she legally can to her foundation and the price she'll pay for it is taking a cussing from you and Suzan and Carl. I'm sick and tired of it. It isn't worth it to me. I don't want the responsibility and I sure as hell don't want any more name-calling from the rest of you. I'm tired tonight, Tommy Lee, and I'm going to bed. I don't care to discuss this with you anymore. I'll talk to my bank in a day or two about making you the loan myself. As soon as Fullerton and Haynes are finished with all the paperwork making me the trustee, I'm appointing Martha to the position." I pushed the END button on my phone and tossed it on a patio table, grinding my teeth in frustration. What I had not told my brother was that the police also had a dish towel with Howard's blood on it, and possibly a bullet fragment from the trunk of my car that would make me look like a murderer to a judge and jury. I lit a cigarette and watched storm clouds move eastward across the lake, leaving behind clearing skies as the late-night shower ended. But my mind wasn't on clouds or weather at the moment—I was wondering what a prison cell would be like.

After Cathy went to sleep I got up and came down to the den for a few drinks in peace and quiet, staring out our glass wall at a night sky alive with the stars above the lake, wondering where my life was headed. A lab report would most certainly land me in jail—Howard's blood was on the dish towel, and Detective Menem impounded my car, looking for fibers or more bloodstains or any other incriminating evidence. I'd taken a taxi home and told my wife another lie, that my car was in for repairs. I could not remember what I'd done with the bullet I took from Howard's chair no matter how hard I tried to re-create events from the night of the twentieth.

Again, I found myself wondering what prison would be like. Most civil attorneys are totally unfamiliar with these things. I knew the names of a few Texas prison units . . . Ramsey, Ellis, The Walls, where murderers are sent to await execution on death row. I might join them in a few months.

It was two in the morning when I called Suzan. A sleepy voice answered the telephone, a child's voice.

"Let me speak to your mother, Jody. This is your Uncle Matthew."

Minutes later Suzan's voice came on the line. "Do you know what fucking time it is?"

"I know. Wake up and listen to me. I saw you at Howard's that night. I was parked down the street. I saw everything, so don't lie to me. Did you park in the alley after you drove past his house?"

"Screw you, Matt. What the hell is this all about?"

"You know damn well what it's about. I haven't told the police I saw you there. They think Tommy Lee killed Howard and that detective from Dallas believes he did it. Martha told me they found a gun at your house, and it had been fired recently."

"Are you recording this?"

"I'm not recording anything. It wouldn't be admissible in court anyway."

A hesitation. "I didn't park in the alley. I was looking for Tommy Lee. When I didn't see his car I drove someplace else and had a drink. I tried to call Carl, but the bastard wasn't at home. He's having an affair with his secretary. We've been sleeping in separate bedrooms."

"What did you do after you called Carl?"

"You're recording this, trying to trick me into saying something, aren't you?"

"There is *no* recording being made. The police took me down for questioning tonight and I'm in shit up to my eyebrows because I had a gun belonging to Tommy Lee in the trunk of my car and I can't prove where I was at the time Howard was killed—hell, I admitted being there. Where did you go after you made the call to Midland?"

Another lengthy pause. "I drove back by Howard's.

Nobody was there." She lowered her voice. "So I picked up this guy I met at the bar and we went somewhere. I screwed his ears off and I can't tell that to the cops, can I? I was getting even for what Carl's been doing to me. My friend Joanna calls it a grudge fuck. Carl hasn't made love to me for months."

"But did you go inside when you went to Howard's either time or did you just drive by looking for Tommy Lee?"

"I didn't stop. I sure as hell didn't want to talk to that son of a bitch Howard. I wanted to keep Tommy Lee from going to jail, that's all."

"The Dallas police will want you to prove where you were," I said.

"I can't. The guy's married. He's gettin' a divorce, but he still lives with his wife on account of his kids. If you *are* recording this I'm gonna swear I was only kidding you about it, because I hate your guts. I *do* hate your guts, Matthew. You've turned into the same kind of dick-head Howard was."

"Forget that you hate my guts for a moment and tell me about the gun they found at your house. Tom Walters told me you could really shoot well, that he taught you how when you were younger. Where did you get the gun? And why was it fired recently?"

"I shot out two of Carl's tires when I found his car parked at a motel. The dirty bastard had the balls to get a room with the bitch right here in Midland. I drove off after I gave him two flats. I laughed all the way home. This is Howard's fault, you know, because he wouldn't loan us the money to buy that ranch in Alpine so Carl could build a deer-hunting lodge. Instead of hunting deer, Carl started hunting other women. But in case you *are* recording this, I didn't shoot Howard. I didn't park in an alley or anywhere else. I screwed a computer salesman an' that's the only thing I'll admit to. Carl had it coming . . ."

"You didn't see me parked near Howard's house?"

"I did see a car, only it wasn't a Buick so I knew it wasn't Tommy Lee. Nobody was in it. I drove right on by. I figured Howard and Diane had company over for some Christmas eggnog, and that would stop Tommy Lee from doing anything. I drove back to the bar and picked up the cute little computer guy. He was horny and so was I. That isn't a crime. If that was your car, how come you weren't in it? Did you go inside and blow a big hole through Howard's penny-pinching head?"

I let out a sigh. Suzan had seen my Mercedes. "The car you saw must not have been mine. The police will be asking you questions. Be careful what you say."

"Why's that? I've got nothing to hide, except I screwed some guy. I wouldn't take advice from you anyway, Matt. You'd be the last person I'd take advice from. For all I know, maybe *you're* the one who killed Howard. It had to be you, or Tommy Lee."

"Or a burglar," I protested.

"Bullshit. Tommy Lee threatened to kill him, more than once according to Martha, and the cops even have a tape recording of what he said. Or you could have killed him. You admit you were there and with Howard dead you're the big cheese with the money."

"And you were there. You had the same opportunity to do it as the rest of us did."

"Screw you, Matt. It won't work, trying to blame it on me. Even if I did it, you'll never be able to prove it."

The phone clicked. I reached for my half-empty glass. I wanted to know what Suzan had seen that night and now I knew. She had seen a car in front of Howard's house, but whose car had she seen?

•   •   •

Cathy came downstairs shortly after dawn. I was seated in my recliner watching the sunrise with a drink in my hand.

"Please tell me what's wrong, Matt," she said, sitting in a chair beside me. "It's more than what happened yesterday with Tommy Lee, isn't it? I have the feeling you're keeping something from me."

"I'm tired of my family's squabbling, tired of hearing about new theories having to do with Howard's death. I'm sick of Tommy Lee's whining over a loan from the estate which I probably can't make. Martha still bitches about contributions to her foundation and Suzan blames Howard for Carl having an affair with his secretary because he was frustrated over not getting the money to buy some ranch in Alpine where he could build a deer hunter's lodge. I'm disgusted with all of them and their attitudes. I've had about all I can take."

"I can't stand to see how this is destroying you, honey. I see you drinking more and more, and at times you drift off into your own private thoughts so you don't hear me when I'm talking to you. It isn't worth it, running Helen's business affairs. I hate what it's doing to you."

Cathy was looking at me as she said this and in my bleary state of mind after a night without sleep and too much Scotch, I almost told her the truth, the whole truth, until I caught myself. "I'm turning things over to Martha as soon as I can. I don't want the responsibility. I never did want it. The problem isn't solved if I get rid of managing the estate. The police still think I'm a suspect in Howard's death and until it's resolved, I'm doomed to more of their questions."

Cathy gave me one of her looks. "You know who did it, don't you? You know Tommy Lee killed Howard and you won't tell the police what you know."

"I swear to you I didn't see Tommy Lee in Dallas. I wish you could believe me."

"Then you saw someone else at Howard's. It has to be Martha or Suzan."

I closed my eyes, resting my head against the back of my chair while I wondered how I would explain things to Cathy if I were arrested for my brother's murder. "You'll have to trust me," I said softly. "No matter what happens, you must believe what I'm telling you now. I did not kill Howard. Even if the police charge me with it, I want you to believe me when I say I didn't do it. I've got plenty of shortcomings and faults, but I'm not a killer."

"I *do* believe you, Matt, but I don't understand why you won't tell them everything you know."

I thought about a way to answer her that might make some sense, knowing I'd be on dangerous ground if I revealed too much. "Anything I tell you will only deepen your involvement in something you had nothing to do with. I suppose I'm asking for your understanding. Let me handle this in my own way. I believe I know what I'm doing."

Cathy reached for my hand. "What you're doing is protecting someone else and they don't deserve it. Your sisters and brother are sick, selfish people."

I opened my eyes. A small sailboat had begun to tack back and forth into winds rippling the waters of the lake. "They are also my family," I said quietly, squeezing her palm. I was certain I could never make her understand.

I WAS ARRESTED BY DETECTIVE SI MENEM AND A female officer at eleven-thirty Monday morning. I was spared the disgrace of being handcuffed in my office. I rode down to police headquarters in the backseat of a Chevrolet where I was shown to another interrogation room on the second floor. Only then was I allowed to call John Albritton from a pay telephone in the hallway. His secretary said he was in court, but she would get him the message right away that I was in jail, charged with the murder of my brother. The plainclothes policewoman had read me my Miranda rights before we left my office although I already knew I didn't have to say anything until John got there. I'd told Betty to call my wife, knowing how much pain Cathy would suffer when she learned what happened, and I'd spoken to Gene, asking him and Mark Herring to handle my cases until I was out on bond—although I supposed there was a chance bond might be denied in my case.

Detective Menem came back into the room with a small plastic bag and tossed it on the table in front of me. I looked at what it contained and closed my eyes. I didn't want to remember how I acquired that small, insignificant-looking piece of lead.

"This is the bullet that killed your brother," he said, his voice echoing off plaster walls around us. "We found it in the back of your car. You aren't required to talk to me until your attorney gets here, as you know. While we're waiting, I'll tell you a few things. Some are puzzling, quite frankly. The lab test-fired two guns. Dallas PD did the tests on a gun Detective Garcia took from your brother Tommy Lee and a forty-five the Midland police found at your sister's. They faxed PMTs of the bullets and none of them match the slug we took from your car. The nine-millimeter Luger wrapped in the bloody cloth is the wrong caliber. Blood typing and DNA tests confirm it is your deceased brother's blood on the cloth and the slug. Detective Garcia is on his way down to drive you back to Dallas, where you will be formally charged with murder. You had motive and opportunity, physical evidence in the form of a blood-stained towel and the fatal bullet found in your possession. There's a recording of a conversation during which you accuse Howard of embezzling. A very strong case, don't you think?''

"It would appear that way," I agreed, feeling dizzy and sick to my stomach. My skin and palms felt clammy. "I don't think I'll say any more until Mr. Albritton arrives. I can recite Miranda for you, if you wish."

"I'm familiar with your rights, Mr. King. If you confessed right now, I doubt anyone could use it. I was simply curious to see what you had to say. I've been a cop for more than twenty years and I never ran across a murderer who killed his brother. An unusual case. I suspect putting you in front of a jury will be like feeding you to the lions, even without a murder weapon. They'll tear you apart. Since you live on the lake I'm having divers sent down, to see if you ditched the gun there. With or without the gun that fired this bullet I can't see anything but a guilty verdict when you go to trial, although I don't think a DA will need the gun. They've got enough right now to convict you."

"Are you enjoying this, Mr. Menem?" I asked, feeling bitter bile rise in my throat.

Menem's eyes became slits. "Not at all," he said hoarsely. "I find it disgusting, not the least bit pleasurable, to be in the same room with a man who'd kill his brother." He picked up the bullet and walked out of the room, leaving me alone with my haunting memories of the night of December twentieth in Dallas.

Detective Tony Garcia came alone to drive me to Dallas, and he seemed almost friendly, though it could have been part of an act to catch me off guard so I'd say something, or admit to the crime I'd be charged with. When we went downstairs I saw Cathy in the waiting room wiping tears from her eyes with a Kleenex.

"Can I have a minute to talk to my wife?" I asked Garcia.

"Of course," he said, moving to stand near the front door.

Cathy rushed into my arms, sobbing, attracting the attention of a roomful of policemen, bail bondsmen, and family members who were there for the same reason as my wife.

"Why won't you tell them the truth?" Cathy asked, gripping the lapels of my suit coat.

"John Albritton will tell me what I can say. He's in court right now, but he sent a junior partner over to tell me John will fly to Dallas this evening and arrange for my bond. I'm not to say anything until I've talked to John."

"But you didn't *do* it, Matt," she cried. "Why are you still protecting Tommy Lee?"

"I'll explain things later, honey. Right now, I want you to trust me. I'm doing the right thing."

"You didn't kill Howard, so why are they doing this to you?"

"They found some circumstantial evidence in my possession. I can't tell you any more right now. Please trust me. All this can be straightened out. Please don't cry."

Her expression changed quickly. "It's this sick family

of yours doing this to you, and you're letting them do it. I can't understand why you'd let them. They're all insane, Matt. You can't deny it.''

"Please, Cathy. I've got to go now. I'll be back on the first available flight as soon as I've been arraigned and my bond is posted. John will handle everything. Tell David I love him. I'll explain everything as soon as I get back.''

I took her hands from my coat and kissed her, then, before I cried myself, I went with Detective Garcia out into the chill north wind blasting past the police building.

"My car's over there, the gray Ford,'' he said, ducking his head. "I won't bother with cuffing you, Mr. King. I'm quite sure you're not the type who'd try to run.''

"I won't run,'' I promised, climbing into a Ford sedan with no markings. When Garcia got in I added, "I'm sure you know I have been advised not to say anything without my attorney being present.''

He started the car. "I understand. We can talk about the NBA, if you like basketball. Or football. The Superbowl was a joke, the Bills losing again.'' He drove away from the curb and turned north on Interstate 35. "Do you have any kids?''

"A boy. He's fourteen and he plays basketball. He's not a great player, but he loves it.''

Garcia changed lanes carefully. "I'll just ask you about a single matter involving the case, Mr. King, and you don't have to answer. Then we can talk about basketball. I like how Houston is playing this year. I want to know if I'd be on the right track if I kept looking for someone else in your family who has something to hide. To tell you the truth, I don't think you did it with premeditation. Maybe it was an accident, a gun goes off during an argument. I don't expect you to tell me what happened, but I was wondering if I'd be wasting my time to keep digging—to see if your sister or brother could have been involved in any capacity. This is strictly off the record.''

"That would be saying I know who killed Howard and I wanted to accuse them or implicate them somehow. I can't answer your question on legal grounds.''

Garcia smiled, watching traffic through his windshield. "I think you gave me my answer. Now, how about those Rockets, eh?''

I was free on a one-hundred-thousand-dollar bond at ten the following morning, after John Albritton argued I was no threat to society and wouldn't leave the country to evade prosecution. I flew back on a noon Southwest flight and caught a taxi to the office, after calling Cathy from the airport to say I'd be home as soon as I could. She told me David stayed home from school, saying he was too upset to attend classes until he talked to me. Burdened with this, I was less than happy when Betty handed me messages from Tommy Lee, Martha, Suzan, and Diane, all wanting to be called back the moment I got to the office. I learned it was my wife who called them all, crying, according to Betty, to demand that whoever I was protecting come forward before I was sent to prison for something I didn't do.

"Jesus," I said when Betty gave me the list of calls. Gene and Mark came down the hall when they heard my voice, presenting me with the need for more explanations. I spoke to everyone gathered around me. "I'm free on bond. John Albritton says I can't say a word to anyone. It's still a circumstantial case without witnesses or a murder weapon. And just so you'll hear my official position on it, I didn't kill my brother.''

Betty handed me folded copies of *The Austin Statesman* and the *Dallas Morning News*. "Somebody gave it to the papers,'' she said gently.

I glanced briefly at both front-page story headlines.

"King Family Heir Charged with Brother's Murder" and "Oil-Rich Matthew King Charged in Brother's Death." I grieved silently for what I knew Cathy and David were going through now. I shook my head and went into my office, closing the door to make my last phone call to my brother, sisters, and sister-in-law.

I called Diane first and said simply, "I didn't do it. I've been advised to say nothing further until my trial. Please don't call me again."

I reached Tommy Lee at home. "This is Matt. My attorney has advised me not to talk to you or anyone else about it. I'll have to stand trial and you'll be subpoenaed. Consult Marvin Miller on everything. This is the last conversation we'll have about it until my trial."

"You didn't do it, Matt, but I know who did. Suzan hasn't got me fooled a goddamn bit. She an' Carl did it. Neither one of 'em can come up with a convincin' story about where they were when Howard was killed. Carl's a loudmouthed jerk. He's still pissed off about that land in Alpine an' Suzan's always been a hot-tempered bitch. They did it, the two of 'em together. I called 'em last night when I heard what happened. Suzan told me to fuck off an' then Carl got on the line, yellin' I was the one who oughta be in jail."

"I can't talk about it, Tommy Lee. Good-bye."

I called Suzan at home. "This is Matt," I said, hoping to get this over with quickly. "I'm free on bond and my attorney advises me not to talk about the case to anyone. I won't call you again and please do not call me until the trial is over."

"You're gonna tell 'em in court, aren't you? You're just enough of a bastard to tell everybody."

"Tell them what?" I asked impatiently.

"About the guy I met in Dallas. You're nothing but a dick-head, Matt, just like Howard was. It's in your blood. I hope they give you the fucking electric chair." She slammed down the phone before I had time to tell her Texas no longer used the electric chair.

I dialed Martha at home and got no answer, nor did she pick up on her cellular phone. The foundation was no longer a working number when I called it.

I poured myself a brimming drink, to add to the three on the plane ride home, and swilled it down like water.

Now, strangely, I noticed furnishings in my office as if I saw them for the first time, after spending a miserable night in the Dallas City Jail before my arraignment the next morning. A forty-thousand-dollar interior-decorating job and for years I'd taken it for granted. I was sure a prison cell at Huntsville would be more Spartan and my nerve-soothing glasses of Scotch would be a distant memory. My license to practice law would be revoked, but more than anything else, I'd miss my wife and son desperately.

I had an alternative and I wondered if I should take it. I couldn't bring myself to think about it now.

Dreading the moment when I would face Cathy and David, I steeled my nerves with another glass of straight Scotch and tried Martha's cellular number one more time.

"Hello?"

"It's me. I'm free on bond and back in Austin. My attorney told me not to discuss anything with you or the others right now. Don't call me. I can't call you either. Let events take their course and I'll see what happens. They don't have the murder weapon or any witnesses. I've got a good attorney and he thinks I can beat it. I'm having you appointed administrator of Helen's estate. I'll get a letter off to Fullerton tomorrow. That's all I can talk about now."

"Oh, Matt. I have to see you," Martha sobbed.

"No. Under no circumstances, until after the trial. Do not call me. My attorney knows what he's doing."

I heard her crying. "Please?"

"The answer is no. Good-bye, Martha. Fullerton will be in touch with you. This *has* to be our last conversation until I go to trial."

I hung up and took a deep breath, hoping I was doing the right thing.

31

BETTY HAD ARRANGED TO HAVE MY CAR picked up that afternoon, after the Austin police crime lab was finished with it, and as I drove home at four-thirty I took my time, sipping on a plastic cup of Scotch, thinking about Cathy and David, wondering if their doubts about me would ever go away. If I stood trial and I were acquitted, would they ever feel the same way toward me? I had my doubts. It would be easy enough for Cathy to believe a fatal flaw in my character had surfaced—I came from a background making such a thing possible. The same form of mental illness afflicting my brothers and sisters might readily show up in me if it were triggered by some event. David would face a different kind of test. His peer group would ask questions. Is your father a murderer? Did he really murder your uncle? How does it feel to have your dad's name on the front page of the paper? I would lose my son's trust and it was already too late to do anything about the damage.

I wheeled into the driveway and got out of the car, fearing this meeting with my wife and son more than I feared my upcoming trial. I would know, within a few minutes, whether or not I'd lost the two most important people in my life. The only ones who'd ever shown me unconditional love and taught me how to love in return.

I walked through the garage door and pulled off my

overcoat, tossing it over the back of a kitchen chair. I saw Cathy sitting in the den with a drink in her hand.

"Hello," I said stiffly, as though I spoke to a stranger. I hesitated on the threshold leading down into our sunken den with my heart laboring. "Where's David?"

"Up in his room," Cathy replied quietly. "I asked him if I could talk to you alone before he saw you."

"I'll make myself a drink," I said, avoiding my usual habit of kissing her when I got home—there was something in her voice warning me this wasn't the time.

She watched me walk to the bar and pour Scotch over cubes of ice. The silence in the room was absolute. I noted that no fire was burning in the fireplace and I wondered if our proverbial home fires had gone out as well.

I crossed to my recliner and sat down, looking Cathy in the eye, and I saw no hint of love on her face. She had a look that might have been fear, robbing her of her usual beauty. "I guess you'd like to hear the whole story," I said, tasting my drink.

"I would, Matthew. I want to hear the story from beginning to end, starting with what happened the night you went to Dallas. I think it's time you told me the truth."

"What I told you was the truth," I began, proceeding carefully. "There are some things I haven't told you, things I can't tell you because they will bring irreparable harm to someone else and I can't live with that. I pray you'll believe me when I say I did not kill my brother, and that should be what matters most to you and David."

"You saw who did it, didn't you?"

"I can't answer that. I won't answer because I love you too much to involve you in any of this. If I gave you the knowledge you want you would be faced with a very serious moral and ethical dilemma . . . whether or not to tell the police or a prosecutor what you know. By my silence, I'm keeping you from having to make the choice, although it hurts me beyond my ability to describe it to know that I have lost your trust, perhaps even your love, by my refusal to answer your questions. I've made a difficult choice, to remain silent. My attorney does not believe they can convict me without a murder weapon or a witness. I'm forced to take the chance that I'll be acquitted. John thinks I have a very good chance."

"But there is a witness. Whoever killed Howard is a witness to his murder."

I nodded and drank more Scotch. "If he or she comes forward with the truth, the case against me will be dismissed. But that choice is not mine to make."

"Why not?"

"Because, as you have already guessed, it's a member of my family."

Tears welled in Cathy's beautiful eyes. "Not one of them would do the same thing for you," she said, tight-voiced.

"Perhaps not," I told her softly. "But I have to live with myself. I'm doing the only thing I can. If you find my position intolerable, I'll move out of the house until the trial is over. It will save you and David a great deal of public embarrassment."

"That's not what I want at all . . ."

"Then I must ask you for one very large favor. Don't ask me to discuss it again. John believes he can push the judge for a speedy trial, in as little as three months. I know it will be very difficult not to talk about it, however it's the only way I think I can get through this in one piece."

She stared at me in silence.

●　　　●　　　●

I knocked before I entered David's room. He was lying on his bed staring at the ceiling. "Hey," I said, closing the door behind me.

He glanced at me and I stood there for a long time, a knot forming in my stomach.

"They let you out of jail," he said, sounding much older than he was.

"I posted a bond, promising I'll be there for my trial."

"Everybody says you murdered Uncle Howard. Bobby's dad is sayin' maybe you were drunk when you did it."

"I didn't do it," I said, waiting in front of the door. I sensed he didn't want closeness now.

"Then how come the paper says you did? How come the cops arrested you?"

"The police found something in the trunk of my car and it makes me look guilty."

"What was it?"

"A bloody cloth and a bullet and a gun."

"But you ain't even got a gun. Whose gun was it?"

"Tommy Lee's."

"How come the cops don't believe you?"

"They are hired to do a job, and part of being a policeman is being suspicious of everyone until they know who committed a crime, until they have absolute proof of who did it."

"They must *think* you did it."

"It's the bullet and the bloodstained towel. On the surface they make me look guilty."

David sat up and swung his legs off the bed, and now he was looking directly at me. "But you'll swear you didn't kill Uncle Howard." He said it like he had a frog in his throat.

"I swear to you I didn't."

"I've been real scared, Dad, since Mom told me they took you to jail. I couldn't go to school 'cause I felt like I was gonna throw up all day."

"Some of your friends will ask you about it, about what was in the newspaper. That'll be one of the hardest parts."

"Yeah," he whispered. "That's gonna be real hard. Bobby kept on askin' me if I thought you did it. I told him to fuck off."

"I wish I could make things easier for you."

"Mom keeps sayin' you know Uncle Tommy Lee did it an' you won't tell the cops because he's your brother. She says maybe you even *saw* him do it. She's been cryin' nearly all day."

"I'm sorry for that too, only I can't change what's taking place until I've had my day in court."

"How long will that be?"

"Three or four months."

"That's a real long time."

"I know. It'll seem like forever."

"If Uncle Tommy Lee did it, an' since he's your brother, how come he hasn't confessed to the cops so *you* don't have to go to jail?"

"I didn't see Tommy Lee do it."

"Then who the hell did it, Dad? Mom keeps sayin' you know."

"I wasn't there when Howard was killed. I got there later, and he was already dead."

"Then how come Mom keeps sayin' you *know* who did it?"

"She thinks I'm protecting someone else."

"Are you?"

I felt like I was forced to lie to him now. I'd never be able to make him understand. "No. I found Howard dead and I didn't see who pulled the trigger," I said. Part truth, part lie.

He got up and came over to me, and when he put his arms around me, snuggling his face to my chest, I came closer than I ever had since the night of December twentieth to calling the police and telling them what actually happened in Howard's study.

32

DAYS AND WEEKS PASSED SLOWLY AS I INSU-
lated myself from the outside world. I changed both my
home and my cellular phone to unlisted numbers, staying
in contact with the office and my law partners by telephone. I sent Tommy Lee my personal check for two hundred thousand dollars, after deciding I wouldn't need the
money in prison anyway, and to stop him from calling the
office every day asking for me. I hadn't heard from either
of my sisters since my release from jail. I existed in something of a vacuum, spending hours alone away from Cathy
and David and everyone else I knew. I went for long
drives, sitting on park benches or at picnic tables at the
lake in the dead of winter when no one else was there. My
mind constantly wandered while I awaited my trial. I drank
heavily day and night, battling two voices inside my head as
though a pair of ancient gladiators fought continually for
control of my brain, and my conscience.

Cathy remained distant. We ate some meals together,
the three of us, but for the most part I sought solitude.
One cold day in February, after Suzan and Martha both left
messages for me at the office that I declined to return, I
drove to Eden to see the ranch. I didn't want to talk to
either of my sisters, or to Tommy Lee, until after my trial.
It was pointless to answer their questions now, and there
were too many things I didn't want to talk about until I had
time to straighten things out in my head.

I stopped at Tom's house and told him I needed a key

to the big house, even though I wasn't certain I'd go in. I was haunted by memories, wondering if somehow I could put them to rest if I went back home, to the place where everything started. Tom did not say much when he handed me the key and I wonder if he sensed something eating me from the inside out, something I didn't care to talk about with him. He knew about the charges against me and perhaps he believed I was my brother's killer.

I drove to the old rock house ruins first, getting out in my shirtsleeves even though it was close to freezing. I walked among the shattered walls, then down to the creek, skipping a few stones across the water as I did when I was a boy. When this activity offered no distraction or satisfaction I got back in my car and drove down to the house, our house. For a time I sat behind the steering wheel looking at its gabled roof and shuttered windows, my mind blank. Later, I got out and walked slowly around to the back where I had a view of my old bedroom window overlooking hills and oil wells to the west. I remembered the years I'd spent staring through those glass windowpanes wondering about my future, hoping, even praying it would be better than the present. What was now the past.

I turned to the hills, shivering in the cold, allowing my eyes to wander from hilltop to hilltop, to one pumpjack and then another. My teeth were chattering.

"It wasn't this ranch or my family's genes that drove us all crazy," I said to the land, focusing on the steel head of a well pump. "It was all this damn oil. We didn't have to behave like normal people because we were rich, rich enough to get away with just about anything. It was the money that drove us crazy. We were all like spoiled children, wanting this or wanting that. Helen gave us everything we wanted, everything we thought we needed. I am not any different from the rest of them. It wasn't Howard's fault he became obsessed with money . . . money was all he knew. The same goes for the rest of us. We never had a chance to become real people . . .''

I stood there a while longer, making up my mind about what I would do when my trial began. I believed I had no choice but to confess now. It would end Detective Garcia's relentless efforts to unmask the killer. In some indefinable way I felt better about myself when I got in the car and started back toward the front gates.

Tom was waiting for me, leaning against the fender of his truck. I knew I had to say something to him. I pulled on my overcoat and got out of the car to return the key, wondering if Tom was the one person on earth to whom I could tell the entire truth.

He stared at me from beneath the brim of his worn felt cowboy hat, totally expressionless.

"I owe you an explanation," I began. "I guess you've read about it in the papers."

"No need," he said gently. "I know you didn't kill nobody."

"I'm grateful that you believe that."

He pocketed the key, still staring at me without the slightest change in his face or in his eyes. "I'm might' near sure I know what you're doin'. I told Bonnie at supper the other night I had it figured out."

"I can't tell anyone about it, Tom. I suppose I'll have to take whatever comes."

I could have sworn I saw a brief flicker of anger in Tom's eyes—maybe it was the sunlight beaming through thickening gray clouds overhead. "You'll be carryin' a mighty big burden, son. Can't say as I'd want to trade places with you. Maybe the one who done it will come forward afore it's too late. I saw that mean streak in Suzan when she was a kid, an' when I taught her how to shoot she acted real strange, like she enjoyed it. She can be like two different people sometimes . . . real nice, or real mean, dependin' on the mood she's in. I know damned well you wasn't the one who shot your brother. Don't matter what them newspapers say."

"No. But I know what I have to do. I'm doing the only thing I can, the only thing my conscience will allow me to do. It's more complicated than it seems . . ."

"I understand, Matthew," Tom said. "I think it's fair to say you're the only one of Miz King's children who has what I'd call a conscience. Me, I call it bein' loyal to blood kin, even if that ain't one of your family's strongest points. You've got a lot of courage, doin' what you're doin'. I never was much of a gamblin' man, but I'd wager neither one of your sisters or your brother would do the same fer you."

I turned toward my car, feeling sad and lonely and more than a little bit afraid of what was to come. "That part doesn't matter to me, Tom." I offered him my hand.

He took my palm and held it a moment, like there was something else he wanted to say. Then he nodded. "Like I told you once before, Matthew Lee, you're more like your pa than any of the others. Maybe things'll work out for you. Always had a lot of respect fer Lee, an' I've sure got the same for you. Let me know if me or Bonnie can do anythin' for you. Meantime, you do what you think you have to. It don't really matter what nobody else does. You're the one who's got to live with yourself."

My trial began on April 19, 1993.

EPILOGUE

I SAT AT THE DEFENSE TABLE WHILE THE JURY filed in and took their seats. My palms were sweating. The jury foreman came over to the bench and handed Judge Wilson a verdict.

Wilson peered down at me through his bifocals. "Will the defendant please rise," he said. I stood up. "In the case styled The State of Texas versus Matthew Lee King, for the charge of murder in the first degree, how does the jury find?"

"Guilty, Your Honor," the elderly jury foreman said solemnly, unable to look directly at me.

I gripped the edge of the table. I was unable to turn around to look at Cathy and David, or Martha. I stared at my hands, revisiting the kaleidoscope of events from the night of December twentieth. Events that had brought me to this moment.

I had seen Martha's car parked at the curb in front of Howard's house and when I found it empty, I knew somehow she'd gotten there ahead of me and gone inside. She must have floored it all the way to Dallas. I guessed she'd decided to warn Howard. I went to the front door and rang the bell several times, getting no answer. I walked around to the garage and discovered a side door ajar. I went in quietly.

Martha was in Howard's study, standing beside his chair. At first I did not notice the pistol in her hands, although I did smell something strange, something acrid that burned my nostrils. I glanced at Howard, and that's when I saw the bloodstains all over his shirt and his desk and the odd angle of Howard's head.

"What have you done?" I whispered.

She looked at me through glassy eyes. "I killed him."

"But why?"

She turned the barrel of her gun on me. "Because I couldn't let him get away with it," she said. I did not recognize her voice. "He robbed me of my life's work to steal money for himself and there's nothing I can do. Except this . . ."

"Dear God, Martha. You'll go to prison. It can't be worth it."

"I don't care. I don't care about him. I don't care about anything anymore."

"You don't care about living? They could give you a death sentence . . ."

"I'm already dead, Matthew. All my feelings are dead. The only thing in the whole world I cared about is gone, gone because of what he did, because of what Helen did." She said this calmly, almost as if nothing had happened.

I came toward her slowly. "Put the gun down. A collection of art and a few antiques aren't worth going to jail for, worth being executed for murder. Why on earth did you think this would solve anything?"

"It doesn't solve anything. I made him pay for what he did to me, to all of us. His stolen millions won't do him any good now. He can't spend any of it."

"Where did you get the gun? I didn't know you had one . . ."

"I showed it to you in my office the other day. It's the gun that killed John Wesley Hardin. I bought some bullets. As you can see, it works perfectly in spite of its age."

"You told me you were coming up here to stop

Tommy Lee from doing this, and now I find you here, standing over Howard's body with a gun in your hands, admitting you killed him yourself. It doesn't make any sense.'' I stopped when I reached Howard's desk.

"It makes a great deal of sense for a member of the King family, Matthew Lee. We aren't opposed to killing. We killed each other's feelings for one another a long time ago. Helen taught us how. We learned to ignore emotions, sadness, and even the suggestion of love. We've been emotionally dead since we were small children. We exist in bodies like bundles of protoplasm held together by skin . . . thick skin. We were taught never to cry unless we did it alone. We did almost everything alone, in case you've forgotten. You ask me how I was able to shoot Howard? It was easy. He's not my brother. He was a thief and a liar who happened to be born to the same mother and father as you and me. He stole from us. He used us. He felt nothing for us and I felt nothing for him.''

"You still can't use that as an excuse to kill him, Martha. Just because he embezzled money and showed no feelings doesn't mean he deserved to die.'' I glanced at Howard's face. "Are you sure he's dead? Maybe I should call an ambulance . . .''

"He's quite dead. He stopped breathing a few minutes ago. I made sure of it.''

"I wish you wouldn't point that gun at me. Or are you planning to kill me too, so there won't be any witnesses?''

Martha lowered the gun, yet she still held it in both hands in front of her. "I won't shoot you,'' she said, her voice almost a whisper. "Of all of us, you are the one I could never cause any harm. We are similar in many ways, Matthew. We have *some* feelings. You were lucky. You found Cathy, someone who understood what we had been through as children. You met someone who could love you in spite of your emotional isolation and it changed you. I've seen you with Cathy and David. You love them, and you're able to show it. I've always envied you that. Ray couldn't give me love or understanding. He was too busy loving himself.''

"I love you, Martha, in my own way, as much as you've let me. You and I were always closer than any of the others, even though we kept our distance.''

"We were taught to keep that distance. Helen made sure of it.''

"I can't bear the thought of you going to prison, or to a lethal injection.''

"I don't care,'' Martha said quietly, without emotion.

I looked at the bullet hole in the back of Howard's chair, and for reasons I did not fully understand at the time, I told my sister what to do. ''Get me a cloth from the kitchen. I'll wipe off all your fingerprints. I'll use his letter opener to get the bullet out of the upholstery. When you get back to San Antonio, wipe your fingerprints off the gun and send it back to the guy in El Paso. I'll empty Howard's wallet and wipe away my prints, to make it look like a robbery. Hurry, before Diane and the children come home. I'll fix things the best I can. Without a bullet, the police can't make a case unless we are seen by someone in the neighborhood. Get going. It's almost eleven.''

Martha simply stood there.

"Get going!'' I cried, feeling my pulse race. I wondered if I had lost my mind completely.

Woodenly, Martha went down a hallway to the kitchen. When she came back she handed me a dish towel.

"Go!'' I said urgently, picking up Howard's bloody letter opener.

"I love you, Matt,'' she whispered. "I think you're the only person in the whole world I've ever been able to love. I didn't know how to tell you . . . how to show it.''

She put her arms around me. We both cried silently a moment until I took her arms from my neck. "Leave now," I said, choking back the rush of tears. "We will never discuss what happened here, as though it never took place. No matter what happens, promise me you will not speak of this to me or to anyone else. Never!"

"I promise," Martha said.

And she kept her promise. As the following weeks stretched into months we never mentioned the events of that December night, not even after I confessed to a crime I did not commit and stood trial for murder.

Judge Wilson looked at me.

I felt my knees tremble.

"Mr. King, this jury has found you guilty of murder in the first degree. Sentencing will be in two weeks. Because of the unusual nature of this case, a brother who kills his brother, I need time to consider your punishment. On the one hand, this is a heinous crime, however we've heard hours of testimony from other family members and friends that relationships within the King family are, and have been, out of the ordinary, to say the least. The bailiff will place you in custody now, pending my decision for sentencing."

A uniformed bailiff came up behind me and I dutifully put my wrists together for handcuffs.

"Let's go, Mr. King," the bailiff said.

As I was about to walk away from the defense table I spoke to my attorney. From the corner of my eye I saw Martha in the back of the courtroom watching me. I said, "Thanks for everything you tried to do, John."

"I'll see you tomorrow," John replied. "After I've had some time to speak with Judge Wilson."

I only heard part of what John said, watching the look

on my sister's face. I couldn't look at Cathy or David now. I was sure I would break down if I did.

Martha stared at me, and I stared at her, and if there is such a thing as telepathic communication we shared it then. I saw the pain in her eyes. She started to come forward and opened her mouth to speak, until I shook my head and mouthed the word "no." I'd made a choice, an agonizing choice, to show my sister I loved her. Descendants of Lee and Helen King are not known for demonstrations of affection—quite the opposite, until today. I was going to prison for Martha, giving up everything I cherished—my wife and my son—in exchange for a lone act of selflessness. My sister and I shared a secret. I admitted to committing a crime I did not commit, for her sake. Cathy and David could never know the truth, even though I knew they would have to live with the shame and hurt of what they believed I'd done for the rest of their lives.

Some will label me a fool. A few might understand the difficulty of my dilemma. Who can be certain that to choose a sister's love over that of a wife and a son is a poor choice?

Unless you've been there it is impossible to understand what it is like to walk in my shoes.

As I was about to be led from the courtroom, Detective Garcia approached me with a curious combination of wry smile and concern on his face.

"I know what you did, Matt. I just can't prove it," he said, his hands shoved into his pants pockets.

"I'm not sure what you mean."

"Of course you do. You're taking the fall for your brother or one of your sisters. I'm sure one of them did it."

"I confessed," I reminded him.

His grin widened. "You had to. I was getting too close to the truth. You might not have been convicted without it.

I keep thinking that if I could find the murder weapon I'd be able to finger the killer. I even sent divers down to the bottom of White Rock Lake with metal detectors, thinking it might be there. But no luck. Whoever did pull the trigger was crafty, careful, making sure the gun would never turn up."

"I told you. I threw it out my car window somewhere on the Interstate. I was upset and nervous."

At that, Garcia chuckled. "Not likely, but since we have no evidence to the contrary I don't suppose it matters. You've been tried and convicted and that's the end of it. I've got tons of other cases waiting for me."

"Justice has been served," I said, wishing this conversation would end.

"Perhaps the guilty party will come forward before you spend too much time in jail," Garcia said. "Let's hope the killer has a conscience. I would hate to think you'd spend time in prison because a brother or sister feels nothing for you. I think your lawyer is convinced he'll get you a light sentence because of the extenuating circumstances, with your brother's embezzling and the abnormal way your family dealt with things. A temporary insanity plea didn't convince anyone. You might get a few years and early parole."

"I'm guilty. I'll face whatever comes."

Garcia wagged his head. "If only I could find the gun," he said. He nodded to me and walked toward the back of the courtroom, scratching the back of his head.

It was as I turned to follow the bailiff to a side door that I caught a glimpse of a familiar figure with a cowboy hat in his hands coming toward me.

"Can I have just one more minute?" I asked.

The bailiff let me stop when Tom came to the defense table. I hadn't noticed Tom at the trial during previous days of testimony and his presence there surprised me. His face, usually a deep tan from a lifetime in the sun, was pale, almost gray, and he looked extremely uncomfortable.

"Hello, Tom," I said. Cathy and David were standing a few feet away. Saying good-bye to them would be the hardest, the most painful—I found I couldn't look either one of them in the eye.

"Howdy, son," Tom said, fingering the greasy brim of his hat in a nervous way, speaking quietly. "Just wanted to say adios, an' to wish you luck, I reckon. Goin' to prison ain't gonna be easy."

"I'm prepared for it, as best I can be," I said, knowing my voice lacked conviction. "Take care of the ranch. Martha will be administrator and she's agreed to let you run as many cows as you think the place needs. She'll write you a check for whatever you need to buy them."

Tom wagged his head. "I won't stay on, Matt. Been thinkin' on it plenty hard. I don't figure I could ride that land no more without thinkin' about you bein' in jail. I'd just as soon live in Eden an' draw my Social Security as to work for a family who'd let a brother go to prison for somethin' he didn't do."

"The jury found me guilty, Tom."

Tom cleared his throat. "That jury never heard the truth. I know you're protectin' the one who done it, an' because it's blood kin I reckon I admire you some for that. Whoever killed your brother has to live with knowin' the truth of things while you sit in a jail cell. Maybe I'm full of old-fashioned notions but I ain't gonna work for nobody who'd let you take the blame for somethin' they did. I'll be movin' to town in a couple of weeks, soon as I can get my stuff cleared out."

"I wish you'd stay," I told him. "The ranch won't be the same without you."

"It ain't the same no more anyways, Matt. There's

blood on them hills now." He offered me his hand and I shook it. There was nothing more I could say.

In a private antique gun collection in El Paso a weapon is on display, a Remington Model 1890 converted to .45 caliber as a single action centerfire. It is said to be the gun City Marshal John Selman used to kill John Wesley Hardin in the year 1895, the most prolific killer in the history of the American West.

Only two people know this same gun killed again in 1992 at a time when it was on temporary loan to a San Antonio museum. One who knows the truth is in prison. The other is currently administrator of a vast family fortune made in Texas oil. The small San Antonio museum closed for a time, although it has reopened now under another name.

You may wonder if my sister finally came forward and confessed to her deed to keep me from going to prison, if she became administrator of the King estate or went to prison herself. We both kept the promise we made that night never to discuss it again. Wealthy families often have secrets, dark secrets, and we have enough money to pay handsomely to keep most of them hidden from prying eyes.

Love is a complicated thing, taking many forms, too complex to be defined by a few words. Sometimes actions do not properly convey deeply felt emotions. We take love where we can find it and give as much love as our set of life experiences allows. As is sometimes the case it is not enough, judged by another standard. But in our hearts we know we have given as much love as we have . . .

ABOUT THE AUTHOR

Frederic Bean is a native Texan who used to raise and train quarter horses. He was formerly editor of a national livestock magazine and he has written more than thirty historical novels, including *Pancho and Black Jack, Lorena, The Pecos River, Hell's Half Acre,* and *Black Gold.* He lives in Austin, Texas.